# Murder
# and
# Romance

Kim William Zerby

For information, contact:
Kim William Zerby Consulting, LLC,
6248 Fay Court, Loveland, Ohio 45140.
KWZerbyConsulting@gmail.com.

Cover Artwork Image by Andrea Baratella from Pixabay.

ISBN:  9798324400798 (KDP)

SECOND EDITION

## DEDICATION

For my supportive and loving wife, Christine.

# Murder
# and
# Romance

# Prologue – Back, Forever

Weather had delayed the company jet out of Dulles making Alexander Gage's long day even longer. Riding home in a limo from the private terminal at the San Francisco Airport, Alex felt every day of his seventy-five years. He knew the back and forth to D.C. in one day would take its toll, but his boss had insisted that he hire the investigator personally. He ached even worse for the wear than he ever imagined possible.

Alex played back in his mind the conversation he'd had with the CEO while waiting onboard the plane. He edited out the crudity of Michael Schowalter's language; a man of Alex's generation and up-bringing couldn't even think that way.

"What happened? Get him signed up?" Michael growled.

Alex didn't pay the tone any mind, he'd gotten used to this and much worse. "Yes sir, I have engaged his services. He will be in your office tomorrow afternoon, any time after three."

"Tell him to be here at four. No later. Got me?"

"I am sure that will not be a problem." Alex kept his voice calm, not letting himself be provoked.

"And what will all this cost me?"

With Michael it was always about the money, so Alex swallowed hard and laid it out. "Three-hundred-fifty-thousand for his services, paid up front before I left, plus expenses. I had to deposit another two-hundred-thousand as a retainer to cover those." Alex had lit the fuse, now for the explosion. He didn't need to wait long.

"What the f-," Alex couldn't say the whole word, even in his mind, "this f-ing guy is charging me over a half-million dollars for one week of work. Are you f-ing kidding me?!"

Alex recognized the younger generations threw the 'f-' word around casually, just another superlative like 'It's f-ing cold out today', but his boss wielded four-letter words like a ninja assassin brandishes his sword. The wounds he aims to inflict, however, were intended to heal much more slowly - they target the soul.

"Your instructions were very clear, sir, 'retain him at any cost'." Alex's voice remained even and confident. He relished the opportunity to throw the man's words back at him. While he hadn't even pretended to negotiate, simply laying open the checkbook, of course he wasn't going to tell his boss any of this.

"G-damn it," more editing in his mind of the tirade, Alex kept God out of this, "I have no idea why I keep you around. You're an f-ing idiot."

"Because I get results." Alex couldn't help taking the dig, he'd finally had it with Michael. Tomorrow, he would tender his resignation. This was his final official act.

He would have told Michael to go to D.C. himself, but Alex wanted to make sure Rock was hired. If his boss was guilty of insider trading - and Alex had his suspicions the man might be - then Robert Stone would ferret it out. The CEO wanted a rubber-stamp inquiry, but Alex had snuck Rock into the line-up of possible investigators. When the Japanese said they wanted Rock, Michael had no choice but to hire him. His boss would lean heavily on Rock to sweep any questions under the rug, but Alex knew this sleuth could not be muscled.

Alex recalled with satisfaction how the line was silent for the longest time after his comment. He could see in his mind's eye the red face on the other end of the call, veins throbbing noticeably above a locked jaw as Michael loaded the next volley of expletives.

Alex wasn't disappointed. His memory simply deleted the one-minute assault that ended with, "Get your f-ing ass back here tonight and be in my office first thing in the morning. This conversation isn't over, you G-damn a-hole!"

The silence when the call ended was heavenly. Alex would be a free man after tomorrow to do whatever he pleased. It was too long in coming, but this just meant the day would be all that much sweeter. He had come to dislike his boss over their ten years together. During the last few months, however, that dislike had turned into pure loathing. Alex realized a long time ago that Michael was not a nice human being, but lately the man had gone beyond being a hard-ass CEO and had become – Alex could view him no other way - evil.

"We're here." The driver's voice brought Alex back to the present. The limo had stopped and Alex was finally home.

"Yes, thank you." It was taking him a second to refocus away from the memory. "What do I owe you, good man?"

"Nothing, sir. Just sign the trip receipt and we'll bill the company."

"Please add twenty-five percent for your tip. It is late and you have been most helpful."

"Thank you. Much appreciated." The young driver swiveled toward the back seat and shared a big smile while handing over the clipboard with the chit attached. "Can I help you into your apartment?"

"No, that will not be necessary," Alex replied, returning the signed paperwork, "you had better be on your way. But I could use a hand getting out." The pain in his back was the worst it had been all day.

The driver promptly had the door open, proffering an arm. "There you go, grab hold."

Alex grimaced and groaned while being extracted from the limo. The pain was nearly unbearable. Sharp knives to the small of his back would have been no worse to bear. The shooting jabs down the back of both legs made attaining his vertical a herculean task. Alex yanked so hard on the driver that he nearly dragged the young man down.

But the boy was strong and had a good hold, so after an extended process of twisting and maneuvering, Alex stood upright breathing hard while leaning heavily on his cane. Like a woman in labor, he took slow deep breaths trying to manage the pain.

Holding on tight, the driver focused on the small beads of sweat that had formed on Alex's forehead. "Are you sure I can't help you in, sir?"

"No, no, I'll be fine from here," Alex assured, mustering the energy to stand straighter while forcing a weak smile. "I have no bags and a private elevator to my apartment. I can take it from here." He motioned the driver to the car. "You've been very helpful, young man, have a pleasant evening." Then turning away, he hobbled toward the entrance.

"Okay, have a nice evening." The driver slipped behind the wheel and a few seconds later the taillights of the limo briefly bathed Alex with their red glow.

Once the car had gone, Alex stopped to regain his strength. The night air was cool but not cold. He found it refreshing and it invigorated him slightly as he stood in the bright moonlight looking at the world below.

His apartment was in the hills with a view of the San Francisco Airport. Planes were landing and leaving with regularity even at this late hour. Further off, the bay glistened from the moon hovering low in the east. And beyond, the lights of the buildings and cars across the water showed the world was not yet asleep. The sounds were so far away. Alex was at peace.

"Well, Millie, tomorrow I retire again. But this time it's for good."

Alex often talked to his dear departed wife. He'd retired when he was sixty-two, full of expectations for the many happy days they would spend together in their twilight years, but her passing a year later ended this. With no children and no job, there was nothing to keep him in New York where he had so many fond memories. He had moved to San Francisco and started working at SBI soon thereafter. He'd needed the distraction, not the money.

"Look at that pretty moon." Always with him in spirit, Alex could feel her hand in his as they took in the beauty of the night. "Well, I'd better get some rest, it will be a big day tomorrow. Poor Del will be devastated when I tell her, but she more than anyone will understand."

Delilah Green had been with Alex since his start at SBI. He'd hired her his first week on the job. She, too, was new to San Francisco, coming there from Nashville at age fifty-five after the sudden loss of her husband. She was smart, energetic, and brought Southern hospitality to the office.

Thinking of Del, Alex remembered he needed to tell her that he would be in late in the morning. He felt terrible from the back pain, and this alone would justify sleeping in. The fact that it would piss off Michael by making him wait to rip into Alex was the cherry on the sundae. This thought cheered him. He dialed Del's office number and left the message.

With this last bit of work completed, he was off the clock. "Come on, Millie, let's get me some rest."

The excruciating shock of pain radiated down both legs with each step. Leaning hard on his staff, Alex shuffled up the handicap ramp into the building then to his private lift. He rented the apartment on the top floor with the luxury of this exclusive entrance. He pushed the button for the ascent and within a minute the door opened onto his foyer.

Alex took two steps, but before completing the third he was hurtling toward the tile, fading fast from a blow delivered to the back of his head. He would not remember the moment when he hit the floor.

\*   \*   \*

Alex became aware of the sound of running water. The mental fog was lifting. Naked and cold, he lay flat on his back on a hard surface. He opened his eyes; his sight was blurry. Turning his head toward the splashing, someone's silhouette appeared. He couldn't make out any details.

Squeezing his eyelids tight, Alex tried focusing his mind. *Where am I? What happened?* Then he tensed, unable to catch his breath at the next thought. *What's going to happen?*

He tried to move.

"Ah, Mr. Gage, still among the living, I see. I thought I might have hit you too hard. I don't want to rush things."

The man dealt out these words slowly, deliberately. He wanted to make sure his victim understood. And was afraid. It was not enough to kill. Some element of torture had to be involved or he wouldn't have any fun at his work. And since this murder had to look like an accident, the torture could only be mental. This was effective. Maybe more so.

"It's you!" Anger mixed with terror in Alex's voice.

"At your service," the intruder replied menacingly.

"Why?"

"Because you've outlived your usefulness." The s's rolled off the assassin's tongue like a serpent's hiss.

"He didn't have the balls to do it himself," Alex scoffed.

"Oh, he wanted to, but he knew I'd do it better. And I would enjoy it more," he replied gleefully. "There, we're all ready."

The water stopped running. When footsteps approached, Alex opened his eyes. Finally able to see, he watched the man he knew - and had hated and feared for a long time - bend down to pick him up.

"Now, now, you queer little fuck, it's time for your bath," he sneered.

Alex tried lashing out, but his hands and feet were bound. All he could do was squirm. This caused him great pain but did nothing to deter his assailant.

Lifting his victim, the executioner mocked, "Aw, baby doesn't want his bath."

His head having cleared, Alex recognized his own bathroom. The approaching tub had been filled to the brim. Driven by the terror that overcame him like a crashing wave, he fought violently, ignoring the pain.

Then his anger, greater than he had ever known, erupted. *"Eat shit and die!"*

Alex surprised himself. The sensation was otherworldly. Those words did not come from him. God had issued the curse. And God would execute judgement.

The attacker stopped, looking wide-eyed at his victim. The impact, however, was merely a momentary pause. The cold-blooded murderer remained undeterred. A sinister grin formed. "I can assure you, it will be you who dies tonight, not I. Goodbye, Mr. Gage. Forever."

With this farewell he dropped Alex into the tub and forced him to the bottom, thrusting him under with arms the old man had no possibility of resisting.

The struggle was brief. Alex held out as long as he could before gasping in liquid. But by then, the white light and calm had overtaken him. The last thing he saw was Millie's loving face carrying him away to a peaceful rest.

Red McGregor didn't need to wait long until the old man's strength failed. He pulled his arms from the water and stared down at the job well done. Reaching in once more, he took the padded restraints off limp wrists and ankles. It doesn't work to make a murder look like a slip-and-fall if there are bruises from a struggle.

This wasn't Red's first rodeo; everything had been staged exactly right. He glanced around to confirm all the props were in place. The actor was on his mark. The theatre was ready for the audience to arrive. Tomorrow, the show would go on.

He wiped his arms and hands dry, then threw the wet towel and cuffs into his backpack. Distracted by the memory of Alex's scream, Red absentmindedly lit a cigarette. He took a long, satisfied drag. While he found Alex's words funny, he took no humor from them. He understood them as they were intended. The old man had cursed his soul.

"Good luck with that," Red jeered, a gray cloud forming from the dual streams he exhaled. The smoke swirled across the water, rising like Alex's ghost to the heavens.

Pinching off the ember, Red shoved the butt into the folds of the damp rag.

After surveying the scene one last time, he zipped the bag then slipped away down the back stairs, careful to leave as he had arrived - undetected.

# Chapter 1 – Rock at Fifty

**[Twelve hours earlier.]**

"Fuck off!"

Undaunted, John slid into the office and strolled toward his boss' scowl. "It's nice to see you too, Rock."

Robert Stone leaned over his desk. "What part of *fuck off* don't you understand?"

"I understand it's your birthday," John quipped, easing into a chair.

"Now you're just trying to piss me off." The springs of a seatback groaned when Rock threw himself into them.

"No, I'm trying to distract you. Or would you rather sit here moping all day?"

"I walked the Mall over lunch," Rock groused.

John glanced at Rock's sweat-dampened shirt and matted hair. "I'm shocked the weather did nothing to improve your mood. Summer is such a lovely time to meander around D.C."

"Is there a reason you're bothering me? I need to get ready for a call."

John scoffed. "Your regular clients won't come anywhere near you today. They circle August twentieth on the calendar in red. *Especially* today. Hell, they've probably highlighted the whole week."

"Asshole. I should fire you right now."

The ends of John's lips curled into a sympathetic grin. "I'll ignore that. Tomorrow you'll apologize - like you always do – and I'll be the best secretary you've ever had."

Unlocking his rigid posture, Rock's "Yeah, yeah," carried a less biting edge. But he appeared no less angry when grunting, "What's the distraction?"

"A gentleman is here asking to meet with you. He won't tell me what he wants, only that it's regarding a week of work for the CEO of a major corporation."

"What the hell," Rock muttered, "send him in."

John flexed to rise, then paused. "Just so you know, he's a squirrely little guy. Looks like someone's accountant. Or lawyer."

Rock didn't hold either of these professions in very high regard, even though the latter was his prior vocation. Waiving toward the door, he huffed, "Give me five."

Hopping to his feet, John hustled from the room.

When the latch clicked, Rock lumbered into his private bathroom. He extracted a neatly pressed shirt from his emergency stash then hung it by the mirror. Unbuttoning the weathered one, his gaze locked on the sullen face staring back. He knew that sad look. It visited him this same day every year.

His attention focused on the streaks of white that had crept into his black sideburns. Before today, he'd been satisfied with the distinguished transformation. Now, on the other side of fifty, it just made him feel old.

"God I hate my birthday," Rock moaned.

He always had. Never could put his finger on why. It wasn't because he was older - or bored - or alone. It just was. Except maybe on this birthday, Rock hated it because he was older, bored, *and* very much alone. It was weighing on his mind like a thousand elephants and every effort to ignore it as successfully as he had the preceding forty-nine was failing.

Splashing water on his face, Rock forced his thoughts to work. He'd had a busy summer traveling through Europe. The continuation of a hectic year for his thriving business.

At first, he enjoyed kicking back in his comfortable office on Pennsylvania Avenue, finally free to relax. But each passing day without a new project made him more and more restless. Being home only made him itch to be on the road. This was the worst possible time for a lull.

Rock loved his business. Maybe a bit too much. He'd started it twenty years before, after leaving his legal practice. Law was an interesting profession for the first few years, but it quickly stopped being a challenge. His stint as a lawyer had followed a jump from multiple science degrees. He hadn't been satisfied with anything until he started his own company.

His business? Obtaining information. A background in technology and law made him very unique - and very much in demand. These days the clients were mostly multinational companies. Rock was known by CEO's and thought-leading scientists at the world's biggest innovators. Even Uncle Sam was a client when the FBI needed help investigating corporate espionage or theft of trade secrets.

What made him so good? He knew how to get information. More importantly, he knew how to interpret it. And when the info needed to be extracted from someone, he could ferret out fact from fiction, truth from lies. Rock could read people. So well, in fact, that some swore he was clairvoyant. An impression he cultivated and exploited. Combine all this with being fluent in five languages and a knack for being able to relate to anyone from any walk of life, and he was able to make a comfortable living doing what he loved.

With half-a-century of history to reflect on, Rock thought of these and many other things while cleaning away the grime from his earlier stroll. Finally giving up on his hair, he tossed the brush.

Planting palms firmly on the counter, he leaned into the mirror. "Son of a bitch, you're *fifty*." Saying it out loud didn't make the funk go away. A rap at the office door pulled him from the struggle.

Rock fastened the last button on the fresh shirt as he made his way to the desk. "Come in."

John eased open the door while addressing the visitor. "Mr. Stone will see you now. Please come in." He held it for the gentleman then left the men to conduct their business.

The bookish, slender, seventy-something man was truly a gentleman. Dressed in an Armani suit, the several-thousand-dollar kind, and carrying a finely-crafted gold-trimmed mahogany cane, he presented a very dapper appearance. By how heavily he leaned on the staff, it was not solely for show.

*Someone's accountant, but a well-paid one*, Rock concluded. He reached across the desk and shook the extended hand of his guest. Nodding to a chair, Rock offered, "Please have a seat."

Dropping with great difficulty into it, the man accompanied the polite "Thank you" with an unintended groan.

Rock grimaced, tensing at the sight. "Would you be more comfortable on the couch?"

"No, but thank you very much for asking. I've learned to live with this miserable back of mine," he answered breathlessly, soldiering through the pain.

Perching rigidly on the edge of the chair, the gentleman focused a stare and continued properly, "Mr. Stone, it is very nice to meet you. Thank you for agreeing to see me without an appointment. My name is Alexander Gage. Please, call me Alex." Though very business-like, his genuine smile displayed sincere appreciation.

"It's a pleasure. What can I do for you?" Rock snapped. The abruptness of the question had come across as impolite, but he didn't care. Rock's mood was making him something other than his usual hospitable self.

If Alex was offended, he didn't show it. "Certainly, I will get straight to the point. I am the Chief Financial Officer of Schowalter Bio Industries. You may know it as 'SBI'. You come very highly recommended to my boss, the CEO, Mr. Michael Schowalter. Do you recognize the name?"

Rock knew this was asked to see how he would react. Pretty much everyone knew the company and its founder - the tenth richest man in the U.S. All new money made by his biotech company over the two decades since he'd created it.

Backing further into his chair, Rock crossed his arms. His low-key reply was tainted with disdain. "Yes. I was just reading about him and the allegations of insider trading in SBI stock. He cashed in a chunk of his shares just before they went south earlier this year. Then he bought back a significant number right before a healthy rebound."

"I assume you're referring to the article in today's *Journal*."

"A very informative exposé." Rock didn't even try to cover the contempt in his tone, provoked by his unshared thought. *Just another case of a greedy man feeling he could never be too rich. And getting caught.*

Alex tilted closer, pressing ahead. "This is exactly what I wish to discuss. Mr. Schowalter would like to hire you to investigate who has been manipulating SBI's stock."

Rock let out a sarcastic chuckle.

"You seem skeptical of Mr. Schowalter's intentions," Alex noted blandly.

"Frankly, I am. I don't like getting into situations where personal agendas dictate action. It seems your boss is looking to stage a show with me as one of the props. Someone to parade around before the SEC and shareholders – and their lawyers - while proclaiming, 'Look, I'm innocent, would I do this if I'm guilty?' Let me tell you, I don't play games for anyone."

Certain that he had ended the meeting, Rock relaxed, glad for having passed on this job.

Alex's grin bloomed beneath taunting eyes. He observed wryly, "Already convicted him of insider trading, have you?"

Rock gaped. He'd been called out.

Leaning away, Rock directed an unseeing gaze toward the ceiling. He hated to admit it, but Alex was right. Rock prided himself on building conclusions based on facts, but here he didn't know any more than what he'd read in the papers. This, plus his personal radar - which he admittedly trusted sometimes a little too much - and he was certain the guy had done everything they were saying.

*Could I be wrong? My gut tells me not likely, but would it hurt to give the guy a chance?* These thoughts were followed by less relevant but more practical considerations. *I have nothing else to do. And I do have the itch.* They sold it.

Rock pulled his focus from overhead to lock on Alex. "You may be right, but I've never been noted for my open-mindedness. Especially when my gut tells me I'm right." Fixing his stare, Rock took the bait. "Your boss wants the best, he's got him. But I don't take orders and I don't come cheap. I call the shots, I hire the help I need, and the minute he wavers even the slightest from one-hundred-percent cooperation, I'm gone."

"Excellent! Mr. Schowalter would not want it any other way. Now, I assume you can be in San Francisco tomorrow. If you'd like, you can fly with me, the company jet is waiting at Dulles. I will happily delay my return a few hours."

Wagging his head, Rock replied, "That's very kind, but I have some prep work to do. I'll take the early morning flight and we can meet at three. Will that be acceptable?"

Rock needed time to organize his resources and prepare dossiers on the key players. His instincts told him at least these would be interesting, even if only half of what the papers reported was true.

"That's fine. I will arrange the exact time and contact your secretary before the end of today."

His eyes narrowing, Rock continued, "But first we must discuss a few details regarding my services."

Alex flashed an easy smile. "Ah yes, the matter of your fees. But of course, please name your price."

Rock decided to test the gentleman's resolve. While he didn't come cheap, for a Mickey Mouse job like this – more beauty contest than an investigation – he needed a lot to make it worth his irritation, itch or no itch.

With a relaxed expression matching his visitor's, Rock laid out his terms. "My time will cost fifty-thousand per day, for a minimum of the week you anticipate I will be needed. That's three-hundred-fifty-thousand up front, non-refundable, before I lift a pencil. I'll also need my expenses paid, plus you will be billed separately for all associates I use on the job, including my secretary's time. To cover these, I expect a two-hundred-thousand-dollar retainer deposited by tomorrow."

Rock scribbled the figures on a slip of paper and slid it across the desk. "These are non-negotiable. John will provide all the information you need for wire transfers on your way out."

He expected to see outrage from the slender gentleman then the back of his head when he stomped away to his waiting plane.

Alex's demeanor didn't waver. "The wire transfers will be completed within the hour."

"Thank you, I look forward to meeting Mr. Schowalter," Rock answered stone-faced, concealing his amazement. Then his brows furrowed. "There's one more matter. All my services are provided on a confidential basis, to protect both your boss and me. There can be no press release or any other publicity regarding my employment. Make sure he understands that this is a very serious point. My standard contract, which you must sign before you leave today, calls this out as a breach resulting in my immediate termination of our agreement. I will keep all fees plus the retainer if this should occur."

"I understand completely. No press." Alex paused, waiting for yet another condition to be added to the growing list. In light of Rock's silence, he concluded, "Have a pleasant trip tomorrow." Hoisting himself gingerly from the chair, he tipped a stiff upper-body bow accompanied by a polite but very formal "Good day", then shuffled from the office.

When the door closed, Rock began muttering. "What the hell am I doing? Am I nuts?" He drew a deep breath, releasing it as a protracted sigh. "I said I'd be there, and I will. But I don't have to like it. Besides, what's the worst that can happen?"

# Chapter 2 – The 38,000 Foot View

Rock woke at four, not so rested and definitely not so eager to be on the road again. The itch hadn't passed, but his only desire at that ungodly hour was to sleep. With eyes half shut, he showered, threw on a robe and stumbled into the kitchen for the much-needed shot of caffeine.

*Early mornings suck.* With this thought pervading his brain, he hovered over the coffeemaker. His phone buzzed, it was a text from John.

*All files loaded. Stop by on way.*

A reply was slow in coming. Rock's fingers weren't awake; autocorrect didn't help. The first attempt at 'Holy crap' got changed to 'Holly grapes.' This made him chuckle. He finally pulled it together.

*Holy crap. You up all night? Be there at 5.*

*Yep. K.* Short and sweet.

The double espresso had cooled. He threw it down like a tequila shot then hustled to dress.

At a quarter to five Rock left the apartment and hopped into the waiting limo. Fifteen minutes later the car pulled in front of his office building. A haggard John appeared carrying Rock's computer tucked under an arm. He slid in and handed it over.

Rock stared. "Wow, you look awful." Disheveled hair and red eyes from focusing all night on computer screens were only a part of the damage John had inflicted upon himself by his sleepless night. "I really appreciate you getting this done, but I've seen cadavers look better than you."

A weak grin accompanied John's fatigued reply. "Thanks. I wanted you to have this for the flight. Frankly, I had fun pulling it together. Well, not the boring SBI financial crap, but the bios are quite the soap opera. I don't want to ruin it, but they include divorces, indiscretions and drug addictions - some wild stuff." His smile broadened. "I've included a couple salacious newspaper articles to spice things up."

"Great. I need something to keep me awake."

Perking up, John continued, "I created dossiers for Mr. Schowalter and SBI as you requested. With a little digging I also pulled together files on the CEO's ex-wife and a few others. You'll have more than enough to peruse at 38,000 feet."

Rock packed the computer in his carry-on then focused on his secretary. "You need to rest. I don't want to hear from you any more today." John readied a protest, but Rock cut him off. "Go home and get some sleep. That's an order. I'll text if I need anything. If you're all set, I'll drop you off on the way."

"No, I need to shut some stuff down, then I'll head home. A little sleep will be nice."

"Thanks again." Rock patted John on the arm then watched while the poor guy practically rolled from the car.

Killing time on the ride to Dulles, he scanned what John had assembled. Rock was impressed. Impressed, but not surprised. John was a wiz at this. It came easy to him, and he liked doing it.

Several years before, Rock had met him on a project. John was bored being a computer genius among all the other geniuses in Silicon Valley. He was ready for a change, so with many promises and a helluva salary, Rock lured him to D.C.

Rock chuckled at the memory of John's first day on the job. Rock had asked, "Would it be okay if I call you my secretary? We can make your title Executive Assistant, or something like that if you want."

John gave a very practical response. "Hell, for the money you're paying me, my title can be Asshole."

Secretary it was.  Since then, John had proven to be the best hire Rock ever made.

Arriving at the airport, Rock checked his bag and passed through security without delay.  Taking off at seven-thirty, he settled into his seat with the low sun chasing him across the country.

Sitting comfortably in his business-class seat, he thought about the poor souls crammed into the tight rows behind, enjoying with guilty pleasure his legroom.  He could have flown economy and paid a lot less, but he had learned a long time ago that the travel gods hated when he flew in coach.  Rock had proven many times a corollary to Murphy's Law.  If you want to work in economy, you will be seated beside Jabba the Hut, and Dennis the Menace will be running up the back of your seat.  Then there was the chatter common in coach.  Business class focused on business.  Some polite hellos followed by even more polite silence were the norm.  Work could be done.

He glanced at the gentleman seated beside him quietly studying a thick document.  Rock relaxed even more.  What he hated beyond the general chit chat was the occasion when a woman seated next to him decided to not-so-subtly hit on him.

Rock was a good-looking man, he could admit this without being conceited.  At six-feet-two and one-hundred-eighty pounds of well-toned muscle, he would attract attention.  But while he wasn't celibate by any stretch of the imagination, he wasn't interested in one-night stands, no matter how easy they would be to come by.

His contented feeling faded as he accepted this could explain why his relationships had been few and far between, and the prospects for any developing in the near term did not exist.  He wouldn't have given it a second thought any other day, but this day, after a painfully lonely birthday, got him thinking more than ever before.

The fasten seat belt sign dinged off.  Wagging his head, Rock chased the gloomy thoughts of personal life from his mind and happily retrieved his computer.  It was time to get to work.

While the computer booted up, the flight attendant arrived with breakfast and, more importantly, coffee.  Coffee, coffee, and more coffee, it was the fuel Rock would be running on this long day.  He sipped the hot brew while tapping keys with one hand, bringing the screen to life.

The first document was a summary of the cast of key characters.  It contained little more than a picture with name, age and address - about enough to pick them out of a lineup. He had intended to begin with the CEO, but his interest immediately fixed on another player.  Lily Schowalter, Michael's second wife, was a stunning beauty.  Rock instantly wanted to know her story, expecting the light fluffy tale he needed to ease into the day.

He scrolled through the other files to reach hers.  Clicking her folder, an AV presentation jumped to life.  As usual, John had prepared a bio worthy of a BBC documentary with pictures and documents parading across the screen, bringing the subject to life through his narration.  Rock had seen him prepare these dossiers on many occasions.  With multiple monitors open, John flitted adroitly from one to another capturing morsels of the person's history, weaving them into a seamless story of their highs and lows.  To Rock's eye, the process looked a lot like the control center for a TV broadcast of a Superbowl.  The end result was just as thrilling in its own way.

Lily's face filled the screen as John's voice announced in the headphones, "Quite the looker, isn't she, Rock?"

He smiled at the intro.

"But she's not a piece of arm candy.  Behind that pretty face is a woman smarter than you and I could ever hope to be."

A picture of a run-down rural town, storefronts boarded up except for a sad little dollar store and diner morphed over her headshot. "She was born in the hills of West Virginia, in one of the many dirt-poor coal mining towns. Her father was killed in a work accident when she was four. Her mother was an alcoholic who took off with a truck driver to who knows where a year later. At the age of five, Lily was sent to Wisconsin to live with an aunt and uncle she had never met."

The video faded to a family – mother, father and young Lily, arms wrapped tight around the neck of a scruffy dog, her face beaming. "But she was lucky. They were a loving couple who couldn't have a child of their own. She was treated like a princess. Or as much of a princess as they could afford on their modest income. They valued education, making sure she learned and thrived from the day she completed their family."

Lily's high school graduation photo appeared. "She was scholastically gifted and her grades earned her admission to MIT. She had scholarships and financial aid, but even the limited bills that remained burdened her family. To relieve the hardship, she worked odd jobs all through her four years."

The picture transitioned to Lily dressed as a waitress. "She toiled long hard hours, all the time never letting her grades falter. During the school year she floated between waitressing and receptionist. I'm sure those jobs exposed her to the never-ending sexism typical for a beautiful young woman in those days," John grumbled. "In the summer, she performed more physically-demanding labor." The screen faded through black to an orange-vest-clad Lily wearing a hard hat. "She worked on Wisconsin state road crews. While it paid well, she sweated to earn every penny doing the same back-breaking tasks her male coworkers did."

Rock's breakfast sat untouched while he consumed Lily's life history.

"She graduated *cum laude* with a B.S. in Biochemistry. She followed this up with a PhD from the University of Wisconsin and post-doctorate research at Stanford. Her first job was at SBI." The hard-hat photo melted into her new-hire pic. "She quickly distinguished herself as a researcher and manager. Promotions came quickly and soon she supervised a group of fifty PhD's developing cutting-edge technology to diagnose a wide variety of genetic disorders." A screen-shot of Lily giving a TED presentation replaced the SBI photo. "Her work caught Michael's eye and he made sure her projects received his personal attention. The close working relationship became more than work, and it wasn't long after Michael's divorce from his first wife until the two were wed."

The video pulled up a mansion, the smiling couple waving from a wide porch. "Their marriage by most accounts is a happy one. By most accounts. But I found the police have responded to domestic disturbance calls at their residence on more than one occasion. Each call came from one of their staff. Charges were never brought. I could chalk one up to a disgruntled employee, but more than one hints at turbulent waters churning beneath the calm surface of this marriage."

Even with his sixth sense, Rock could not divine that by the end of the day he would be swept up in this torrent.

# Chapter 3 – Mr. Average, Old Money, New Talent

Lily's video bio ended and John's one-page written summary appeared. Rock did a quick scan of its contents, for the most part a black and white version of the presentation he'd watched. Reaching the bottom of the page, however, he realized that John had obviously expected him to view Michael's file first. The document contained a curious footnote he didn't understand.

**She was the other woman the first Mrs. Showalter found Michael with the night he received his lead injection.*

He couldn't wait to pull up Michael's dossier.

The plane was passing over Rock's old Columbus stomping grounds when he clicked on the folder. A shot of the CEO sitting behind his desk at SBI faded in while John's narration began.

"Michael grew up an only child of a lower-middle-class family in an economically depressed town near Pittsburgh. His formative years were uneventful - not a great student but not a poor one either." A scrawny kid, bat in hand, crouched at home plate. "In high school he played football and baseball all four years, and he had lead roles in plays with the drama club." A more mature lad in full Hamlet attire, skull in hand, replaced the ballplayer. "His SAT scores must have been good because he got into the University of Michigan." The Buckeye in Rock chuckled at the thought of telling John to call it *That School Up North*. "He graduated with a B.S. in Chemical Engineering, a solid 3.40 average in a difficult program, and was immediately hired by a small company in Los Angeles. It was there that Michael's ordinary life became interesting."

Rock paused the video to down half a cup of coffee. Thinking about Michael's life being generally normal until he moved to California reminded Rock of a quip one of his law school professors had made. He had described California as the 'granola state,' full of flakes and nuts. Rock's experiences since then pretty much validated this assessment, which just one trip to Venice Beach will confirm for any average person. So with this view of Californians being outside the norm of Main Street America, Rock wasn't surprised to hear that Michael's life picked up the pace once he hit L.A.

Rock returned the drink to the tray-table and hit play. "In the course of five short years, Michael met and married his first wife, bought and sold the chemical company that had hired him, started SBI with a small team of biotech geeks, and prepared for a messy divorce."

John interrupted his narration while a montage of pictures spanning those eventful five years flicked one after the other across the screen. To Rock, this looked like a lifetime of living for a lot of folks, except in California.

"Michael's meteoric rise from entry-level engineer to business mogul was not unassisted. While he possessed raw untapped business savvy, he would have stayed Mr. Average without the help of two people." The video lingered on an attractive debutante while John announced, "His first wife, Anna, was his financial angel." Her picture morphed to a young Asian man in a white lab-coat. "The second was Sam Reed, the nucleus of the biotech experts at SBI."

With this introduction to Michael's first wife, John's presentation automatically opened her file. A picture of a more mature woman who showed signs of having had work done popped up. "Anna funded Michael's good fortunes. To say she came from a wealthy family would be a gross understatement. The money for Michael to buy the chemical company was a wedding present from her family. She also arranged the business connections needed to make the company extremely profitable. These same contacts provided venture capital to start SBI."

The couple's wedding picture faded in. "Their union was rocky right from the start. Contrary to her meek and mild-mannered sounding name, Anna was far from little miss devoted and supportive wife. I know it takes two to tangle, but if only half the things rumored that she did were true, I almost feel sorry for Michael. She frequently took being a bitch to a level never before attained. Here's just one example."

A newspaper piece by a Bay Area gossip columnist entitled "Mrs. Schowalter Drives Home Her Point" filled the monitor.

Rock nibbled at a croissant, perusing the article with great amusement.

Last Friday afternoon, patrons in the parking lot of the exclusive Bay Golf Club were entertained by a public airing of Mr. and Mrs. Michael Schowalter's scheduling differences.

Mrs. Schowalter (formerly Anna Belaire, of the Beverly Hills Belaire's) confronted Mr. Schowalter (CEO of the successful biotech company SBI) about not being home preparing for that evening's theatre engagement. Mr. Schowalter, accompanied by several Japanese businessmen following their round, tried convincing his wife the theatre was the following night. Mrs. Schowalter punctuated her displeasure by smashing his 3 Wood through the front window of his brand-new Porsche 911 Turbo.

Unable to remove the club, Mr. Schowalter drove the car to the dealership to have it extracted. He groused to the inquisitive mechanic who asked what had happened, "I'm going out to the bars and this is my designated driver!" He also reportedly told the shop manager,

"When you get the damn thing out, have it gift-wrapped and sent to my wife with the note, 'Up Yours'."

The couple had no comment for reporters who spotted them at the theatre - the next evening.

When done reading, Rock clicked 'continue' and John's commentary resumed. "I've documented in my written report more examples of how their relationship continued to crumble. Their path to divorce reached its end a few years after the start of SBI. When it came, Anna made sure she got her pound of flesh. And for good measure, she also extracted a couple pints of blood. Literally. She shot Michael in the arm during one of their weekly clashes. What set this row apart from the others, aside from the more than usual amount of blood-letting, was Anna had found Michael and the future Mrs. Schowalter in a compromising position."

Rock chuckled to himself. *The footnote. Anna didn't care to see the couple coupled before she was done with him.*

"Instead of pressing charges, he told the police that he accidentally shot himself while servicing the gun. Michael leveraged the incident to obtain Anna's consent for a quick end to the marriage. More importantly for him, he used it to get out of the union financially unscathed."

A picture of Michael with his arm bandaged in a sling faded to a recent newspaper clipping showing Anna dressed to the nines walking a red carpet for some charity event. "Anna didn't leave the marriage poor. She came from a wealthy family, and money knows how to make more money. After the divorce, she stayed in the Bay Area dabbling in the distractions of the social elite. She never remarried. I was unable to confirm it, but I came across speculation that her experiences with Mr. Schowalter had changed her partner preference from AC to DC, as some might say."

Clicking past John's written summary for Anna, Rock opened Sam Reed's folder. The same lab-coat-clad shot of Sam from earlier filled the screen. John started by announcing, "The catalyst for Michael's amazing success with SBI was a first-generation Chinese-American named Sam Reed. Sam was adopted as an infant out of a Chinese orphanage and raised in a small burg located in a narrow Pennsylvania valley. Like Michael, Sam's early childhood in a lower-middle-class family was uneventful. But unlike his boss, his genius was apparent at a young age. He accelerated high school and entered Stanford's Chemical Engineering program at sixteen on a full scholarship." The video flashed a photo clipped from a magazine article showing Sam standing on the Stanford campus looking more like a middle-schooler than a college freshman.

"Stanford apparently underwhelmed Sam. He breezed through his curriculum with a nearly perfect average at the top of his class. However, with only a semester to go before graduating, he dropped out and headed south to L.A. He was asked a few years later, in an interview for a story on the then start-up SBI, why he had never finished his degree. Sam replied, 'I'd learned all I could there. I was bored.' Sam's boredom quickly dissipated in L.A."

The cover page for the annual report of Michael's first company rolled onto the screen showing Michael and Sam inspecting a manufacturing line. "Sam applied for a job not long after Michael had acquired the place. His interview for an entry-level job went well, to say the least. Sam was hired, instead, as the Director of the development team for the next generation of products. Apparently, Michael's business acumen includes genius for identifying talent. Putting the then twenty-year-old Sam in charge of the new products development team was a hell of a risk. No management experience, no corporate experience, no experience, period, he could have screwed up that company's business for years to come. Instead, he orchestrated the two dozen researchers into one of Southern California's most creative and innovative teams."

The monitor morphed to an industry magazine cover with Sam below the moniker 'Wonder Kid.' "Sam's foresight included recognizing the vast possibilities presented by getting in on the ground floor of biotechnology. He taught himself everything about genetics and genetic engineering, and while his opportunities to fully exploit his vision were limited by being in a chemical company, his developments made Michael boatloads of money. This experience and Sam's vision for what could be accomplished with research focused on bioengineering convinced Michael to start SBI."

A grinning Sam behind the wheel of a Lamborghini filled the screen. "Sam benefited not only intellectually but financially. Michael was very generous with him. He recognized the value of motivating key employees with a capital interest in his companies, so Michael gave Sam lucrative stock options and stock bonuses. These made Sam a millionaire several times over before he turned thirty."

Rock gaped when a mug shot of a disheveled Sam replaced the auto. "But as you can probably guess, Sam's lack of experience included lack of experience with the ways of the world. The narrow valleys of central Pennsylvania could never have prepared him for the wide-open lifestyle of the West Coast. Fast cars and faster women, booze, and cocaine were already taking control of his life by the time he was launching SBI to stardom. Within three years from the start of SBI, soon after this police photo was taken for a DUI arrest, Michael canned Sam. From all reports, it was for good reasons. Sam had become so lost in his *hobbies* that the young SBI R&D group lacked direction."

A legal document headed *Sam Reed vs Michael Showalter* popped up. "Sam didn't take his discharge lying down. He sued Michael and SBI, and a bitter, hard fought, and expensive court battle ensued. Two years later, broads, drugs and attorneys had sucked Sam dry, financially and emotionally, and he dropped the suit without collecting a dime."

The narration paused on a picture of a sullen Sam sitting on a folding chair in a circle of sorry-looking men. A banner on the gym wall read, 'Just say no!' Rock stared at the shot wondering why John had bothered to include Sam's bio. There had to be more to his story, but Rock couldn't imagine what.

The fasten seatbelt sign pinged on. He ignored the flight attendant's announcement to prepare for landing and clicked 'continue.'

"After hitting rock bottom, Sam got serious about taking control of his life. He spent more than two years in drug rehab working hard to put his past behind him. During this time, he picked up consulting jobs. The success he was having with companies brave enough to hire him got back to Michael. This was lucky timing for Sam. About then, SBI's R&D was faltering. Michael axed the V.P. for R&D and, to the amazement of industry analysts, hired back Sam. Michael apparently didn't let his emotions interfere with his business judgement, and by all reports rehiring Sam was a good move. Sam turned SBI's R&D organization around in less than a year."

A recent shot of the two men looking uncomfortable while inspecting a lab for a magazine article bloomed from a dark screen. "The two never kissed and made up. One industry analyst wrote about their odd alliance: 'Colleagues still don't leave the two alone with sharp objects.' "

Rock closed the laptop. Reflecting on Sam's unique bio, one word came to mind as the plane's wheels kissed the runway. *California.*

# Chapter 4 – First, A Little Fun

As the limo turned onto the 101 Freeway, Rock looked forward to relaxing in his room until the four o'clock meeting. He was headed to a small boutique hotel on Market Street, within walking distance of SBI's offices. This lodging wasn't as grand or historic as the Palace down the street, or as cavernous either, and didn't have the spectacular views of the Mark Hopkins up the hill. What it did provide, however, was the feeling of a home away from home.

Thinking of the Mark Hopkins got him reminiscing about one of his favorite movies, *Bullitt* starring Steve McQueen and the supporting cast of muscle cars. The movie shot a scene in its lobby. Rock had seen the flic as a kid and the car scenes thrilled him. The Mustang became his favorite car. He needed to wait another ten years before he could even think about driving one.

Rock shuffled uncomfortably in his seat feeling he'd been born too late. He had an old soul. He loved muscle cars - the Mustangs and Chargers and GTOs - and he loved 50s and 60s rock music. He shuddered at the memory of disco and then the hair bands. By the time he could drive, all he could choose from were the wimpy fuel-efficient cars. He took some comfort, however, from not having just turned sixty or seventy.

Forcing thoughts to more pleasant matters, he anticipated the comfortable accommodations awaiting him. He appreciated the hotel's spacious rooms, impeccable service, intimate bar, and excellent food. As if on cue, the limo slowed to a red canopy covering the entrance with its revolving access.

The wheels had barely stopped before the doorman opened the car door. "Welcome back, Mr. Stone! We're so happy to have you staying with us again."

Rock beamed. He liked being known at the places he stayed. He traveled so much, he enjoyed a familiar face. "Hi, James, good to see you again. Sorry your Giants are having a so-so season, but they still have a shot at the Wild Card."

James was a diehard fan who lived for baseball season. Rock had become his favorite guest when he gave him two tickets to a playoff game, seats just twenty rows behind home plate. James swore he could have called a better game from there than the umpire had.

"They'll make it. You gotta have faith," James encouraged heartily, taking Rock's briefcase while he exited the limo.

"That's the spirit," Rock answered, concealing his doubts. "Could you help the driver with my bags? Please have them sent to my room when it's available."

"Your suite is ready now, sir. We saw you were coming so housekeeping made it up first thing. It's your favorite, of course. I have your key right here."

Rock accepted the cool metal with an appreciative nod. A real key, one he left at the desk when he went out, like in the old days. He liked that touch. "That's why I keep coming back. You guys are the best."

Slipping it into a pocket, he extracted his wallet and passed out tips. Both men thanked him effusively even though neither was so impolite as to glance at the amount. Another reason Rock liked the place. Big tip or small, the staff showed genuine appreciation and unwavering service.

James held the hotel door for Rock to escape the heat of the city. Entering the lobby, Rock heard a woman squeal, "Rock, over here!"

His smile exploded. Turning, he spied a pretty young thing vault from a chair, launching herself at him.

"How have you been?!" she gushed while wrapping arms around his neck, pulling him into a hug before she finished the sentence.

He shuffled his feet to keep from stumbling backwards. Talking into long black hair, Rock answered, "I didn't expect to see you until tonight." With her thick locks draped across his face, he drew a deep breath. She smelled wonderful. Not like perfume or soap or anything he could put a finger on. She just smelled... good.

Rock pulled away, focusing a tender gaze on her dark eyes. "Here, let me get a proper look at you. Yep, still as lovely as ever."

She bounced energetically, like a kid on a sugar high. "I couldn't wait to see you. John said you were getting in early so I took the afternoon off."

"I have the key, we can head up. You can fill me in on how you and your mom have been." He wrapped a caring arm around her shoulders and guided her toward the elevator.

Rose Chow was the daughter of a law school classmate. Her father, Jeff, and Rock had spent many a late nights briefing cases and preparing outlines for classes. And several afternoons hitting the bars on High Street in Columbus instead of being in Civil Procedure class.

Jeff landed a job practicing law with a firm in San Francisco right out of school. Soon thereafter he met Rose's mother and they were married within the year. Rock was best man at their wedding. He had been close to Rose when she was growing up, but after Jeff died suddenly when she was only twelve, Rock took on the role of her surrogate father. Now twenty-five, she loved him like one.

He took in the delicate features of her face as they rode to the top floor. Rock couldn't imagine a more beautiful thing in the world.

"What are you looking at? You're staring at me like you haven't seen me in years. Have you forgotten what I look like since you were here in April?"

"Nah, I thought I saw a zit," he teased. "It's just a big hairy mole. You get that when you're as old as you are."

"And you wonder why I never introduce you to my boyfriends."

"You mean you have one? Finally bagged one waiting outside the blind school?"

"You should try it. But I doubt you'd get lucky even there, they're just blind, not deaf and dumb too!" She gave him a playful jab.

He laughed even as he feigned being insulted. "Well, aren't you the ungrateful little brat. Boy, I've missed you." Rock wrapped arms around her, squeezing her tight.

The elevator door opened. An elderly couple stood looking in at their embrace. The old prune of a woman huffed, muttering something about, "The management shouldn't allow such goings on in this hotel." The little old man gave them a feeble apologetic look as they exited arm in arm.

Rock didn't need to be clairvoyant to know what the guy was thinking: 'Sorry for my stupid ass wife. You wanna trade? Please? At least tell me where I can get one like you got!'

Rose and Rock laughed the whole way to the room. "That poor guy," he snickered, opening the door to his suite, "I bet the only way he can get that old bat to go down these days is in an elevator."

"You're terrible!" she replied, smacking him playfully. "But you're probably right."

He threw the key on the desk. "You've sure made this boring day much more pleasant." Settling into a chair, Rock motioned to another. "Have a seat."

They spent the next few hours happily chatting over their room service lunch. Work, travel, hobbies… their lack of relationships. They talked freely about everything and nothing.

When Rock glanced at his watch, the time was already two-thirty. Frowning, he announced, "I hate to break this up, but I need to get ready."

"John said you might need help while you're here. Can I? I'll rearrange my schedule at the flower shop to be available whenever you want." Rose's energetic voice carried a hint of pleading.

"Calm down, don't pee your pants. I'll look for something, but unfortunately right now I don't have anything." Watching her deflate, he added, "Don't worry, I'm sure something will come up."

Her gloomy look softened. "That would be great. Thanks."

"You'd better get going. I'll call you and we'll have dinner if it's not too late." Rock helped Rose from the chair and led her to the door.

Pausing in the doorway, she sighed, "I hope I'll see you tonight."

"Me too." He gave her a peck on the cheek then watched her bounce down the hall until she disappeared around a corner.

Rock thought about Rose while readying for the meeting. He couldn't figure her out. Why would she work in a flower shop when she is so smart? She graduated with a political science degree from Berkeley. He'd encouraged her to go to law school but she said it wasn't for her. Rose had seen the pressure the firm put on her dad and she blamed the heart attack that killed him on that stress. She had received several job offers from companies in other cities over the years but turned them all down. Her mother meant everything to her; Rose would never abandon her. And since mom would never move from the Bay Area, she wouldn't leave either. Rose was happy at the flower shop so Rock was happy for her.

He walked the long way around to SBI headquarters, meandering to the end of Market Street then ambling along the bay towards Fisherman's Wharf before doubling back.

The fresh air, the water, the hills, everything about the city reminded him why Rose and her mother loved the place too much to move.  Before his first visit, Rock had wondered why anyone would want to live on geological faults. Afterwards, he wondered how anyone could leave.

# Chapter 5 – To Work

Rock arrived at the SBI reception desk at ten minutes before four.

A large man standing nearby strode over. Proffering a beefy hand, he announced, "Mr. Stone, I'm Red McGregor, V.P. for Corporate Security. It's a pleasure to meet you."

Taking Red's overly firm handshake, Rock grinned. *Asserting his dominance.* Sensing the man was anything but pleased, Rock squeezed out a polite response. "It's nice to meet you, too. I'm here for my four o'clock with Mr. Schowalter."

Rock had skimmed Red's dossier. While it spanned fifty-five years, there wasn't much to read. He had grown up on a farm in rural Kansas then joined the Army after high school. All of his life from then until he joined SBI eleven years before had been spent in the military.

John could find very little on what occupied his time in those days. Government records weren't very illuminating. 'He was either in the Green Beret or Special Ops, or a member of the Mickey Mouse Club,' John noted, wryly summing up the little he'd found.

From other sources, John unearthed reports of the man showing up now and again in bad places where bad things were happening. Rock smelled the scent of the CIA. John did too, but he failed to confirm anything. That seemed to Rock to make it all the more likely.

Rock had predicted he wouldn't like the man. Having met him, he decided he wouldn't trust him either.

Turning from his guest, Red lumbered away, throwing over his shoulder, "Follow me. I need to check you in and get you your security badge." He led Rock through the lobby to a large office with Red's name and title prominently displayed on the door. Once inside, he made his way behind an oversized desk. Forcing a welcoming expression, Red offered curtly, "Have a seat. It will be a minute until my folks handle the paperwork."

Rock recognized the stall tactic. Everything would have been ready that morning. Red wanted time alone with him.

The burly man reached into a drawer and pulled out a pack of cigarettes. Lighting one, he sucked a deep drag into his barrel chest. Exhaling a gray cloud, Red muttered, "Mind if I smoke?"

Resisting the urge to cough, Rock answered, "No, go right ahead. But I thought I saw a sign when I entered saying this is a non-smoking building?"

"Oh, it's allowed in here," Red scoffed, scowling below furrowed brows.

Rock had expected this response. And the attitude – the man felt entitled to do whatever he damn well pleased.

Holding out the pack, Red flicked up a brown tube. "You want one? It's a special Turkish blend I have shipped from Istanbul. I got onto them when I was in the military in the Middle East."

"No thanks." Rock didn't smoke, but even if he had, he wouldn't have taken one. A pile of burning tires smelled better.

Deciding to see how much he could learn while they waited, Rock plowed right in, testing what some provocation might produce. "It sure looks like your boss is guilty of insider trading. Do you think he is?"

Setting the square jaw that consumed the bottom third of his square head, Red snapped, "That's not possible. I know everything that goes on in this company. If he was up to something like that, I would have heard about it asap. No, I think that investment-analyst bitch that writes so many articles about SBI is behind this. She's trying to make Michael look bad, making it appear he did something he didn't. Julie Burrows, you've heard of her, right? That's who you need to investigate."

"Why do you think that?"

Red rubbed a broad palm across his bristly flat-top of carrot-red hair. "She's had it in for Michael for a long time. He sued her a couple years back for libel when she wrote some pretty nasty, personal things about him. All lies. Very unprofessional."

Rock's bullshit meter was pegging the needle. This sounded so very rehearsed, and Red wasn't going to win any Academy Awards. "Really?"

"Yeah, check it out, their lawsuit made all the papers. She's had a hard-on to get back at him ever since." Red's ruddy cheeks formed into a grin. Leaning back in his chair, he drew a long pull from his smoke.

"Okay, thanks for the tip."

He played along, but Rock already knew the rest of the story. Ms. Burrows had pointed out that newspapers were reporting Michael was seen several times with various women, not his wife and of questionable character. The dossier on Michael documented the stable of prostitutes he had kept over the years. She correctly noted SBI's business was being negatively affected by the adverse publicity. Michael brought the suit but quickly and quietly settled without Ms. Burrows ever retracting her statements or apologizing. It was an open secret that he simply dropped the suit rather than suffer further embarrassment by all the sordid revelations sure to come out at trial. To top it off, all this had happened more than ten years ago. Revenge may be a dish best served cold but this had been left in the freezer way too long. Rock couldn't see any of this as motive for some Machiavellian revenge plot.

Further probing was interrupted by a knock. Trudging over, Red huffed through a partially opened door, "Yeah?... Oh, okay." A hand thrust something to him. He snatched it away then turned to Rock. "I've got your ID badge. Make sure you wear it visible at all times in the building."

With those terse instructions, Red handed over a red-trimmed nametag then held the door open. "We'd better be getting up to the Executive Suite."

Making their way down the hall, Rock peered at the brightly-colored badge. 'VISITOR – Robert Stone.' While attaching the clip to the pocket of his suit jacket, he chuckled, "I love these things."

Red glanced over looking mildly surprised. "You do?"

"Yes. I have a collection of these in my office for just about every major company in the U.S. They're better than the keys to the front door and the alarm codes."

"How so?" Red's reply signaled minimal interest.

Entering an elevator, Rock explained casually, "Most security systems are set up expecting espionage by the back door, middle of the night intruder. Actually, the best and easiest way is through the front door in the middle of the day. I prefer just after lunch when there's a lot of traffic into the building. Slip one of these babies on, walk like you know where you're going, and no one ever questions you. You're in and out in no time with whatever you want, and nobody is the wiser."

"What would you do about our surveillance cameras?" Red punctuated his dismissive question with a poke of the button for the top floor.

"Oh, no problem. That's why after lunch is the perfect time. With a little pre-work to identify where the cameras are located, a properly adjusted hat or newspaper or tall employee all work great to shield you from the prying lens. You're in without a trace. Once inside, there aren't any more. You have nothing else to avoid until you make your way out with the crowd at the end of the day."

"It would never work, and certainly never here at SBI," Red scoffed, staring at Rock like he was an idiot.

As the doors parted, Rock gave a one-word response. "Kiss."

Red stopped mid-exit, shooting Rock a shocked look. "What did you say?"

"K-I-S-S. Keep It Simple, Stupid. *Kiss*. I've found it to be the best approach to any problem, and what I've told you is more than theory. I've used it successfully on several occasions."

Rolling his eyes, Red wheeled away, leading down a long corridor.

Falling into step, Rock continued, "My favorite time was just for fun. I was having a conversation very much like ours with the president of a major corporation. He was very proud of the security measures he had instituted. Surveillance cameras, picture IDs for all employees, visitor badges with bright colors so they'd be easily identified, state-of-the-art alarm system – the works. He thought I was nuts suggesting I could get anything out of his building, let alone something of value."

A shallow smile crept onto Rock's face. "The following day, I walked into his office and laid the plans for his next major product launch on his desk. I did what I just described to you. He couldn't even find me on the videos until I pointed myself out. Afterwards, I felt a bit bad about having done it when I found out he moved the V.P. for Security to managing the janitorial staff."

Glancing to his host, Rock thought he wouldn't have felt the same remorse if it had been Red.

"Could never happen here," Red grunted, "I'm a hundred percent certain."

Rock let the topic drop. He'd seen enough in his ten minutes to observe SBI's second-rate security and conclude Red was the perfect pompous ass to believe otherwise. He appreciated that Red's value to the company lay elsewhere, likely as the CEO's personal bodyguard. Michael had not changed his ways after the lawsuit, but the pesky newspaper articles about his dalliances hadn't reappeared since Red came on board.

Rock made a mental note. *Red must be doing his real job very well.*

# Chapter 6 – Into the Lion's Den

Red tapped his badge to the security panel for the executive suite. The lock clicked and the entrance swung open. He motioned his guest through with the jerk of a thumb. "After you."

Entering the ornately decorated lobby, Rock stepped onto a plush Persian rug. A half dozen offices, each guarded by a strategically placed executive secretary, ringed the expansive space. Located on the far side, the CEO's office dominated a corner of the building, the one with a view of the bay and beyond.

A scowling woman hurriedly approached. Placing her ample body in front of Red, she forced him to halt. "Have you talked with Alex yet? I'm worried. He would never miss a whole day without letting me know."

Glaring down his nose, Red growled, "Del, can't you see I'm with a visitor? You're holding us up from our meeting with Michael."

"Hi, Del, I'm Robert Stone. It's nice to meet you," Rock interjected politely, shaking her trembling hand. "Alex had a very busy day coming to see me yesterday. I'm sure he's just at home getting some much-needed rest."

"Oh, I hope you're right, but it's so unlike him. Thank you for your kind words." She turned toward her desk shooting Red a vicious stare.

Red didn't see it, already plodding toward the CEO's office. Rock followed wondering whether Del's concerns were justified. His six sense was aroused.

Nearing the door, Michael's assistant leapt from her cubicle to block their path. "I'm sorry, gentlemen, but Mr. Schowalter cannot be disturbed. Please have a seat over there. I'll tell you when he's free."

While her sentences contained polite words, there was nothing courteous in the way she delivered her command. And her countenance was so rigid, she would have broken her face had she tried to smile.

Jaw tensed, Red replied gruffly, "This is Mr. Stone, Michael's four o'clock. Let him know we're here. We'll wait in the conference room." Red pivoted, diverting Rock to the nearby space. "This way."

Mildly amused by Red's fuming, Rock suppressed the snicker that tried to form. He sensed the big man hated taking orders from anyone, especially a woman.

Red moved to the door next to the CEO's. Shoving it open, he muttered, "We'll meet with Michael in his office. You can use this room afterwards to review documents."

Rock wandered in. His host followed, stopping in the doorway. Peering back, Red offered loudly with a noticeable edge, "Do you want some coffee or a pop? I'll have Nancy get it for you."

"No, I'm fine." Rock wasn't going to play Red's games.

Moving to a wall of windows, Rock focused on the outdoors. The view was toward the city, but he could readily see the bay and Coit Tower. A tip of Alcatraz Island was visible farther away through the summer haze. He concentrated on the vista, trying his best to ignore the troll in the room rocking noisily in a chair.

The door creaked, pulling Rock's attention from the distraction. Standing squarely in the opening, Nancy barked, "I need you to wait out here. When Mr. Schowalter is ready, I'll show you in." This was not an invitation. These were marching orders issued by the general of the executive assistants.

Red groused, "Come on, we need to get out there."

Rock pulled himself from the view thinking, *What a dysfunctional group.*

While they returned to the lobby, the door to the CEO's office opened and the participants of a meeting began exiting. Michael appeared first, partially turned toward his guests while continuing a conversation. "Thank you again for coming on such short notice. I hope you agree this has been very useful. We can continue our discussion in the morning. That should give us both enough time to check the numbers."

A man out of Rock's sight replied, "Yes, it has been most helpful. We will review more details tomorrow."

Rock recognized the voice speaking with a pronounced Japanese accent. He craned his neck to peer around Michael.

An older Asian gentleman emerged. He glimpsed the waiting men then paused mid-stride. Pivoting to face Rock, a broad smile bloomed. "Mr. Stone, what an unexpected pleasure it is to see you again!"

Each man gave a respectful bow.

"Konnichiwa, Sato-san. It's so nice to meet again. This *is* unexpected." Rock tossed a sideways glance at Michael.

Swiveling his head from his guest to his consultant and back, Michael displayed the appropriate amount of surprise. "You gentlemen know each other?"

"Yes, Mr. Stone did a project for me a couple years ago. He did a most excellent job. If you want the best, he is your man." Mr. Sato offered Rock a satisfied nod. "Had Mr. Stone not steered us in the right direction, my product launch would have been a financial disaster. And a personal embarrassment. By revising our plans based on his report, we beat the competition."

"Thank you, Sato-san," Rock responded, "it was my pleasure to assist you and your exceptional company. I'm glad you found my work acceptable." He remembered the project well. It was intellectually challenging, financially rewarding and the employees had been easy to work with. That trifecta was hard to come by.

Mr. Sato eased closer to Rock. "Please let me know the next time you are in Tokyo. I would like to arrange a celebration dinner. I never had the opportunity to properly express my company's appreciation."

"I certainly will. And please say hello to your lovely wife for me."

"Ah, she will want to attend the dinner. She does enjoy talking with you."

"And I with her. But I'm holding you up," Rock added, turning toward the onlookers. "I'll let you and Mr. Schowalter finish your business."

Mr. Sato looked to Michael. "We are done, right?"

"Certainly. I hope you don't mind, but Mr. Stone and I have a meeting. I will leave you in the very capable hands of my Executive Assistant to arrange transportation to your hotel." Turning toward Nancy standing her post, Michael directed the overly-polite request, "Can you please take good care of Mr. Sato for me? Thank you so much."

"Of course. *Happy* to help, Mr. Showalter." She accompanied this most accommodating and compliant reply with a grand welcoming expression. She understood who signed her paycheck.

"Please follow me, Mr. Sato. I will escort you to the lobby and get you a limo. Can I offer you something to drink while you wait?"

These were the last words Rock heard the toady speak while guiding the gentleman and his team toward the exit. Turning his attention to Michael, Rock was tempted to call him out for staging this chance meeting but he decided against it. He had learned something about Michael's plans. What, exactly, he wasn't yet sure, but he was confident John could piece together the link between Michael and Mr. Sato. That would reveal more than the man would ever admit by confronting him.

"Shall we go into my office?" Michael stood back allowing Rock to enter first. "Have you worked for many Japanese companies?"

"Quite a few, actually. In Japan, as I'm sure you are aware, if you do a good job you get many opportunities by personal referrals."

"Yes, that is true. You certainly are held in the highest regard by Mr. Sato. I've heard the same about you from others. That's why I insisted on Alex personally hiring you. Thank you for agreeing to do this little project for me."

Motioning to plush chairs near the windows, Michael offered, "Please, have a seat. We'll be more comfortable talking over here. Would you like a drink? I have some very good single malt Scotch."

"No, thank you." Rock never liked Scotch, bourbon was his spirit of choice, plus alcohol would only make him sleepy and his day was not close to ending.

Red had followed the pair into the office.

Michael waived a hand clutching a half-full tumbler in his direction. "Mr. Stone, I hope you don't mind if my head of security joins us. I asked him to be here to provide more information about my current situation should you desire it."

Rock's eyes narrowed but he forced out, "That's perfectly fine." This was Michael's show and he didn't feel the need to push back. He highly doubted, however, that the lump could provide any assistance beyond removing oxygen from the room.

As the other men moved to their chairs, Rock settled into his contemplating the minutes that had passed since he first met Michael. He believed in first impressions, trusting his gut more than reasoned evaluation. While he always learned more over time, what a person said and did later almost always reinforced his initial feelings.

Rock's first thoughts? Regarding his appearance, Michael looked his mid-forties age. His oval head had masculine angles at the jaws and the chin jutted slightly, but not enough to be considered pointy. A full head of brown hair graying heavily at the sides framed the top of his face. Except for a high forehead that drew attention to piercing dark eyes, the rest of the face was handsome but unremarkable. He stood straight-backed, extracting every inch from his roughly six-foot body. A trim build suggested a wedge shape based on narrow hips capped by broad shoulders. He was in excellent shape and carried himself with apparent self-assurance, with his overall demeanor bordering on arrogance.

Beyond the physical, he was a very smooth, polished – maybe too polished - businessman who knew how to turn on the charm and make people like him. He was confident, possibly to a fault, and used to having his own way. Rock couldn't put his finger on the reason why, but something about Michael felt slimy, likening him to a very successful used car or insurance salesman.

Bottom line? This was not a man to turn your back on or let your guard down around.

Regretting more and more his decision to take this job, Rock relaxed into his seat hoping he'd seen the worst of SBI. Still, he couldn't shake the nagging feeling that he hadn't.

# Chapter 7 – Clenched Fists

Michael slid into the chair opposite Rock. Crossing one leg over the other, he commenced the meeting. "Mr. Stone, as Mr. Gage told you yesterday, I'm in a bit of a bind. My predicament arose from allegations that I've been involved in insider trading. I need your help unraveling the tangled circumstances which led to these charges so I can resolve this matter."

Rock looked him straight in the eyes. "Well, you could start by trying to convince me that I need to investigate someone other than you."

The edges of Michael's mouth curled up ever so slightly. "Fair enough. I'll start by telling you that both the sale of the stock and purchase of the shares were planned by me years in advance. I have documentation to prove this. The sale was timed to give me cash to exercise an option to buy from my ex-wife some real estate property she was awarded in our divorce. Because it is income generating, she was allowed to own it and take the profits for a number of years. I was able, however, to purchase the property earlier this year. I always planned on exercising this option, but since the cost was significant and I keep my money in my company, naturally I had to sell shares to make the payment."

Rock interrupted. "You say you have documentation. Will I be able to look at this?"

Michael turned to Red. "You put the folder that Alex prepared in the conference room, right?"

He responded with a military-style, "*Yes, sir.* All there for Mr. Stone to review when we're done."

"Thank you." Pivoting to Rock, Michael continued, "You will find original documents. You may review them and, if you wish, have copies made of any you want to look

48

at more carefully later. Mr. Gage's secretary will be staying late to assist you."

"There's also substantiation for the stock you acquired?"

"Absolutely. The circumstances surrounding that purchase are really very straight forward. Annually, I am granted stock options by the company. Several years ago, I was given the right to obtain ten million shares of SBI stock with a price per share at that time of twenty dollars. I exercised that grant as soon as I could a few months ago."

Michael observed Rock, allowing him time to do the math. "That's right, Mr. Stone, two hundred million dollars to exercise the option on shares that, while lower than earlier in the year, were still trading at twenty-two dollars. Anyone in his right mind would have exercised that option and acquired stock worth twenty-million dollars more than he paid for it."

"Assuming all this is true, it still doesn't prove you didn't commit insider trading. If you knew of information that was going to impact the price of SBI's shares, and that information was not publicly known when you traded the stock, that's insider trading."

"I agree," he replied, revealing no hint of concern. "You will also find in the records that I had always planned to do these stock transactions. They were preprogramed and pre-authorized, even if it meant I'd lose money."

Michael leaned closer to Rock. "You see, I need to own a certain percentage of SBI's shares to be assured of control of the company. I recognized years ago - when I arranged to buy the real estate from my ex-wife - that the sale of my shares to raise the cash would put me in a vulnerable position. By prearranging to exercise the stock option later in the year, my strategy included reacquiring enough shares to protect my control. The shares I bought replenished a significant chunk of those I'd sold so my ownership of the company is again on firm footing. It all worked because revenue from the real estate I purchased provided the cash I needed to exercise the stock option."

Relaxing into his chair, Michael concluded, "Financially it all fit together nicely, exactly as I had planned years before. It is all completely legal and makes perfect sense. Doesn't it, Mr. Stone?"

Rock sat silent for the longest time, playing the different motives and angles that might contradict the story but none seemed to implicate the man of insider trading. "It does, but then why are you being investigated? And I'm still wondering why you hired me? I have no one but you to consider."

Michael nodded. "The investigation by the SEC has taken on a life of its own, due in part to some powerful shareholders who lost a lot of money pressing for it. They seem to think I'm guilty simply because I'm the one who profited the most, relying solely on the baseless assumption that the stock fluctuations were too coincidental not to be related to my activities."

"Well, I must agree with them. If it walks like a duck and quacks like a duck. But if not you, then where should I start looking?"

His expression darkening, Michael confided, "I suggest you look into the activities of the stock analyst who follows my company. Julie Burrows. She issued some very suspiciously-timed reports on SBI that started the stock moving both times. I have my reasons to believe she is motivated to put me in a less than favorable light. I know this is a very serious allegation against her, but it all fits."

"Red told me you had a run-in with her. I recall having read about your lawsuit, but this goes back many years. That's an awful long time to hold a grudge." Rock let his skepticism show. "Have you two had any more recent clashes?"

"That was just the most public of our disagreements. We've had many since, but they've been more one-on-one fights. I need to talk with her frequently because she's considered an expert on SBI in the investment world. Very often we don't see eye-to-eye on the direction for my business strategy. While it's true that all companies have critical analysts to deal with, I can assure you, she has made this personal."

Rock sighed, wagging his head while feeling like he was being sent down a blind alley. "It's not much, but it's a place to start. I'll begin looking into her tomorrow. But if you don't mind, when we're done here, I'd like to look through your records."

"Of course. I have nothing else. Unless there's another matter you'd like to address, you're welcome to begin. The documents are next door."

"That does it for me." While it all seemed too rehearsed to be believable, without other avenues to explore, Rock was content to end the meeting and dig into the paperwork.

While Michael rose from his chair, a gentle knock came at the office door. Before he could answer, it opened and in walked a gorgeous brunette.

Rock recognized the current Mrs. Schowalter from her bio. The pictures didn't do her justice. With tanned skin accentuated by a casual white dress, she was a thing of beauty. Then he caught the scent of her perfume. She was intoxicating.

"Hi Michael," Lily greeted cheerily, "I finished up early at the homeless shelter, can I give you a ride to our five o'clock meeting?"

Realizing Michael was not alone, Lily stopped after two steps. "I'm sorry, I didn't know you were busy. I can come back later when -"

Michael didn't let her finish. "God damn it! How many fucking times do I need to tell you to not bother me at work!" He was yelling so hard his voice cracked. His face had turned bright red; the veins at the temples throbbed noticeably. "Where the hell is Nancy?!"

Tears welled up in Lily's hazel eyes. "Mrs. Johnson isn't out there. I was in the neighborhood and thought I would stop by to see if you wanted to join me." Her gaze fell to the floor.

"You thought? God damn it, bitch, that's your problem, you never think. Don't you have a brain? Just get the hell out of here so I can take care of business." Michael stormed past her, making her jump out of his way so he didn't knock her down. Pushing the office door fully open he shouted, "Nancy!"

From the far end of the lobby came a harried reply. "Yes, Mr. Schowalter?"

At the top of his voice, he screamed, "Where have you been? Did you know my wife is here?"

"No sir, I just got back from showing Mr. Sato off." Her terrified voice quivered while she scurried to the office.

Michael wheeled to the room. Glaring, he demanded through a tightened jaw, "Lily, get the hell out of here. And if it's not too much for your feeble brain to remember, *don't* bother me at the office ever again."

With her head hung low, Lily squeezed past her husband who was blocking most of the doorway. In a hushed voice, she offered, "I'm so sorry, gentlemen, I didn't mean to interrupt your meeting." Raising her focus, she looked Rock in the eyes. "Please forgive me."

While only a passing glance, he saw in it the scars of the many such abuses that had preceded this one.

Then she was gone.

Michael slammed the door. Giving every appearance of a man who had just cleaned up dog shit, he growled, "I'm so sorry for that interruption. Let's get on with our business."

Rock clenched his fists. It took every bit of his restraint to not punch the guy's lights out.

With as much outward composure as he could muster, Rock answered curtly, "I'll be going to the conference room now."

# Chapter 8 – A Quiet Evening

Rock spent the next two hours scrutinizing SBI documents. He hadn't reviewed everything, but he'd seen enough. They supported Michael's story. A massive headache squeezed his brain. While he tried to focus, he couldn't dislodge the memory of Lily. It was time to call it a day.

Opening the door, he peered across the lobby into Del's cubicle. Well past seven, she remained at her desk waiting patiently.

She raised her head when he walked over.

"Hi, Del. Looks like we're the last ones here. Has Mr. Schowalter left?"

"Yes. He said he had an important meeting. Red left with him," she added with unveiled disgust. "He said I was to stay until you're done. Is there anything you need?"

"I'm finished. I hate to ask, but could you copy the files in the conference room and send them to me? I think he only wanted me to take a select few, but I'd like to review them all tonight when I'm more relaxed. Would that be a problem?"

"I thought you might ask so I did that earlier today. Here's a flash drive, if that works for you. Otherwise, I'll need to print them out which will take a while. I can have them sent over to your hotel when I'm done."

Rock shared a tired smile. "That's perfect, thanks for being so efficient. Alex is lucky to have you working with him."

Del's expression turned grave. "You know, I still haven't heard from him and I cannot reach him either. I'm really worried. And that asshole, Red – excuse my French – is no help at all. But that's not surprising, he never is."

"Maybe Alex decided to take the day off and felt he didn't need to bother you."

"That would be very unlike him. Plus, he said he'd be in today, only just a little late. I saved his voicemail. Would you like to hear it?"

"Yes," Rock replied kindly, pushing aside his exhaustion and desire to stretch out in his hotel room.

She hit the speaker button on her desk phone then dialed up the message.

Alex's voice began speaking. "Hi, Del. I wanted to let you know I'll be in later tomorrow. It was a tough trip to D.C., I need to rest my back before coming in. I got the investigator I told you about. Please pull the folder from my office and put it in the conference room. Oh, and I hate to ask, but could you plan to stay late? He'll likely want copies of some of the documents so I need you to hang around until he's done. Sorry and thank you so much. Bye."

Del hung up, focusing her grim expression on Rock. "You see why I'm worried. I just don't know what to think or what to do."

"I understand your concern, but there isn't enough to warrant calling in the police." He scribbled on a slip of paper. "I'll tell you what, here's my personal cell number. If you can't reach him by tomorrow morning, give me a call and I'll go with you to his place. I have a couple questions now that I've looked at the documents. Hopefully he won't mind me tagging along to ask. But I'm sure you'll reach him before then," he added reassuringly. "When you do, could you schedule a time for us to meet? I hope this helps you sleep better tonight."

"Thank you, Mr. Stone. It will."

"Please, call me Rock. Now that we have a plan, let's get you home to rest."

"I am pretty beat. It's been a draining day." Sighing heavily, she handed him the electronic files. "Here you go. If you're ready, I'll walk you out so security doesn't tackle you."

"All set. Let's call it a day."

She gathered her things then they shuffled in silence to the exit where they said their tired goodbyes.

Walking to the hotel, Rock called Rose.

Her chipper voice greeted him, "Hi there! Ready for dinner?"

"I'm sorry, but I need to beg off tonight."

"I understand. You've had a full travel day. It's already late for you."

Her disappointment made Rock feel worse. "I can do it tomorrow night if you're free."

"I'll make it happen," she assured.

"Great, I'll text you in the morning with the time and place."

"Works for me. Now get some rest."

"Night."

"Bye."

Staring sullenly at the phone, he pushed the 'end' button.

The shadows were long in Rock's suite by the time he settled in. He ordered room service, put on sweatpants, and started his evening exercise regimen, at least everything he could do in the room. The forty-five minutes on a treadmill would have to wait until the morning. He finished by the time dinner arrived. Having worked up a sweat, the suite smelled like a locker room, but that didn't hinder his appetite.

In the old days - his younger days - the meal would have been a burger or steak with fries or a loaded bake potato as the side. If there was a salad, it would be dripping with a high-calorie dressing. Tonight's meal was more in line with the health consciousness that had set in when he saw his fifties on the horizon. Grilled salmon, asparagus with the splurge of a dab of butter, and a side salad with low-cal French dressing. The glass of pinot noir was another indulgence, but only a glass not the whole bottle. Good for his heart in moderation, he told himself. No bread or other carbs darkened the table.

Eating in silence, his mind wandered to the day. Meeting Mr. Sato was not a coincidence. Rock wasn't buying the surprise Michael expressed at hearing he had worked for Sato-san. Michael had staged this, but what was his endgame? For some reason he wanted to impress Mr. Sato. Was it to make a sale, or did they have a bigger deal cooking? Rock's gut told him it was the latter. He'd have John work his connections to shake out what the rumor mill would reveal.

Then his thoughts turned to Lily. Rock's blood boiled anew recalling the way Michael had berated her. He found it surprising that the big prick didn't give a shit about doing it in front of witnesses. Red hadn't batted an eye; he'd seen this before.

But Rock was also pissed at himself for not speaking up. He tried convincing himself the reason was because he'd been caught by surprise. It was over so fast he didn't have time to react.

This was a lie. He had let it slide because the guy was a client. Then a truly troubling question struck him. Who was worse, Michael for doing it or him for letting it happen? For the first time in a long time, Rock felt ashamed.

He could see Lily's face as clearly as if she were standing in front of him. So helpless, her pained expression painted a pitiful picture of her inability to defend herself. Rock played Michael's belittling in his head. "Don't you have a brain?" dripped with irony. *Yes, she has a brain and she knows how to use it.* Her college transcripts made her husband's mediocre academic performance pale by comparison. *And not only does she have a hell of a mind, she has a hell of a body to go with it. She's the whole package. He doesn't deserve her.*

Rock wondered why she took it. Was it because Michael has all the money and a pre-nup? He couldn't accept this knowing her history. She clearly had her act together in all other aspects of her life, so why did she get involved with such a slimy lothario? Had abandonment as a child made her too ready to commit to anyone who could provide a comfortable existence? That seemed too simplistic.

After considering all the why's, Rock decided, *The heart wants what the heart wants.*

# Chapter 9 – Quiet Interrupted

Rock had long since finished dinner when a gentle tap on the door interrupted his solitude. His first thought went to Rose. Hadn't he told her they couldn't get together? Would she have come anyway? Maybe there was a problem.

While easing himself from his chair, there was another soft rap. This time a quiet voice carried through the door. "Mr. Stone, it's Lily Schowalter. Can I talk with you?"

Rock froze. Did she come to rat on her husband? Not likely, the show today made it clear he doesn't tell her anything about the business. Did she come to cry on his shoulder? He had given her a sympathetic look. Maybe she was looking for more than a shoulder. That would be a problem.

While he weighed the possibilities, Lily knocked a third time. Her sweet voice bore an insistent edge. "Please, Mr. Stone, may I come in?"

Exhaling slowly, Rock pushed the room service table from his chair and walked to the door. With the handle in his grasp, he paused. But he'd abandoned her earlier by not coming to her aid, he wouldn't fail her again.

Swinging away the barrier, he found her standing with her shoulders bowed in the same white dress from earlier. "Good evening, Mrs. Showalter, this is a surprise."

The hazel eyes Lily shared were red but dry. She glanced to the hallway before focusing an uncertain stare. "I'm sorry for disturbing you," she said softly, her voice shaky. "Thank you for allowing me to see you at this late hour."

"That's perfectly fine. Please, come in." Rock motioned to the closest of the chairs. "Have a seat."

Lingering a beat, Lily tilted her head then trudged into the room. On reaching the chair's cushions, she lowered herself wearily into them.

Rock settled into the space opposite. "Can I get you something to drink?"

"No, thank you," she answered slowly, deliberately, her head angled down as though looking for something in the hands folded lightly on her lap.

"How can I help you?"

Silence filled the room.

He didn't press for a reply. Seated close to the woman, he marveled at her exquisite beauty. She was thirty-nine, and in many respects she looked her age. But the contour of her toned body, the slightly bronzed color of her skin, the shine of her brown hair – all this and so much more gave her a more youthful appearance.

The weight of her burdens, however, were taking their toll, creasing a face quick to share joy with lines etched by pain and worry.

Rock would have been comfortable sitting across from her all night staring, but the evening was getting late. As he leaned in to speak, she raised her gaze.

Keeping her head slightly tilted to the side, still uncertain about engaging, Lily looked Rock in the eyes. "I know you're wondering why I stay with such a person."

He shifted in his chair but didn't respond.

She sighed. "The simple answer is fear. I'm terrified I wouldn't know how to live on my own again. No, not the fear-of-the-dark afraid of being alone, it's the fear of not having someone to share my life with."

Lily searched Rock's expression for a reaction. He remained stone-faced.

"I guess I can't expect you to understand." She bent her head, focusing once more on the hands in her lap.

Groaning softly, Rock hushed, "I was married once."

He struggled to pull the history into his thoughts. Speaking the memories openly caused him physical pain. Dredging them up felt like a punch to the gut.

"Briefly, after graduating from law school. It wasn't a particularly bad marriage, we rarely fought. No, the problem was we didn't have much emotion in the marriage either way. I had the bar exam and a new job consuming all my time. She was a new lawyer as well, making the same climb into a successful career. We had little time for each other. After a year of not working on our relationship we decided to go our separate ways. I remember vividly the thing most difficult about the divorce. My fear of being old and alone. That has never gone away."

When Lily didn't react, Rock continued, "But aren't you alone now, even with him?" As soon as he'd said it, he cringed.

Her head snapped up. She blurted out, "*Yes,* I am. I didn't say I was being rational. Most fears aren't." Burying her face in her hands, she sobbed, "God, I don't know what to do."

Tilting toward her, Rock encouraged gently, "You must realize you're very attractive. You wouldn't have any trouble meeting men." Trying his best to be comforting, he was out of his depth.

Folding away her concealing palms, Lily offered a look that told she appreciated the effort but her wagging head signaled he just didn't get it. "I don't want to meet someone new. I want to find my soulmate. I don't want a lover, I want a friend, a companion, someone to share my life with. I thought I'd found him with Michael. I was wrong. What if I'm wrong again? Or worse, what if that man doesn't exist?"

The sadness in Lily's voice tugged at Rock's heart. Sliding to the edge of his chair, he leaned close. "I don't have the answers. Nobody does. I'm sorry, I know that doesn't help you feel better but there are no certainties... no guarantees. There's only yourself, and your life is what you make of it. If you don't control it, someone else will. Then it's not yours anymore. Don't let Michael steal your life."

A table lamp on the desk in the far corner of the room offered the only light. Even in that dim glow, Rock could look deep into the hazel eyes staring back and see a woman who wasn't sure if she still had a life to live.

Deep in thought, Lily didn't move. Then, abruptly, she stood. "Please excuse me."

Scurrying away to the bedroom, she disappeared into the bathroom.

# Chapter 10 – Passion or Revenge?

"Great, what do you do now?" Her surprise move had Rock muttering to himself. "The wife of the guy you're working for just locked herself in your bathroom."

Rock had been in many difficult situations over his life, but this was a first. And while he had imagined beautiful women readying themselves in his hotel room, this reality was more out of a horror story than a fantasy.

His primary thought, however, was concern. Was she in there gathering herself? Or throwing up? Or contemplating suicide? This last one almost panicked him. Wasn't he just telling her she was losing her life? *You're such an idiot!*

At first, breaking down the door seemed a little drastic, but the longer the silence continued the more seriously Rock considered it. He relaxed some when he heard water running in the sink. No scenario he conjured up involved washing before a suicide.

He settled onto the edge of the bed facing the door. *Give her some time, she'll come out when she's ready.* When she did, he planned to politely but firmly send her on her way. She could sort everything out on her own. She would be fine.

*Who am I kidding. It won't be that simple.*

He was in deep and he knew it. How much deeper he would go, Rock couldn't imagine.

Lily had been ensconced in the bathroom for fifteen minutes. Other than the brief time when he heard running water, the only other sound was the constant purr of the exhaust fan. He accepted that his best course of action was to be patient, but his patience was nearing its end. Then the lock clicked.

Rock tensed. The door handle turned. A sliver of light escaped the narrow opening; a snap extinguished the glow. The purring fan went silent.

Ever-so-slowly, the barrier to the darkened room swung away. Aided only by the dim glow from the sitting room, Rock strained his eyes for a first look. Would she be composed and ready to leave? Or would her face reveal more drama was still to come?

Rock thought he was prepared for anything. He was wrong.

Stepping into the doorway, the soft amber light illuminated her. She lingered at the threshold, naked except for a camisole suspended carelessly by two tiny straps over slender shoulders.

From where he sat, Rock could make out every contour of her body. The sheer top hugged her nipples like a second skin. The light-colored silk ended above an almond-shaped navel, accentuating her tanned stomach. A few inches lower, the skin was creamy white. Hips, slim and well proportioned, completed the hourglass figure. Her stance, with feet slightly apart, revealed a closely-trimmed brown mat. The V-shape pointed down, directing Rock's attention to the muscular legs he'd admired in the office.

He stared, embarrassed but unable to look away. He didn't blink, fearing if he did, she might be gone.

Hesitating in the doorway, Lily waited until Rock's focus returned to her face before stepping into the bedroom. She eased close, halting in front of him.

Rock's gaze locked on hers. When she reached out, he took her ice-cold hands into his.

Leaning to his ear, she whispered, "Come here." Her warm breath caressed his neck. With a gentle tug, she urged him to rise.

He paused a beat. Was this passion… or revenge? Every rational thought screamed this was a bad idea. But reasoned thinking had already yielded to animal instincts. Rock willingly complied.

Once he was standing, Lily released his hands. Grasping the bottom of Rock's workout shirt, with one effortless motion she slid it over his head. Her body was pressed tight against his bare chest before it hit the floor. Her silk top was the thinnest of barriers.

Looking into his eyes, she reached one hand to the small of his back. The other moved to the nape of his neck. He wrapped both arms around her, drawing her tight. She quivered. Sliding her hand higher, she tipped his head to her waiting lips. They shared a passionate kiss.

When Rock raised his head, they loosened their embrace. Lily reached to his waist, finding a draw string. Tugging the knot, his pants fell freely to the floor revealing everything he had to offer.

Rock's embarrassment had passed. He proudly shared all.

Lily gave him a sneaky smile. "I guess I still have it."

"Beautiful, I can't imagine you ever losing it," he chuckled.

Reaching to the bed, he grabbed the covers. With a forceful tug they flew to the floor. Rock began leading Lily onto the mattress.

She resisted, hushing, "Lie on your back."

Obeying, he lowered himself atop the cool sheets.

Lily remained standing. Her eyes moved slowly from the shared gaze down his body. They lingered briefly on his firm stomach before stopping their exploration just below. A grin with a hint of coquettishness blossomed. She allowed the suspense to build. When her look returned to his face, she gave him a broad schoolgirl smile.

He was grinning too. His whole body tensed with an excitement he'd not felt in years.

Then Lily's expression turned serious. Moving onto the bed, she knelt beside him. With one swift motion, she swung one leg over his body. Straddling his chest, she supported herself with both arms fully extended, hands on his shoulders. From the full limit of her reach, she looked down on him. Arching her back, the camisole fell away giving him a clear view beneath.

Tilting his vision downward, he watched her thighs lower into firmer contact. The hairs of his chest disappeared in her brown mesh. Swaying from side to side, Lily pulled her shoulders back while thrusting herself ever harder against Rock. While her quiet groans built, he pressed tighter to add to her pleasure.

When the volume of her joy became exclamations, Lily leaned forward releasing some of the tension. Bending her elbows, she lowered her face close to his. Their eyes locked. Holding the visual embrace, Lily slid her hips along Rock's body, maintaining contact across his stomach while venturing lower.

With her face nearly touching his, they exchanged steamy breaths that came in rapid succession. They kissed. Lightly at first, then with more and more urgency. Their mouths opened; tongues probed the narrow channel.

Easing her body lower, Lily advanced slowly but without any hesitation. Rock tilted his head, sustaining their kiss. Her hips bore down; he forced his against hers. Gently but firmly, they eliminated all remaining space.

A decision was to be made. They couldn't stop. They didn't stop.

# Chapter 11 – What Next?

Rock came out of his slumbers through a pleasant fog. The memory of his time with Lily flashed by during the dawning of his consciousness, leaving him with the same satisfied feeling. Rolling toward her side of the bed he was disappointed but not surprised to find it empty. His wish for her to stay until morning was foolish.

The clock on the end table showed one o'clock. The energetic love-making combined with his jet lag had put him right out once they'd achieved nirvana. Rock was amazed he hadn't slept straight through until the next afternoon. Lying there semi-conscious, he was about to turn over and give in to his desire for the much-needed rest when something struck him as not quite right.

Fighting the urge for sleep, he focused his mind. A sound - a faint background noise - jumped out at him. The bathroom fan was on. Had he forgotten to turn it off? Had she when she left?

Then a powerful thought struck him. What if she hadn't gone? Could she still be in there? That possibility both pleased and alarmed him.

Straining his memory, he tried to recall seeing her leave. He'd fallen asleep around midnight. He knew this because he'd glanced at the clock when she left the bed. While she headed into the bathroom, he lay his head on the pillow.

If she was in there, an hour had passed. That struck Rock as a very long time. Maybe she had headed home. But if she hadn't, the fear that she might hurt herself leapt again into his mind. Sleep would wait; he needed to check.

He rolled out of bed. The exercise pants were on the floor where they had fallen. Slipping them on, Rock lumbered to the door. Only the purr of the fan could be heard as he reached for the knob.

*Hold on, you idiot, what if she's in there just doing her hair? Calm down, everything is fine.*

With those rational thoughts finally making their way through his sleep-deprived brain, Rock backed off.

Knocking lightly, he called, "Lily, are you in there?"

Nothing.

Another rap, this time more firmly, accompanied his announcement, "I'm coming in."

No reply.

Rock grabbed the handle and turned. It was unlocked. While a good sign, he didn't relax. Giving the knob a gentle push, the barrier swung slowly away.

"Lily?" His entry remained unchallenged.

He scanned each part of the room as it appeared. The counter, then the sinks, then the space in front of them came into view. He looked to the floor. No body in sight.

With the door nearing its limit, Rock spied a filled tub at the far end of the room. Lily's white dress and shoes lay bundled carelessly in a pile beside it. He could see the water's surface. He couldn't see her.

The adrenaline surge doubled his heart rate. Rushing into the room, with two long strides he reached the bath. Through a thin layer of old bubbles, he discovered Lily. Her face was submerged; her eyes were closed. His heart skipped a beat.

Rock dropped to his knees beside the tub. Plunging arms into the water, he heaved her from the bath, clutching her tight to his chest. "Lily!"

What he expected was a lifeless body. What he held in its place was a squirming shrieking naked woman.

"What are you doing?!" she screamed into his ear.

Loosening his grip, he eased her away, returning her to the water. His expression shared a mixture of confusion, relief, and lingering fear. All painted over a look of utter embarrassment.

Finding his voice, Rock blurted out, "I thought you were dead!"

Lily paused a beat before recognition set in. But instead of yelling that he had scared the hell out of her, she started laughing and crying at the same time.

"I'm so sorry." Rock repeated his apology over and over, hoping she would stop wailing. The tears just kept flowing. "Did I hurt you? Are you okay?"

While smiling, Lily continued to cry.

Rock became quiet, staring with a questioning look.

Finally, Lily choked out between sobs, "No, no, I'm fine."

Dumbfounded, Rock wagged his head. "Then why are you crying?"

A few more stuttering breaths were needed before she answered, "I've never had anyone come to my rescue before. I didn't think anyone cared about me, but you do. I'm just so very happy." The smile grew and the tears subsided.

Relaxing, Rock leaned away. "You may be happy, but I feel like a complete fool." His red face said it all.

"Don't be embarrassed," Lily soothed. Stretching up, she kissed him tenderly on the cheek. "That's the sweetest thing anyone has ever done for me."

"Well, I'm still sorry. I never will understand women."

"Rock, someday I'm sure you'll need to understand only one woman and she'll be a very lucky lady for sure."

Feeling a bit better, he rocked onto his heels and began to rise. "I'd better go."

Lily caught his hand, halting him. "Please don't. Join me." Her eyes invited him even more than her words.

Every fiber of Rock's being wanted to say yes, but he forced out, "I'd better not."

"Please. I'll tell you what I know about Michael's business dealings."

"That's a tempting offer, but conducting an interview while naked would be damn distracting. How about you get dressed and we'll discuss it on the couch?"

"In the tub or I'm leaving." Her tone was definitive. "Look, I don't want more sex. I only want to enjoy being the most relaxed and content I've been in years a little while longer. Please join me. I promise we'll just talk."

Rock flashed a devilish grin. "If I join you, I may not be able to keep it to just talk."

"Please?" She shared a charming smile.

The opportunity to get what Lily knew about Michael's activities was too big a prize to pass on. Dropping his pants, Rock muttered, "I must be nuts."

# Chapter 12 – A Different Light

Rock slid into the warm water facing Lily, wrapping his legs around her hips. She rested her feet gently on his thighs. The relaxing smell of lavender hung in the moist air. The bath felt so good on Rock's tired body.

Looking him in the eyes, Lily sighed, "You must think I'm batshit crazy."

He raised an eyebrow but stayed silent.

"My therapist has taught me all the medical terms, but I prefer to call myself troubled."

*Must be a tough life being married to a billionaire.* Rock bit his tongue to keep from blurting this out.

Leaning forward, she waived a hand above the water. "This is not me... and *that*," Lily motioned toward the bedroom, "I *never* do that."

"Really?" He hadn't intended to let this slip.

Lily blushed. "You're right. I assume you've heard about that night."

Rock nodded.

"Of course you have. Everyone has. I'm just glad Aunt Mary and Uncle Bill had passed before that happened. They'd raised me better."

"I'm sorry, I wasn't judging."

"I was such an idiot. I'd resisted him for nearly a year, then that night I finally gave in." Chuckling wryly, she muttered, "Alcohol should come with a bad judgement warning."

"We've all done things we've regretted while under the influence," he replied sympathetically.

"Still, it's no excuse. We'd worked until late in the office preparing for a board meeting. I was exhausted and hated the thought of making my one-hour drive home for a few hours of sleep only to return early the next morning. I accepted his offer to use the corporate suite at the hotel next door. Playing the card that he needed to make sure I got there safely, Michael walked me to the room. When we got there, he had a couple more thoughts on how we could improve the handouts. Like a fool, I invited him in. One nightcap led to another and before I knew it, we were in bed with his wife waiving a gun around."

"That must have been pretty scary."

"You can't imagine. Anna burst in shouting she was going to kill me. Michael intercepted her before she got close enough to take the shot. Trying to stop her, he grabbed the revolver and it went off. She dropped it and ran. I called nine-one-one and tended to his wound until the police arrived. By then, Michael had convinced me to go along with his story that he'd accidentally shot himself. I was in a daze from all that had happened, and he was still my boss, so I went along with it."

"Some pretty gullible police officers to buy that," Rock quipped.

Lily scoffed. "You know how the world works. Throw enough money at something and black becomes white, up becomes down. The officer who wrote the report probably didn't need to work another day in his life."

"I've seen the file. I can't imagine how anyone could believe that was what had happened."

"It didn't matter to Michael what anyone else thought, he only cared that he had leverage against Anna to get favorable terms in their divorce. I was exposed in the news as the woman at the scene because I'd stayed to take care of him. Anna's name, however, was never mentioned. Michael made sure of that. He called in all the favors he was owed by the press to make that happen. But everyone who knew us knew the real story. I was mortified. My reputation has never recovered."

Rock wagged his head. "So that was your first night together. Some start to your relationship."

She shrugged. "I've begun wondering if Michael arranged for Anna to find us. I'm sure he didn't expect her to show up armed, but he'd been trying for a long time to push her into ending the marriage. They'd been living separate lives for a couple years and he wanted out, but he feared he'd lose too much - possibly even control of SBI - if he drew up the papers. I wouldn't put it past him to have tipped her off hoping this might finally get her to pull the trigger on filing." Lily gave a sad laugh. "Sorry, bad joke. My therapist says I manage my pain with humor."

"And yet you married him."

"Worst mistake I've ever made," she snapped. "In my defense, back then Michael was nothing like he is today. He was sweet and considerate, a real charmer. And I was in love. I knew about his carousing but I'd convinced myself that once we were married, he'd be the perfect faithful husband."

Reacting to Rock's furrowed brows, Lily added sarcastically, "I know, pretty gullible of me, but I think most women tell themselves this lie. How else could so many of us willingly enter into indentured servitude?"

"You know there's a solution to that," Rock noted in a tone that carried more of an edge than he'd intended.

Lily hung her head, drawing a deep breath. "I didn't tell you the whole truth earlier."

Rocks eyes narrowed. "How so?"

"About why I haven't left him." Exhaling shakily, she confided, "I'm going to tell you something I've never told anyone except my therapist. Not even Michael knows this."

Rock leaned in, one-hundred-percent focused.

"You seem very familiar with my history. I assume you know about my childhood… about my father dying and my mother abandoning me?"

"Yes. Your father's sister and husband took you in when you were five."

"They were saints," she answered, voice cracking. "They saved my life."

He tipped a nod. "The little I know, they loved you like their own. They certainly changed your life for the better."

Brushing away a tear, Lily sighed, "I'm sorry, I don't mean to get emotional. I've discussed what I'm about to tell you with my therapists a hundred times. It's been a long time since I've cried while doing so."

"It's okay if you don't want to tell me."

"I know. But for some reason... I can't explain it... I want to."

Rock sat motionless, unsure how to respond.

"You'll never guess what my first childhood memory is."

"I can't imagine."

"Hiding in a dark closet clutching my baby doll while a stranger searched my bedroom."

Eyes wide, his mouth gaping, Rock gasped, "What happened?"

"He found me."

"Holy shit."

"I started screaming and crying. I can still see his shocked expression."

Rock swallowed hard. "Who was he?"

"He was the landlord, Mr. Colliopoulos."

Lowering his voice, he asked hesitantly, "Did he hurt you?"

"No, he didn't. He didn't know what to do. Fortunately, he was the sweetest man."

"Then why was he in your bedroom?"

"All that I know about what happened, Aunt Mary told me when I turned eighteen. Even then I wasn't ready to hear it," Lily moaned, giving a slight shuddered.

"It was just after my mom had run off. He was there to bug her, yet again, for at least some of the back rent. If I'd seen him before that moment, I don't recall. What I remember is he opened the closet door and was as surprised to find me as I was to see him. He didn't come in after me. Instead, he sat on the floor and tried comforting me.

"I don't have any memory of exactly what he said, I just remember he had the most soothing voice. He pulled out a chocolate bar and offered it to me. I was starved. I snatched it away like a snake catching a mouse. To this day I can't see a candy bar without feeling a melancholy thrill."

Shaking his head, Rock growled, "Your mom left you there? All alone?"

"For nearly a week," Lily replied, wiping away another tear. "She abandoned me without telling anyone. I'd been in the apartment living off the little bit of stale food I could find until he found me. To make it worse, the power had been cut off so I was in total darkness at night. I'm lucky Mr. Colliopoulos showed up when he did. I was malnourished and dehydrated. When he finally managed to coax me out of the closet, he took me to his home where he and his wife cared for me. Even after Child Welfare got involved, they kept me until my aunt and uncle drove down from Wisconsin to take me away."

"No wonder you don't remember. That was traumatic."

"I'm thankful I can't recall any of it. But on some subconscious level, I'm still aware of what happened. An army of shrinks has tried for years to rid me of my abandonment issues. I've gotten to the point where I can recite every detail Aunt Mary told me in detached clinical detail. That's why I'm surprised I'm having such an emotional time telling you," she confessed, blinking back tears.

"Thanks for sharing. I didn't know."

She swallowed hard. "No one else but my analyst does. I'd like to keep it that way, if you don't mind."

"I promise, this will stay a secret."

Her demeanor softening, she sighed, "I hope you now understand why my fear of being alone keeps me from leaving Michael."

"I do." Rock felt foolish about having shared his divorce worries. They paled in comparison to what she was struggling with.

"One good thing has come from all of this," Lily noted, her tone less strained, "I've been motivated to help needy families. I like to think my charitable donations and volunteer work have made a difference for the less fortunate. I get great joy from working at the homeless shelter, especially when I see a family create a stable home for their kids. I don't want any child to suffer as I had."

Rock touched Lily's hand. "I'm sure it has meant a lot to many."

"Every now and then I come across a little girl who reminds me of me. When I do, I give her a doll hoping that she'll find as much comfort from it as I found in my little Dolly. She was a present from my aunt when I lost my father. Aunt Mary said she named her after Dolly Parton because my daddy would play Dolly's songs for me at bedtime. I still have her in my bedroom watching over me. I had hoped that someday I could pass her down to my daughter,... but I guess that will never happen." Tears flowed freely.

Rock eased away, suddenly feeling very uncomfortable. "I'm sorry, this was a bad idea. I should go. But please stay as long as you like."

He began to rise when Lily grabbed his arm. "Don't leave. You may not believe me, but telling you all of this has been more cathartic than two decades of psychoanalysis." Her damp cheeks gave him a sweet smile. "I should hire you as my therapist."

"I'm glad I could help," Rock replied, sliding back into the tub.

Lily splashed some water onto her face, washing away the tears. "Okay, you wanted to ask me questions about Michael's business affairs. Still interested?"

"Very."

75

"I'll tell you everything I know after I get this bath warm." She turned on the hot water then eased back, relaxing with eyes closed while warming waves rolled over their legs.

Rock looked at Lily, seeing her in a whole new light.

# Chapter 13 – A Most Unusual Interview

Lily sat up and dialed the faucet handle. The hot stream faded to a trickle before halting. She stirred the warmed tub with fingertips. "Much better."

Switching to his business mode, Rock began, "Shall I start?"

"What do you want to know?" she answered, making herself comfortable in the scented water.

His eyes narrowed. "First, one more personal question, if you don't mind."

A surprised look accompanied, "Sure, what is it?"

"Why are you still here? Won't Michael be wondering where you are?"

Her relaxed demeanor flipped to a pinched frown. "Michael doesn't know where I am most of the time. He's out almost every night with his customers or investors. Or his hookers. He sees a lot of them, I assume you know. That used to bother me. Now I'm just numb to everything he does. If he cared, he'd assume I'm at home. Until tonight, he would have been right."

Rock couldn't decide whether sorrow or anger dominated her tone. "Then you know he's not there now?"

"Yes. I got a message he was going out with some Japanese investors. Michael won't be home until late. I learned a long time ago that 'until late' was code for all night. Maybe he'll stop by in the morning to shower and change clothes. More than likely he'll do that in the office." Lily's sadness had returned.

He hesitated to continue, but her answer offered a tantalizing possibility for information he couldn't gather any other way. "So, Michael said he was going out with the Japanese. Would that be Mr. Sato?"

"That's right. I cannot understand how such a nice person could want to do business with a man like Michael. But I guess business is business. Strange bedfellows and all."

"Do you know what they're discussing?" John might not need to shake the grapevine after all.

"Some big deal. An investment or possibly a merger of some kind between their two companies. I don't have any details, sorry, but I know it's something really important. Michael has been courting Mr. Sato for a year now. It seems like they're getting close to finalizing whatever it is they have planned."

"Anything else?"

"No, that's pretty much it, except it must be huge because I've not seen Michael so nervous about a deal. Especially before all that insider trading stuff first came up, before he sold the stock and the shares tanked, he gave me the impression the negotiations were falling apart. He's never been a pleasant person but all that put him in a dark, dark mood. I could tell when things had gotten back on track when his disposition improved."

"And when was that?"

"About the time the stock rebounded. While it raised more insider trading allegations, that didn't seem to bother him. Evidently the deal was on again because Michael was as happy as a clam."

Rock found this interesting, even if he didn't have all the pieces of the puzzle to understand what it meant. "Do you think Michael is guilty of insider trading?"

Stirring the thin layer of old bubbles, Lily pondered before answering, "He would do about anything to be a success, I have no doubt at all about that. But break the law? I just don't think Michael would do that. He has control of SBI, more money than he could ever spend - pretty much everything he has ever wanted he already has. I confess, while I don't put anything past him, I can't see any reason he'd take the chance."

"Did you notice him acting any differently when he sold or bought the stock?"

"Not at all. In fact, I didn't even know he'd gotten rid of as many shares as he did until I'd read like everyone else about the SEC investigation. Michael buys and sells SBI stock all the time, I know that, but the size of these transactions, especially the sale, are surprising. If anything, I'm shocked he wasn't more concerned about the number of shares he gave up."

Rock had heard this story from Michael's perspective. Maybe Lily's would be more informative. He feigned ignorance. "Why so? He got a whole lot of money. That would have made him very happy."

"I just don't see him being excited about the money, he already has lots of that. Sure, it was a significant chunk of cash, but the risk Michael took by selling so much stock just doesn't make sense."

"What risk?"

"Of losing control of SBI. Michael protects his ability to run the company as he sees fit more carefully than anything else. Honestly, I'm amazed he wasn't more freaked out after the sale than he was."

"I'm still not following you."

"The number of shares he sold put him at risk of losing enough votes to keep control. I remember once before, a number of years back, when he had to sell far fewer shares. Michael was crazy concerned about losing the company, and I really do mean crazy. Not this time. He was totally relaxed, which is very odd. The purchase of the shares, the other transaction under investigation, that makes total sense. It put him back on very safe footing."

"Any chance you missed his concern? He was nervous but didn't let on?"

"No, Michael wears his emotions on his sleeve, especially when he's stressed. He takes it out on me. Not his whores, but on me," she spit out with unveiled disgust. "Everything was completely normal. Well, no better but no worse," she sighed.

This was consistent with Michael's narrative but Lily's observations colored the transactions differently. Rock had another piece to the puzzle but the picture remained obscure.

There was one more matter Lily might be able to illuminate. "Michael told me the person I should be investigating is the analyst specializing in SBI's stock. A woman by the name of Julie Burrows. Do you know her?"

Lily's eyes widened below raised brows. "I know her well. She and Michael have had a number of disagreements over the years, some pretty heated ones, but Ms. Burrows has always struck me as being very professional. In almost every instance, my impression is Michael was the one out of line."

"He's blaming her, saying she's determined to get back at him for suing her. Does that seem reasonable? Or has there been anything since then that might have her gunning for him?"

"That was years ago," Lily scoffed. "Nothing of any significance comes to mind more recently. In fact, I thought they had buried the axe ever since she got close with his ex."

This raised Rock's eyebrows. "What do you mean she's close to his ex?"

"Rumors only. The scuttlebutt is they're an item. But this is San Francisco and any two women who appear to be friends generates speculation that they're something more than just that."

"So, are they friends? Or more? Have you ever seen them together?" Rock couldn't create another piece of the puzzle based solely on gossip.

"Never have. But as you might understand, Michael's ex and I don't have a close relationship," she quipped, giving a derisive chuckle, "or any relationship, really. I think she's a B, and I'm sure she feels the same way about me."

Rock was about to put a pin in this as an interesting rumor, and only that, until Lily added the off-hand comment, "Well, all I know is I've heard Michael talking with his ex about her. Telling Anna to pass along some off-the-record things to Julie. Seems to me the two must be pretty close if Michael would ask Anna to share that with her."

"And you've heard him do this?" This could be a big puzzle piece. Maybe two.

"More than once."

"Does he talk with Anna often? I would have thought with their past they'd avoid each other like the plague."

"Oh, they're not best buddies, but the divorce left them with several financial entanglements. Money is more important to both of them than any emotional baggage they carry from the marriage. And money trumps hate in their world." Frowning, she continued, "Frankly, back then it pissed me off how often they talked. I guess I should be glad I don't care anymore or it would be eating me up inside."

While all this was interesting, it was now very late and Lily was starting to fade. Rock decided to wrap up the questioning. "Has this been going on for a long time or is this more recent?"

"They've always kept in contact, but not daily until about nine months ago."

"Just before the stock sale?"

"Yep, that's about right. But as you've likely been told, Michael was selling the stock to buy real estate she owned, so maybe this isn't too surprising."

"Maybe." Rock's ESP wasn't so sure.

"Thank you. You've been very helpful. I think I can chalk this up as the most unique interview I've ever done." Grinning broadly, he added, "And frankly, the one I've enjoyed the most by far."

"If I think of anything else I'll let you know, but this tub water is freezing and I really should be going." Sharing a sneaky smile, she asked, "Who first? Or are you afraid George Costanza was right about shrinkage?"

Rock chuckled. "I see you're a *Seinfeld* fan. I'm sorry to tell you but I'm a grower not a shower, so shrinkage is just a part of my everyday life."

"Well, I've got nothing to grow and you've already seen my complete show, so I'll go first."

Hoisting herself from the tub, Lily twisted her body over the side to reach a towel. Her back turned toward Rock. Beneath a glistening sheen, black and blue bruises colored her skin from shoulder to shoulder.

Rock's rage exploded. "I'll kill the bastard!"

# Chapter 14 – No Help to be Given

Lily slid into the tub facing Rock, sinking into the water in an effort to hide the marks. Speaking barely above a whisper, she moaned, "They look worse than they feel."

His muscles flexed; his eyes narrowed. Tension gripped his voice. "I mean it, I'll kill him. He can't get away with this." Eager to spring into action, Rock pressed his fists hard against the top of the tub.

"Rock, no," she hushed, tears moistening her lashes. "There's nothing you can do."

"I sure as hell can!"

"You know you can't. You shouldn't know."

"I don't care. He's not getting away with this."

Speaking with her head down, she sighed, "I'm going to leave him. I've made up my mind. I should have done it a long time ago, but now I'm certain. I'll need a couple days to get a lawyer and arrange to move out. Confronting him will only make things much more complicated."

"But…"

"You know I'm right," she interrupted.

He did. That pissed him off even more. The prick would get off scot-free.

Looking up, she focused sad eyes on Rock's angry stare. "Today was the last straw. It's ironic, really. The reason I stopped by his office was to make sure he joined me at our marriage counseling session. He agreed to do them when I threatened to walk out a couple months ago. At first he attended regularly, but recently he's been finding excuses to miss them more times than he's come. It's finally obvious to me that he's just humoring me, stringing me along."

"Why would he do that?"

"For now, I have value to him. I make him look like a devoted husband instead of the whore-chasing bastard that he is. Part of the corporate persona he cares so much about, especially while he's courting Mr. Sato. After that's done, he'll kick me to the curb."

Tears dripped from Lily's nose making tiny ringlets in the water where they fell. "I don't know how I didn't see this before. Maybe Michael is right, I don't have a brain," she sobbed.

Rock fought the urge to scream at her that it isn't her fault. She's the victim. Michael is the asshole; she is the saint. But he'd seen enough battered women in his times to know she shared the same trait so many of them have. They'd been brainwashed into believing they somehow deserved it. What she needed wasn't his anger but his help to begin a new life.

"I'd better go," Rock groaned, lifting his deflated body from the bath. He scurried from the tub, water crashing in a wave onto the floor. Reaching to the shelf under the sink, he grabbed two towels. One he slung over his shoulder, the other he hastily secured around his waist.

Pulling another from the pile, he handed it behind his back. "Here, you'll need this."

When Lily had taken the offering, he hustled toward the bedroom, foot-sized puddles forming on the tile with every step. Pulling the door closed when he exited, Rock continued a few steps before halting. Shaking with rage, he gave a few perfunctory swipes with the towel then grabbed the closest shirt. Yanking it on, the fabric stuck to his damp arm. The sleeve tore. "God damn it!"

He flopped onto the edge of the bed, his heart pounding, his face beet red. Inhaling deeply, Rock let the air escape as a protracted hiss. "Relax," he growled.

Several deep breaths allowed him to focus on how he could help Lily. She was right, confronting Michael was a bad idea. But Rock knew plenty of great lawyers and, if she needed it, he could provide protection. For now, however, all he could do was offer support and be a friend. Giving a frustrated huff, he let his body fall onto the bed.

After ten minutes the door opened. Lily stepped from the bathroom backlit by its lights. Rock had dressed and was sitting on the edge of the mattress, his attention focused on her. She looked to the floor, avoiding his gaze.

"How will you get home?"

"I'll get a cab," she answered, sounding defeated.

"No, the hotel will take you. It will be safer."

She replied weakly, "All right. Thanks."

Rock pushed his weary body from the bed then wrapped an arm tenderly around her shoulders. Guiding her to the other room, he soothed, "Sit on the couch and I'll arrange it. They won't be long."

Lily slumped into the cushions while he hastened to the desk. Flicking on the ceiling light, Rock glanced to her. The bright light illuminated a broken woman. His heart ached. He wanted to fix everything for her, but this fight was hers. The best he could do was play a supporting role.

The front desk answered on the first ring. "Good evening, Mr. Stone, how can we be of service?"

"I'd like the limo to take a friend home."

"Certainly. I'll have it brought around immediately."

"I'll escort her to the lobby. Night."

Hanging up, he turned to Lily. She sat with her head bowed, motionless except for the trembling hands resting on her lap. "The car is ready. We can leave whenever you want. I'll walk you down."

She didn't move.

Grabbing the pad on the desk, Rock scribbled then tore off a sheet. Moving to her, he held the slip in her gaze. "Here's my cell number. Call me any time, day or night." His voice carried a hint of pleading.

She took the paper without raising her head. "Thanks. I can't tell you how much I appreciate all you've done for me tonight. I'll admit it, I'm a mess. But you've helped me make some important decisions. Tough ones I would have never faced without you."

Folding the sheet, Lily exhaled deeply while sliding the square into a pocket. "I promise I'll call if I need help, your support means a great deal to me. But you know as well as I do, I can't lean on you too much given the circumstances. And that's fine, I need to own this. The first steps on my path to a new life... to my redemption... I must take by myself."

Rock sat beside her. Gently touching Lily's chin, he turned her head so she had to look at him. "You're not alone."

Hugging him, her tears trickled under his collar while she buried her face against his neck.

"We'd better go," he muttered, helping her to her feet then to the limo.

Rock's prayers that night were for God to give Lily strength and keep her safe.

# Chapter 15 – Morning

The cell phone urged Rock to rise as directed at seven, but his brain was successfully shutting it out. The seconds went by and its persistence was paying off. Recognition began to dawn. Lying on his side facing the source of the attack on his blessed sleep, with eyes closed he slapped at the insistent beeping. His palm landed hard but the nuisance remained. He took another shot, this time forcing an eye to participate. Through the blur he found his target and the assailant was dead a beat later.

On the verge of returning to fitful dreams, the smallest of things roused him. The sweet scent of lavender wafting from his skin triggered memories of the not-so-distant evening.

Rolling onto his back, Rock muttered, "What the hell was I thinking?"

He'd decided years ago that on-the-job relationships were taboo. Females had a way of messing with his ability to make good decisions. Rock equated getting close to a woman with holding a magnet near a compass – both screwed up his sense of direction. Until last night he'd never violated this rule. Now that he had, how would he proceed?

The new day prompted the same concern he'd struggled with before going to bed. Could he trust her? He desperately wanted to say yes, but was this his heart and not his gut talking? Undeniably, they had shared a spark. He couldn't allow that to become a flame.

But Rock was finding this easier said than done. He revisited every emotion he felt in the span of their few hours together. Confusion, fear, desire, and pity all jumbled together. Then came anger - by far the strongest.

The anger stayed, driving Rock to push aside any remaining urge to return to sleep. He couldn't confront the prick but he could work his damned hardest to prove the guy was a crook.

Last night before falling asleep, he'd spent the longest time pondering what she'd told him. At first, he wondered if his feelings for her were clouding his intuition. After all, he had seen documents that supported Michael's story. Slivers of facts, however, existed in Lily's answers. Those breadcrumbs were urging him down a path away from the obvious. He'd shot off a message asking John to arrange a day pursuing these leads.

While only seven-thirty in San Francisco, the day for John in D.C. had passed mid-morning. Rock checked his phone for a reply. Efficient as usual, John had already responded. Anna's personal assistant had confirmed a ten o'clock meeting at Anna's estate. Sam was scheduled to have lunch with him at twelve-thirty. Rose would join him for dinner at seven. The afternoon was held open in the hope that Del would arrange a meeting with Alex. The day was coming together nicely. All Rock needed was the energy to face it.

"God, give me strength," he huffed, forcing himself from the bed. It was more of a chant than a prayer. Rock said it often to give himself the nudge he needed to face many a hard day. Today more than ever he needed the encouragement.

A long hot shower caressed his aching body. When he emerged, his eyes came to rest on the pile of soaked towels bundled on the floor. In his exhausted state he grew sad at their sight, much more so than he expected. Shoving the memories aside, Rock found a fresh towel and dried off at a leisurely pace, loitering in the bathroom to enjoy the lingering smell of lavender.

While dressing, there was a knock at the door. His breakfast had arrived right on time. He answered and a waiter wheeled a serving cart into the room. "Good morning, Mr. Stone, I hope you had a pleasant night's sleep."

Rock answered with the polite lie, "Yes, thank you."

The gentleman laid out an attractive table, with fresh cut flowers joining the bowls of cereal and blueberries, pitcher of low-fat milk, and carafe of regular coffee. A meager looking breakfast that was his usual. The coffee again constituted the key ingredient for the start of this day.

After the man exited, Rock took his seat and poured the first of the many cups of caffeine he needed to survive the schedule. He took a sip and perked up, a good first step toward facing the day.

While mixing the blueberries with the cereal, his cell phone rang. Rock answered on the second ring without looking at the number. "Hello, John." He was startled when Lily's voice responded.

"Rock, is that you?" she fumbled.

"Lily? Yeah, it's me. Sorry, I was expecting my secretary. Is everything okay?" She didn't sound upset but the unexpected call had Rock concerned.

"Everything is fine," she assured, her voice relaxed.

Before she could say anymore, he cut her off. "Any problems with Michael? Was he there when you got home?" These questions had weighed on his mind all night. Hearing her voice brought them to the surface.

"Honestly, I'm fine. As I expected, he wasn't around when I got here. He won't be back until later today. That's partly why I called. I think I have some additional information relating to a question you asked me last night."

"Oh, that's great to hear," he replied, his relief unmistakable from the tone of his voice. Rock surprised himself with how obvious he was being. He quickly added, "Did you remember something?"

"No, I learned something. The aviation group that flies the corporate jets has a policy of sending a notice to emergency contacts of all passengers on a flight. I found one in my email this morning informing me that Michael flew late last night to Seattle. He's coming back this evening."

Perking up, Rock replied, "Really? Was he with Mr. Sato?"

"Michael said he was going to be with the Japanese all evening so I assume Mr. Sato went with him. But the message didn't say who else was flying. I'm just guessing."

Rock had a strong suspicion she was right. He knew far more than she would about a possible connection. "Would Michael have any reason to go to Seattle?"

"No. SBI has a lot of competitors in Washington but Michael doesn't do business with any of them. I don't remember him being there for many years. I'm not sure I ever recall him going for business."

She couldn't know it, but Lily had just given Rock an important puzzle piece. "Thank you, this is interesting. I do appreciate you calling to tell me. Is there anything else?" Rock was finding the balancing act of being businesslike without coming across as impersonal to be tricky.

"No, that's all."

"Please be careful and call me again anytime. Even if it's only to talk." He paused, holding back the thought he couldn't share: *So I can hear your voice.* "But I don't want you to risk any trouble with Michael."

Taking her time, like searching for more to say, Lily concluded, "I will… I'm glad I could help… Have a good day. Bye."

Hoping there would be more, Rock hesitated before saying goodbye. Even then, he lingered over ending the call. He sensed she had too, but she hung up leaving him looking longingly at the phone.

With the call ended, Rock poked the screen.

After the first ring, John answered, "Hi there. Did I miss something?"

"Are you at your computer?"

"Where else would I be," he chuckled.

"Do you sleep with it?" Rock kidded.

"Only if she talks dirty to me."

"You're a disturbed little man."

"That's why you love me."

"Ask your girlfriend to pull up the files from three years ago. The job we did in Japan for Mr. Sato. Do you remember that one?"

"Yep, what do you need?"

"Find the corporate summary. I'm looking for his division in Seattle."

Following the sounds of John engaging the speaker and putting the phone down, the line went quiet until he answered, "Got it."

"Can you search whether it's still operating there."

Soft tapping preceded a few seconds of silence. "It's still there. Looks like it's grown a lot since then. It went from a couple hundred researchers to a couple thousand PhD's. Bunch of new buildings added to the campus."

"That doesn't surprise me. Mr. Sato had plans to grow the group by leaps and bounds. This is his baby."

"I can tell. He's poured a boatload of money into this subsidiary."

Rock nodded. "Mr. Sato was exceedingly proud of the research they were doing. He set them up to focus exclusively on cutting-edge genetic engineering problems. Even back then they were cranking out patents at a fast and furious pace."

More typing came through from the other end of the line before John responded, "I'm looking at the patent filings for all of Mr. Sato's companies and this division is outpacing the rest by a wide margin."

Jotting some notes on a pad, Rock replied, "He was excited by the group's creativity, but he was equally frustrated by the inability of the rest of his businesses to commercialize their inventions. He was sitting on a goldmine he had no ability to cash in on."

"So you think that's why Mr. Sato is talking with Michael?"

"Make's sense, doesn't it? I remember Mr. Sato saying he knew he'd eventually have to sell the subsidiary if he ever wanted to see it succeed. Since it's his brainchild, he has a special passion for making sure whoever acquires it will continue to nurture it. Getting this group would be huge for Michael and SBI."

"Based on SBI's commercial focus, it would be a great fit," John agreed heartily. "But if it's such a perfect opportunity for both companies, why haven't they sealed a deal?"

"I think they've been working on this for more than a year. It doesn't surprise me that it's taken this long. The legal complexities alone are significant. But there's likely another reason for the protracted negotiations. Mr. Sato is extremely cautious, and like all Japanese businessmen, he values personal relationships as much as the financial terms for a deal. Because this lab is a big part of his legacy, I'd expect him to want to feel one-hundred-percent comfortable with the promises he'd be getting from Michael. I can imagine Michael's sketchy personal history has to be making Mr. Sato very nervous."

"I'm following you, but why does this matter for our current job?"

"My gut's telling me these negotiations have something to do with Michael's stock transactions. While there's nothing about the deal that makes those trades illegal, I'm smelling the scent of desperation coming from them. This acquisition would mean a lot to Michael, enough to explain why he'd do something illegal."

"You know I've learned to trust your instincts, but you'll need more than this to convince others," John cautioned.

"First, let's nail down that Michael and Mr. Sato went to Seattle together. I've gotten a tip that their private jet flew there last night."

"From the same source who's had me making appointments for you since early this morning?"

92

"Yep."

"Care to share?"

"Nope."

"Well, okay then," John answered cheerily. "A well-connected mystery informant. I'll add that to my to-do list."

"Just find me the plane info," Rock groused.

"The flight info is the easy part. Who was aboard gets trickier. Must I play by the rules?"

"Nothing illegal," Rock chided.

"How about the gray areas?"

"No."

"You insist on making my work harder than it needs to be."

"If it were easy, you'd get bored. I have every confidence you can find all of this out without breaking... or bending... the law. Oh, and by the way, can you get me this by the end of the day?"

"Geez, the pressure," John joshed, "but for you, I'll get it done."

"I know you will. Thanks. Talk with you later."

While Rock was putting the cell phone down, the room phone rang. The limo had arrived to take him to his meetings. He threw on a tie and grabbed a coat. Crossing the sitting room headed for the exit he spied the untouched breakfast. Rock left the room hungry but very satisfied with how the day had started.

# Chapter 16 – The Anna Mystery

Anna's 'country estate', as Rock learned it was called, was located an hour outside of San Francisco. She owned a mansion in the city but used it only on weekends. It was more convenient for her active social life. During the week, she stayed at the country estate, a luxurious twenty-five-thousand square foot villa constructed to blend in with the forests close to Muir Woods.

The limo moved at a slow but constant speed across the Golden Gate Bridge, a break for Rock or he would have been late. His ride pulled to the gate guarding the mile-long drive off a country road with five minutes to spare. "Mr. Stone to meet with Ms. Belaire," the driver announced to the intercom.

This introduction was all it took to cause the rustic-looking barrier to open. Rock marveled at how completely it blended in with the surroundings, suggesting nothing of the grand house at the end of the tree-lined lane. He arrived at the front door at exactly ten.

When he approached, the entrance opened revealing an attractive woman in her mid-thirties holding an electronic notepad. She greeted him with a polite but rigid, "Thank you for being prompt, Mr. Stone. Please follow me to the solarium. Ms. Belaire will join you in a few minutes."

Rock fell into step beside her while she led him toward the back of the building. The broad hallway had white walls and ceiling, and the white marble-tiled floor was variegated ever-so-slightly with black. Framed paintings, large and small, covered most of the vertical space. They were colorful expressionist works, not at all Rock's taste in art. Each had an engraved gold plaque providing the name of the piece and its artist. He didn't recognize any, but he could tell they were worth some money by the sophisticated alarm system protecting them.

This interior was not what Rock had been expecting from the home's exterior. Modern in design and furnishing, the rooms were huge, almost to the point of seeming cavernous. The long brisk walk to the solarium passed a living room and dining room furnished in minimalist fashion with furniture no human could sit in comfortably.

While pleasant to look at, it all lacked any hominess. If Rock were to describe it to someone, he'd call it sterile. This was such a disappointment. A home designed so beautifully on the outside with nature in mind needed to have a country feel inside. Rock's imagination transformed the interior into a pastoral setting something like Ballynahinch Castle, an 18th century manor house he'd visited in the western countryside of Ireland. That place provided elegance with country charm.

After a weaving trek, they eventually arrived at the sunroom. It was the best room in the house. Glass walls and ceiling let in abundant light filtered by nearby trees. The furniture consisted of comfortable overstuffed chairs and couches arranged to provide a view of the lily pond garden outside the windows on the long side of the space. Several delicate vases held multicolored flower arrangements strategically placed to maximize distribution of the wonderful scents. It was a large room that still managed to feel cozy. Rock sensed a guiding hand other than Anna's in its ambiance.

Motioning to the chairs, the assistant invited Rock in. "Please have a seat anywhere you wish. Would you like some coffee while you wait?"

"That would be great," Rock replied enthusiastically, easing into a cushion near the windows. He'd managed to finish only one cup in the hotel before Lily's call had interrupted breakfast. Starving, he hoped against hope the tray might include a biscuit or two.

"Certainly," she replied, continuing across the room to settle in at a desk where she focused on her tablet.

His prayers were answered a few minutes later when a servant in a very proper butler uniform appeared with a silver platter bearing a plate of scones and the obligatory silver pot. The cup and saucer were fine china decorated with delicate red roses. Rock downed a cupful and two of the pastries in the blink of an eye and was pouring his second when Ms. Belaire arrived.

"That will be all, Jill. Thank you for entertaining my guest while he waited."

"Yes, Ms. Belaire," she answered, looking to Rock for the first time since they'd arrived.

Rock watched the young lady exit into a dimly-lit room. He found it curious that instead of closing the door she left it slightly ajar.

"Good morning, Mr. Stone. I'm sorry to have kept you waiting but I already had a busy morning scheduled before my assistant added you to the calendar. She tells me your secretary was quite insistent to arrange a meeting for today." While she spoke, Anna settled into a chair facing him.

"I do appreciate you finding time for me. I assure you, we will be finished as agreed by eleven."

He produced a small notepad from his jacket and pulled a Mont Blanc pen from his shirt pocket. Rock was comfortable with all forms of electronic devices, but when it came to taking notes at interviews, he was old-school. While organizing these tools, he took the opportunity to size up the lady of the manor.

Anna was in her mid-forties, but behind her pink lip-gloss and red cheeks was a face that had been worked over so much Rock wasn't sure he could have guessed her age had he not known. Some adjustments achieved the youthful appearance she desired but most seemed to have accomplished just the opposite. The taunt skin of her neck and the pulled-back hairline made Anna look anything but young. He had seen pictures of her in her youth and she was very attractive. She would have aged gracefully had she allowed nature to evolve her beauty. Anna's manners were impeccable, as was her overall appearance, but Rock's first impression pegged her as cold and aloof. The sterile design and furnishings throughout the manor mirrored the lady's personality.

Rock flipped the notepad open. "As I presume you've been told, Mr. Schowalter hired me to investigate the circumstances surrounding the allegations of insider trading being made against him."

"Michael informed me you'd be contacting me. I'm aware of the accusations."

This led Rock down the path of his first line of questions. "Do you talk with Mr. Schowalter frequently?"

Her eyebrows shot up. "Oh no, we rarely talk. As I'm sure you've researched our history, our brief marriage was somewhat stormy. It ended less than amicably but our business interests have remained somewhat entangled, forcing us to speak every now and then. Beyond that, we allow our assistants to handle such matters."

He scratched a few notes and put an asterisk beside them. A reminder to follow up. This wasn't consistent with Lily's observations. Who was telling the truth, Rock couldn't be sure. While he wanted to believe Lily, it was still one person's word against the other.

"Certainly understandable," he continued. "You say you are aware of the allegations. Have you ever spoken with him about them?"

"Never. While I still own a significant number of SBI shares, this has nothing to do with me. I'm just another shareholder. The SEC and lawyers will sort it all out."

Rock sensed a hint of defensiveness in her response. "Do you think he did what is being alleged?"

Wagging her head, Anna answered emphatically, "Certainly not. Michael is a hard-driving shrewd businessman, but he would never break the law."

Leaning in, Rock confided, "He seems to think he's being set up. He blames the SBI stock expert, Julie Burrows, for all of this. Michael contends she has a vendetta against him. I presume you know her. Do you think he's right about her having a reason to set him up?"

Anna's eyes darted toward the room with the open door, accompanied by a barely perceivable shift of her weight in the chair. "I cannot believe that," she countered. "I have met Ms. Burrows on a number of occasions. She never struck me as someone capable of such actions."

"But you're aware of the many run-ins they've had over the years?"

"I'm very familiar with those. I just don't think she'd retaliate because of any of that," Anna replied dismissively, her look again flitting in the direction of the room.

"No doubt in your mind?"

"None."

"Michael told me the stock transactions involved some business matters resulting from your divorce. The timing for these were all prearranged and independent of anything happening with the price of the stock at the time. Is this correct?"

Relaxing into her chair, she replied, "I only know about the sale of the stock. That involved real estate we both had interests in from our marriage. The second transaction, if I understand what I've read, involved stock options. This had nothing to do with our divorce."

"Yes, that's correct, thank you for pointing that out." Rock could see she was pleased with herself, feeling more in control of the interview. He wanted to keep it that way.

"And did you talk with him about the sale of the stock or the real estate transaction, before or after either occurred?"

"The lawyers handled all that. As I said, I rarely speak with him. What he did to get the funds to buy the property was his business. If he wanted to put his voting shares at risk by selling so much stock, that was his choice to make."

Rock made the notes and dropped another asterisk. She seemed unusually familiar with the sale for not having discussed it with him. She might have seen some of this in the news, but how did she know that Michael had put his control at risk? Another lie?

He decided to not press Anna further. Her story was she knew nothing and she'd stick to that. But before Rock ended the interview, he decided to test one more thing.

Looking toward the open door, Rock pretended he'd heard something. Watching in his peripheral vision for how Anna would react, he saw the telltale look of fear. She'd been discovered. She quickly erased the expression, appearing undisturbed when he turned back.

Rock acted as though it was nothing. He'd obtained all he expected and then some out of this meeting. Anna had told him a lot by telling him nothing.

Wrapping up the meeting, he rose saying, "That's all my questions. Again, you have been so kind to meet with me on such short notice. I'll let you get back to the rest of your busy schedule."

"Thank you for being efficient," she replied while pulling out her phone. With the press of a button, Jill reappeared, not from the adjacent room but from down the hallway.

Rock carried one thought to the waiting limo. *Interesting.*

# Chapter 17 – Time to Review

At exactly eleven the limo passed through the rustic gate onto the country road. Rock had an hour and a half before lunch to ponder the meeting and consider the implications. His immediate attention, however, was focused on the mystery of the open door. He hadn't heard any noise. Whoever was in that room hadn't betrayed a thing. But Anna had.

Who was it? The list was short. First and most obvious was Jill, but that left the big question 'why?' Also, she'd reappeared from the hallway. Misdirection? Possibly, but the question of why she would be eavesdropping was too troubling for Rock to make her his top candidate.

Next, Michael. He would have been first on the list if Lily hadn't said he was in Seattle. Was he back early or was it possible he never left the city? Lily might be able to provide some answers, but he may be deceiving her as well. Hopefully the information John would dig up about the flight to Seattle would help.

Then there was Michael's surrogate, Red. If Michael had left town and wanted to have a reliable pair of ears in that room, Red was his man. Again, Lily may have more information. John's info might also provide an answer.

An additional possibility was Julie, Anna's rumored girlfriend. She seemed the least likely, mainly because he couldn't find a good motive for her to be listening in. Maybe she'd heard Michael was blaming her and she was interested in hearing about it first-hand. Anna, however, could confirm this to her without all the drama of hiding in the other room. Another less dramatic option could also explain Julie's presence. She happened to be visiting and was curious.

Finally, maybe Jill had just been careless. Nobody had been listening in. This was a very rational explanation but it ran contrary to all of Rock's instincts.

The limo was merging onto the 101 when he decided to chance a call to Lily. The coast should be clear for her to talk. Either Michael was in Seattle as she thought or at Anna's as Rock suspected. His cell phone signal strength had returned now that he was back to civilization. Finding Lily's number, he hit the redial button.

She answered after one ring. "Rock?"

"Hi Lily, I'm sorry to bother you. Are you able to talk now?"

"Yes, I'm in my bedroom. Michael is still not back and the servants can't hear me in here. What's wrong?"

"Nothing. I just finished talking with Anna and needed some assistance rather urgently with a couple things."

"Sure. I hope I can help."

Rock could hear the tension in her voice ease. "Great, thanks. First, how sure are you that Michael went to Seattle and is still there? Any chance he stayed in the city?"

"I'm as certain as I can be. The notice I received says he's to land at the San Francisco Airport around six tonight. The aviation group that runs the flights is a contractor regulated by the FAA. I cannot imagine they'd risk their business or their reputation by sending me false notifications. Plus, if Michael wanted to stay in town with one of his sluts, he stopped hiding that from me a long time ago."

This was as much as he could expect her to provide. The details on the flight schedule would help John. Rock moved to his next question. "Do you know if Red went with him?"

"I have no way of knowing, but my strong assumption is that knuckle-dragger joined him. Michael hasn't traveled anywhere without Red by his side in years. The guy is his pimp and protector. He's especially good at making sure none of Michael's adventures are made public. The press gives Red a wide berth after he beat the crap out of a reporter a couple years back for getting the drop on Michael coming out of a whore house. The only way he wouldn't be with Michael is if he's dead."

"Okay, that helps. Finally, are you sure that Michael and Anna talk regularly. Any chance you could be mistaken about this?"

"No mistake. I'm positive. A long time ago Michael began treating me like I didn't exist. I'm invisible to him. He's gotten so skilled at tuning me out that he never paused to consider whether I was nearby when he made those calls. Not that I hang around waiting to catch him talking with that witch, but he'd just call her from his study with the door open and the speaker on. It was pretty easy for me to hear he was talking with her when I walked by. I figured he was doing it to stick the knife in me a little more. He knows how much I loathe that woman."

"Just double checking. That's all the questions." He let the conversation sit in silence a few beats before, "Are you all right?"

"Getting by. Thanks for asking."

"Good. I'm sorry for interrupting your morning. It was nice talking with you. You've been very helpful once again."

"You're welcome." A pause. "Any time." Another beat. "I miss you."

These last three words caught Rock off guard. He blurted out the first rote response that came to mind. "Okay. Call me any time. Bye."

He heard a quiet "Bye" while reluctantly ending the call. Yes, every urge pulled at him to say he missed her too, but this was a feeling he couldn't have.

The limo's wheels inched through the traffic jam on the Golden Gate Bridge heading into the city when his call reached John. The conversation was brief. John assured him he'd do his best to confirm Michael and Red were in Seattle, but he couldn't promise anything. His best bet, maybe only bet, would be some subterfuge. A call to the airport they'd be flying from or the hotel where they stayed, checking if they were there in order to get a message to them. Rock groaned a bit at this tact but gave in.

Relaxing while taking in the breathtaking view of the ocean from the bridge, his phone rang. It was a number he didn't recognize. He hesitated before answering. "Hello?"

"Hi, Mr. Stone, it's Del. Alex's assistant."

"How are you today?" he asked cautiously, hoping she was having a better day than the one he'd witnessed yesterday.

"Not good," she sighed, "that's why I'm calling. I still haven't heard from Alex and I'm really worried. I hate to bother you, but I decided to accept your offer to go with me to check on him." Her voice, lowered to a hush, cracked as she confided, "I'm afraid what I might find."

"Del, this is no problem at all. I'll go with you. I'm sure we'll find him sitting in front of the TV drinking a bottle of wine while binge-watching his favorite show."

"Thank you so much. I hope you're right."

"I'm sure I am," he replied, struggling to prevent his own doubts from coloring his tone. "I have a lunch meeting, but how about I call you when I'm done. Are you in the office today? I can swing by in the limo to pick you up and we'll go to his place together. Will this work for you?"

"Yes, I'm in the office. That would be so kind of you to take me there. I'd be a nervous wreck driving to his place."

"Perfect. That will give me a chance to ask my questions about those documents he gave me. I'll see you in a couple hours. Until then, please try not to worry too much. Everything will be fine."

"I feel better already. Bye, Rock."

"See you soon."

Rock slumped into the seat, actively forcing his brain to think about something other than this project. He had fifteen minutes of down time before he arrived at the restaurant, precious little time to recharge his batteries, but he happily took whatever he could get.

# Chapter 18 – Lunch with a View

The heavy traffic stretched the fifteen minutes into a half-hour before the limo pulled in front of the restaurant. Enjoying every minute of the solitude, Rock didn't mind the slow pace one bit. With the building in sight, he drew a deep breath, gearing up to question Sam, SBI's head of all R&D.

The driver dropped him off under the canopy at the front door. Situated in a historic building not far from Golden Gate Park, he had dined in this restaurant many times. It combined views of the Pacific Ocean with unsurpassed food, making it one of his favorites.

Rock hustled inside. The host instantly recognized him, greeting him warmly, "Mr. Stone, welcome back. Nice to see you again."

"Good to see you, too, Andre. I'm here to have lunch with a client, Sam Reed. Do you know if he's arrived?"

"I directed him to the bar. I'll take you there." Andre turned to the young lady standing nearby silently observing the exchange. "Becca, please take over while I escort Mr. Stone and his guest to their table."

The host led Rock for the short walk to the lounge. The strategically placed bar provided a spectacular view past the bartenders to the ocean. The windows sat at the very edge of a cliff where the surf crashed against rocks a hundred feet below.

"Mr. Reed, Mr. Stone has arrived." Andre provided this introduction while Sam swiveled to face the gentlemen.

"Mr. Stone, it's nice to meet you," Sam replied, flashing a relaxed smile.

"Please, call me Rock."

"And I'm Sam." He reached out and shook Rock's extended hand.

Rock had a much better feeling about Sam than Michael. *Good vibes*, as Rock liked to say when he met a person he instantly liked.

"This way to your table," the host announced.

Andre led the men to his best booth at the far end of the dining room. It hugged the corner windows so tightly you felt suspended over the waves. Not a table for anyone with a fear of heights, but for those who didn't, it was an unforgettable view that would include an unforgettable meal.

"Thank you, Andre, this is perfect."

"Enjoy," he responded, turning to resume command of the host desk.

"Wow, this is amazing," Sam gushed, leaning against the glass. "I've never been here but I've heard many good things about this place. I just didn't take the time to come to this side of town. I need to get out more." He craned his neck to watch the surf pound granite far below. "Beautiful!"

"Yes, it is." Watching Sam enjoy himself, Rock was now sure he liked the man.

Sam finally pulled his attention to Rock. "I'm sorry, I know you asked me here to talk, but this is so cool. I just can't stop looking."

"Not a problem. Take it all in, we'll have plenty of time to chat." Rock relaxed into his chair, turning his head in the direction of the approaching waiter.

"May I get you gentlemen a drink?"

"I'll have a beer," Rock replied. He couldn't opt for his usual bourbon, not when the jet lag was already starting to get the better of him. "Do you have any hefeweizens?" Rock was never a fan of the bitter hoppy-tasting IPAs. A good wheat beer, especially an unfiltered German hefe, he could enjoy all the time.

"We have a locally brewed one on tap. I think you'll like it. I can bring you a sample."

"That won't be necessary. I'll have a pint. Sam, anything for you?"

"Just a water for me."

Once the waiter had retreated, having gathered his guest's attention Rock started the interview. "Thanks for meeting me today. I realize my secretary arranged this on short notice. You're aware that Mr. Schowalter hired me to do some research for him, right?"

Sam's joy instantly evaporated. "Michael told me he hired someone to prove he wasn't guilty of insider trading," he answered, his voice dripping with contempt. "If you don't mind me asking, you seem like an okay guy, what the hell are you doing working for a scumbag like him?"

Rock raised an eyebrow.

"Yes, I appreciate the irony," Sam noted, giving a wry chuckle. "I know why I sold my soul to the devil. I'm just curious why anyone else would."

Rock didn't mind the question. It was the same one he'd asked himself several times since he signed the contract. Only one answer could be given. "Morbid curiosity."

This provoked a puzzled look from Sam.

"Your CFO came to me and said Michael wanted to prove his innocence, could I help him? I said 'no' because frankly I think he's likely guilty. Alex basically called me out as prejudiced against Michael because he's rich, so I decided 'what the hell, let's see why a guilty guy would hire me to prove he wasn't.' Simple morbid curiosity. That… and a whole lot of money," Rock concluded, sharing a sly smile.

This drew a laugh from Sam. "Well, at least I know you're honest."

The drinks had arrived and Rock made the toast. "To honesty."

"To honesty," Sam echoed.

Settling into his chair, Sam picked up the conversation. "What would you like to know?"

"Do you think Michael is guilty?"

Sam inched closer. "If you know anything about our history, you know I hate the bastard. I think he's the lowest form of human being."

"I won't argue with that."

"But I can't see any reason why he would do it. He has more money than God, he's built a very successful business, and he's getting all the pussy he wants. Why in the world would he risk everything by taking the chance? No, I just can't see it."

This answer surprised Rock. He had expected Sam to say the worst about the man he so despised. Rock figured he'd stir the pot a little by taking a risk on what he thought he knew. "Not even to buy the Seattle subsidiary from Sato-san?"

This violated the cardinal rule Rock had learned his first year of law school: never ask a question you're not certain you know the answer to. But while he didn't know for sure, if he was right, he would learn a whole lot more by making Sam think he knew everything.

Sam's eyes lit up. Leaning across the table, he spoke urgently, barely above a whisper. "Keep your voice down! How the hell do you know about this? Only a handful of people at both companies know. I can't believe Michael would tell you. What the hell?!" he snapped, shaking his head.

Grinning, Rock responded, "You're right, Michael didn't tell me. You see, I'm very good at what I do."

Sam slid into his seat, mouth gaping. "I'm impressed."

Rock pressed his advantage. "Now that you know I'm aware of Michael having such a big prize in his sights, does that change your answer? To me, this seems like a very big motivator for him to do just about anything."

"Look, I agree this is a major deal for Michael. And yes, potentially an incentive to do whatever it takes to get it done. I truly believe, however, there are limits to what he would do. So blatantly breaking the law seems to be on the other side of the line for him."

The returning waiter drew Sam's attention. Rock signaled they needed more time.

When the man had withdrawn, Sam continued, "Michael is far from a saint, but I stand by what I said before. He has too much to lose and he's too smart to risk everything, even for something this big."

Rock accepted this as Sam's honest opinion, but he was less certain. He pushed a little harder, using what he suspected from the info Lily provided. "But the deal was falling apart in the spring right before his first stock trade. Could that have pushed him over the edge?"

Sam looked at him with disbelief and a hint of admiration. "The talks had been called off by then. But as far as I know, the deal and the money Michael made from the sale are unrelated. The negotiations hadn't hit a roadblock because of money."

Two for two. Rock was pleased with himself. "Oh?"

"No. You know the Japanese, they put a lot of value on relationships and Sato-san was not comfortable dealing with Michael. I don't know exactly what happened to cause that. Maybe he finally figured out what an asshole Michael is, but whatever it was, the negotiations were terminated."

"So what restarted them?"

"Beats me. It took a couple months of Michael begging Sato-san before they met in Japan. Michael never told me what he did or what he'd discussed, but it did the trick. The talks were back on. I got pulled in after that and all I heard - hinted at really - by one of the Japanese negotiators was that Michael had sweetened the pot by offering Sato-san something that wasn't a part of the deal. Apparently, some personal *quid pro quo* based on a promise that doing this deal would lead to another."

Rock tipped closer, ready to speak, but halted when the waiter approached. After waiving the server away again, he pivoted his attention to Sam.

Before Rock could ask, Sam said, "I know your next question, and no, I have absolutely no idea what that other deal might be. Frankly, I'm skeptical of the story. My best guess is Michael was able to persuade Sato-san that the deal was too good for his company to pass on. That Seattle group is a perfect fit with SBI. We're offering a lot of money up front, cash he knows he cannot generate by his own commercialization efforts, and there's a fat revenue stream from continuing royalties and profit sharing built into the terms. His company will make a whole lot of money for a long time to come. Like I said, too good to walk away from."

"But the deal isn't done yet, is it? If it's so good, why wasn't it wrapped up soon after their meeting?"

Drawing a deep breath, Sam sighed out, "I just don't know. All I can do is blame the lawyers." He shrugged, sharing his frustration.

"I can tell this deal means a lot to you, too," Rock offered sympathetically.

"It really does. But unlike the quest for profits motivating Michael, I foresee huge benefits for society from producing products that will help a lot of people. If only I can get the two R&D groups together."

"A very noble goal."

Sam eased away, relaxing into the cushions. "There you have it. I'm sorry I can't give you any more information but I just don't know anything else. My views on what Michael is and isn't capable of are just that, my views. I may be right and I may be wrong. I'll leave it in your very capable hands to determine which it is. Now, unless there's something else, could we please get some lunch?"

Motioning, Rock called the patient waiter over and they proceeded to order.

Settling into a pleasant conversation, the men enjoyed each other's company while taking in the scenery and good food. Rock managed to work in his questions about Anna and Julie, each separately then asking about the possibility of them being a couple. Sam had heard the rumors but couldn't confirm their relationship.

Rock also explored whether Michael and Red were in Seattle. Sam was no help there either. He confessed to being generally out of the loop regarding the day-to-day negotiations, being called in only when discussions involved technology. However, Rock did find useful Sam's confirmation that Michael would have taken Red with him if he did go.

This moved Julie to the number one suspect for the mystery person lurking behind Anna's door. Rose would have a job to do tonight.

At last dessert arrived. Sam had ordered peach pie. It came warm with a generous scoop of vanilla ice cream. He dug in with unabashed joy. "I love peaches and these are great."

Rock paused from his hot cup of caffeine. "You know what peaches have in common with Cincinnati?"

Sam answered between bites, "No, I thought Georgia was the peach state. How does Ohio fit in?"

"I'm a font of trivia. Here's a piece I learned from my days growing up there. A guy by the name of Stephen Gerrard sold fruits and vegetables in Cincinnati at the beginning of the nineteen hundreds. An inventive and industrious gentleman, he saw opportunity in providing fresh produce across the country. He developed refrigerated railcars and shipped perishable products, including peaches, from coast to coast. His foresight helped make him a fortune. So, a century ago if you were enjoying this tasty dessert, you'd likely need to thank Mr. Gerrard for getting those fresh peaches all the way here from Georgia."

"I'll file that away in my memory for the next time I'm at a trivia night," he mumbled with his mouth full.

"Kinda sad for the guy, a real rags-to-riches-to-rags story. He became a millionaire then lost it all in the Great Depression. But he built a beautiful mansion during his better times that still stands today. If you like great architecture, you'll love this place. It looks like a castle with stone walls and stained-glass windows. It even has a couple of gargoyles on the roof. Inside there's beautiful woodwork including a pipe organ that's a piece of art in itself. The house and organ are both on the National Historic Register."

"Sounds like something I'd like to see. I get to Cincinnati now and then on business. Is the house open for tours?"

"No, but the owners are good friends. Let me know the next time you're going and I'll arrange a visit. I may join you. I haven't seen them in a while."

"I'd like that very much."

The last of the pie had evaporated from the plate and it was time for both men to get to their next meeting. With very satisfied bellies they said their goodbyes and went their separate ways.

# Chapter 19 – The Audience Arrives

Rock proceeded directly to SBI headquarters to pick up Del. He sat facing her in the back of the limo trying to shake the bad feeling in his gut. Turning off the 101, they headed into the hills overlooking the airport. They'd soon be at Alex's apartment.

He glanced at the time as they circled the garden island fronting the building. Just past three o'clock. Mid-afternoon was always the worst for Rock's jet lag, and after lunch and two beers his energy was flagging. He had to fight through it. The uncertainty of what they'd find provided the necessary boost of adrenalin.

"Well, we're here. Let's go say hi to Alex," he offered, trying his best to sound upbeat.

Del may have appreciated the attempt, but her anxious look told him she wasn't buying it. With his help she slid from the car.

They entered the lobby where she led the way to the elevator at the back. "He has this private lift to his apartment on the top floor. I have the codes for it and his security system. I watch his place when he travels," the proper lady added, her tone making it clear she didn't want Rock to misunderstand her relationship with her boss.

"Okay, we'll buzz him first to see if he answers. No sense giving the man a heart attack by popping in unannounced."

"I agree. Here's the intercom." Del pushed the buzzer.

No reply.

She tried again, holding the button longer.

Still nothing.

Rock cut off the protracted third try. "Time to go in. Please enter the code for the elevator."

She focused on the adjacent keypad. Her entry yielded access to the lift. Their stop at the top was barely perceivable when the doors opened effortlessly to the foyer.

Moving onto the tile, Rock halted to look about. "Everything seems normal. Is there an alarm system?"

"Yes, but it would be beeping if it were on. We can go in." She slid past him, calling, "Alex, are you here? It's Del and I have Mr. Stone with me."

She directed her introduction to the open space in front of them. The living room was brightly lit by sunlight streaming in through the east-facing wall of windows.

Hearing no reply, they moved toward the light. After a couple of steps, Rock gently tugged Del's arm. "Hold on a minute."

"Why, what's wrong?"

"Likely nothing, but let me take the lead." He'd not successfully concealed his concern, triggered by the faintest whiff of an odor.

She hung back, allowing him to venture in first.

Entering the room at a cautious pace, Rock studied the space to understand the layout of the rooms. The open floorplan permitted him to see across much of the apartment. A formal dining table positioned for a spectacular view filled the area beyond the living room. Further along, he spied a kitchen through a wide doorway. The table was neatly set and the pillows on the long couch were properly ordered.

Pointing down a hallway, Rock asked, "This way to the bedrooms? How many?"

"Yes, two. The master is at the far end."

"How about you wait here while I check out the rest of the apartment?"

With brows furrowed, Del hesitated before answering, "Okay."

Rock started down the corridor, his senses on high alert. "Alex, are you here? It's Rock and Del. We've come to check on you. Is everything all right?"

He strained to hear a reply. Only his footsteps on the hardwood broke the silence.

The guest bedroom was open. He gave it a passing glance. His focus was on the interior of the master suite.

The odor was growing more pronounced, intensifying with each step. Reaching the doorway at the end of the hall, Rock entered the chamber with a tentative stride. Everything was in its assigned place. The bed was neatly made. A collection of framed pictures filled the side tables.

Pausing, Rock called, "Alex?"

Receiving no answer, he hastened across the room. The bathroom door stood ajar. On arriving there, he halted to listen. Silence. Rock peered through the narrow gap. Nothing but a portion of the countertop was visible.

With a nudge, the barrier drifted open. His eyes focused immediately on the full tub. The blue flesh of Alex's corpse colored the surface.

Rock froze, surveying the scene. At first glance, everything appeared as it should be for an accidental drowning. Something troubled him, however, when he scanned the space more closely. Looking the place over a third time, Rock spied tiny inconsistencies that told a different story.

Alex had been murdered.

Del's scream shook the bedroom like an explosion, jolting Rock from his inspection. Whipping his head around, he discovered she had followed. He rescued her as she swooned.

The living room was no longer brightly lit. Even this early in the day, the sun had crept beyond the western hills and shadows enveloped the building on their march toward evening. Rock sat on the couch cradling Del in his arms.

She began to stir.

"Just sit still a bit longer, you'll be okay," he soothed.

Her eyes told she did not recognize where she was. "What happened?"

"You passed out. I've called for an ambulance. It will be here soon."

A horrified look appeared; lucidity had arrived. "Oh my God. He's dead!" Del buried her face in her hands, sobbing uncontrollably.

Holding her closer, Rock hushed, "I'm sorry. I wish you hadn't seen that."

Del leaned into the embrace.

After a minute of comforting, she eased herself away. He gently restrained her. "Lay back, you've had quite a shock."

"Thank you, but I'm fine," Del stuttered between sobs. Trying to stand, she stumbled and Rock caught her. She relented, crying quietly until the paramedics arrived.

The medics took their time checking her. Her blood pressure and heart rate were well outside of normal. With Rock's help, they convinced her to go to the hospital.

When she had gone, he turned his attention to the police waiting impatiently in the lobby. He had convinced the FBI to stop them from entering the apartment.

After his 911 call, Rock contacted Special Agent Tim Fuller of the FBI, an agent he'd gotten to know on a previous job. Rock suspected the FBI was assisting with the SBI insider trading investigation. While Tim wouldn't confirm it, the ease with which Rock succeeded in getting some attention convinced Rock he'd guessed right. Asserting that Alex's death might somehow be related to the investigation peeked the agent's interest. Telling Tim the death was a homicide convinced him to intervene.

The local police were not happy to cool their heels. By the time Agent Fuller arrived, the CSI unit had gathered with them in the building's lobby, adding more irritated bodies to the crowd. Rock successfully held everyone at bay, ensuring Tim entered the bathroom first.

"Thanks for coming," Rock welcomed when Tim stepped from the elevator.

Looking particularly unpleasant, the agent responded pointedly, "What makes you think this is a homicide? The sergeant caught me and he's pissed as hell at being held back. He claims this is a straight forward slip-fall accident and you're just wasting everyone's time. Tell me why he's wrong."

Rock turned toward the hallway, throwing over his shoulder, "I can't tell you, but I can show you. Come on, nobody has touched a thing. I made sure of that. See for yourself."

He led the agent to the bathroom doorway. "Stop here. Does anything look out of place?"

"There's a dead body in the tub. Did I get it right?" Tim snapped, clearly as edgy as the cops.

"Wrong. Two things. First, look at where the cane is. It's by the sink, not the tub."

"So he put it there and went to the tub. That's why he fell. Case closed."

"No, I know for a fact he never could have made it over there without the cane. I met with him earlier in the day and he could barely walk even with it. I'm sure the driver who brought him to the apartment from the airport two nights ago will confirm this. He's been dead since that night, I can see and smell that from here. You know I'm right."

The agent craned his neck. "Yep, he's been in there a while."

Tim focused narrowed eyes on Rock. "You said there are two things. What else?"

"Below the tub, what do you see?"

Pivoting his attention, Tim studied the space around the feet of the antique claw tub. "Nothing," he concluded, looking to Rock for help.

"Look more closely, that little gray pile by the closest right foot. Do you see that?"

"So the cleaning lady hasn't been here, is that what you're saying?"

"I'll bet everything that's cigarette ash. I checked with his assistant and she's positive he doesn't smoke. The killer left that behind. This is a professional hit, I doubt you're going to find a hint of anything else. I can only hope this clue gives you a lead. The man in the tub was a good guy and I'd hate to see his killer get away with murder."

Agent Fuller groaned. "I don't know. Seems pretty flimsy."

"It's not a lot, but it's enough to warrant handling the death as a possible homicide."

"Anybody else but you and I'd say you were full of shit." Tim drew a deep breath, taking a long look at the gray powder.

"Hey, it's getting ugly down there," Tim's partner called, entering the bedroom.

Wheeling around, Agent Fuller barked, "Joe, get the lab guys in here right away. I need pictures of everything. But first, have them bring a sample bag. There's something I need analyzed asap."

"Sure thing, Tim."

# Chapter 20 – A Bump in the Road

Michael and Red sat alone in the luxury of the corporate jet. Michael tipped himself a generous pour of forty-year-old single malt Scotch, the second in the hour since they took off from Seattle. Red had already finished his fourth beer.

Less than an hour remained until they landed in San Francisco. Up until then, Michael had been content sitting in silence scheming his next steps for the negotiations with Mr. Sato. Overall, he was happy with the way the last few days had gone. He had pleased Mr. Sato by hiring Rock to look into the insider trading matter. A calculated risk that was paying off nicely.

Mr. Sato had steadfastly resisted meeting with Michael at his facility in Seattle until last evening. The invitation to go there on such last-minute notice was a much-welcomed surprise. The meetings today went well and progress was being made, but Michael had to admit the finish line was still nowhere in sight. He pushed all this aside as just another example of how maddeningly slow negotiating with the Japanese can be. But he was feeling more confident than ever that they would eventually seal the deal. It would just take time. *Patience, Michael.* This was the mantra he kept repeating to himself since the start of the negotiations.

He roused himself to talk outstanding business with Red. A couple of matters required the privacy provided by forty-thousand-feet. "Are you sure that Stone guy got to see only the stuff we wanted him to? I'm still pissed by the two checks you found in the folder that idiot Gage pulled together for him."

"I looked through the paperwork twice. Aside from those checks you sent to Anna, everything else pointed squarely to the story you told Stone. I pulled those from the folder first

119

thing yesterday. He never saw them, I'm positive about that."

"I hope so, they could have been a problem. Not only that I'd given her two five-million-dollar checks around the time of the trades but then she was dumb enough to countersign them over to her Burrows bitch. What an idiot. And how the hell did Alex get those? I specifically told him to only dig through the corporate files. The guy was too damn thorough. I'm glad that problem has been solved. By the way, when do you think they'll find the body? I need to get going on hiring another CFO, this time someone less detail-oriented."

"Should be anytime now. If his secretary doesn't make it happen, the neighbors will soon be complaining about the stench. I'll make sure someone finds him tomorrow if I need to. Okay?"

"Make it happen."

The plane started its descent and Michael's cell phone jingled, alerting him to new messages. They were finally in range of a cell tower and he was back in contact with the electronic world.

"Looks like you can take that off your 'to do' list. I just got an urgent message from Nancy saying they found Alex's body. Shit! She also says they're investigating it as a murder. What the fuck? How'd you fuck this up?!" Michael intended his glare to burn a hole through Red.

"That's not possible. I made everything look like Alex fell. Let me see that." Red pulled the cell phone from Michael's hand and read the text. "God damn it, that fucking Stone guy has got everything stirred up. He's even involved the FBI. I can't tell what tipped him off but I'm positive it's nothing that will link this to me."

"You mean to *us*." Stabbing the air with an accusatory finger, Michael barked, "Get on it as soon as we land. I want to know every detail by tonight."

"Yes sir."

The phone sounded once more. "Now what?" Michael snarled. Finding a voice message alert, he growled, "I got a call. Looks like it's from Anna. What the hell could she want?"

He pressed the play button and listened. His face grew redder as the message rolled. Spearing the end button, Michael turned his ire on Red. "Those stupid bitches! Anna says Burrows is going off the deep end. She listened in on the questions Stone had for Anna. Burrows is talking about going to the SEC. Says this has gotten to be too much. Anna didn't sound too in control of herself either. Can't they keep their mouths shut. I expected ten million dollars would be enough to buy Burrows' silence. And Anna, she got so much more out of the deal. *God damn it!*" Michael screamed.

"You know we need to get rid of her, too. That Burrows bitch. I can make another accident happen. Just give me the go ahead and I can get it done tonight." Red had the gleam of a psychopath in his eyes.

Michael didn't respond. While Red's thrill of getting away with murder made him truly a master of his craft, this involved more than staging a perfect crime. "Seems too risky, so soon after Gage."

"Nobody will connect the two. It will be a totally different accident and she's not you're employee." Leaning in, the fire of desire burning in his stare, Red urged, "You know you gotta do it."

Coldly considering his options, Michael sat motionless until replying, "I know we do, but do it right this time. No screw ups. And if possible, leave some clues so if anyone starts digging it will look like Anna was involved. We'll hold that over her head to make sure she keeps her mouth shut. Any chance you can work that in?"

"I already have the plan in mind. Don't worry, Burrows won't be around by tomorrow and Anna will be sworn to silence."

"Excellent!"

Michael took a swig of the Scotch, draining the glass as the wheels of the jet screeched their arrival into SFO.

# Chapter 21 – A Rose with Dinner

Already into the evening when he arrived at his hotel, Rock had half-an-hour to freshen up and relax before Rose would get there. He was dog-tired and would have canceled had the dinner been with anyone else. A quick shower helped renew some of his strength. He threw on clothes and dropped into one of the sitting room chairs with fifteen minutes to spare. He was asleep in one.

The knock jerked Rock awake. "Coming," he replied automatically. Shaking his head, he struggled to clear his mind. "Coming, Rose," he called as the fog lifted. Extracting himself from the chair, Rock wiped a hand across his face while trudging toward the door. He swung the barrier away.

"I'm so sorry, you were sleeping. Do you want to cancel?" Rose's crestfallen expression showed the magnitude of her disappointment.

"I'm fine. You caught me taking a catnap. Come on in, give me five minutes and I'll be ready to go." Leaving her waiting in the doorway, he hurried to the bathroom.

Standing in front of the sink, the cold water streaming, Rock splashed his face several times. It didn't ease his tired body but it did perk him up. Staring into the mirror at his dripping-wet face, he flashed back to a pleasant childhood memory - his dad teaching him this trick to wake up when Rock was five. It was just the first of his dad's many practical lessons, a legacy more valuable than gold.

The soaking and thoughts of a quiet evening alone with Rose revived Rock. He toweled off then hustled back to the sitting room. "Ready to go?"

"Yes, lets," Rose answered cheerily.

Rock appreciated that John had anticipated his exhaustion and made the reservations in the hotel. Efficient and insightful as always, qualities that led Rock to hire him.

The luscious smells that greeted them when they walked through the dining room reminded Rock that he was hungry. Seated side by side at a corner table, they looked out onto the beautifully decorated space. Perfect for chatting while they ate.

The waitress arrived. "Can I get you a drink?"

"I'll have a diet Coke," Rose replied.

"And you, sir?"

Rock planned to keep the calories in check after his heavy lunch, but he needed a drink after the grueling day. "A glass of your house pinot grigio."

While the waitress slipped away, Rock swiveled his attention to Rose. "Sorry I was asleep when you arrived. It's been one hell of a day." He proceeded to give her the abbreviated version of the two interviews and then the discovery of Alex's body.

"You mean you think he was killed?" Rose gasped, excitement underlying her shocked reaction. "That's terrible. The poor man."

"Yes, it is. Definitely a professional hit. The FBI won't find anything more than those ashes. Pretty sloppy for a pro, I just hope it's enough to find the killer."

"I hate to break it to you but that's not much of a lead. Only maybe a million smokers in the city?"

"You're probably right, but sometimes longshots pay off. The chemical analysis might turn up something unique. But maybe as important as knowing who did it is that it was done at all. All my instincts say this is related to the job I'm working on. There are some big prizes at stake and likely some big secrets to protect." Rock couldn't tell her anything about the acquisition deal that was foremost in his mind.

"I don't know, coincidences happen all the time. Sorry, Rock, but I think your gut may be leading you wrong on this one."

"I hope so. Before this happened, I was thinking about giving you an assignment tonight. Now I'm afraid it's too risky to get you involved. At least not until I'm sure Alex's murder has nothing to do with my investigation."

Rose groaned. "Come on, you're just being overprotective. They aren't related. Admit it, there's nothing behind your concerns except your gut. I can handle myself, and I'll be extra careful. Let me do it. Please."

Rock wasn't sure if it was her logic or pleading that convinced him to reconsider. "Fine, you're hired, but only if you promise to be extremely cautious."

"Yay!" She clapped her hands gently in triumph. "What is it? Do I get to start tonight? Thank you, thank you, thank you!" she gushed, beyond thrilled.

"You'll start tonight. But before you get too excited," Rock knew that ship had long sailed, "I need you to understand it's likely going to be pretty boring. All I need you to do is sit outside Julie Burrows' apartment and see if Anna comes to visit. That's all. No pictures, no eavesdropping on any conversations, you keep your distance and watch. If Anna shows up, report back to me. And I don't want you there all night. When it looks like Julie has gone to bed, you go home whether or not Anna stopped by."

Rock could see this took some steam out of her zeal for the job.

"You're right, that does sound boring. But you need it done and I'm the one who can do it. When do I start?" she replied, appearing more stoic than enthusiastic.

"After dinner. We'll call your mom and tell her you'll be home late. I'll assure her it's an easy, safe job. Don't mention anything about the murder, she'd be worried sick until you get home."

"Perfect."

125

"Okay, now let's get you something to eat. I can't have your stomach growling while you're waiting for Anna to show."

Conversation throughout dinner was light and happy, and business didn't come up again until after the bill was paid. "Here's the address of Ms. Burrows' apartment. Stay in your car, keep your cell phone by your side, and leave at once if you have even one ounce of concern for your safety." Rock held back the slip. "Promise?"

"I promise."

# Chapter 22 – Prying Eyes

Already dark when she arrived, Rose found the perfect place to park in the shadows between two street lights. The one at the corner across from the building illuminated the comings and goings. She had a clear view to the front entrance.

As Rock had instructed, she stayed in the car, ready to get out of there if anything appeared out of the ordinary. "Don't take any chances," was his stern parting direction.

With little activity to entertain her, Rose's mind wandered. She fiddled with her cell phone until it flashed 'low battery'. Popping open the storage box, she extracted a charger cord. Caught up in the lid, she fumbled it to the floor.

Stretching below the dash, Rose groped the darkness for the wayward cable. A car rolled up in front of the building. With her focus directed below, she missed the opportunity to check out the lady who darted into the lobby. The glimpse, however, made Rose think she could have been Anna.

"Rock's going to kill me! One simple task and I screw it up."

Leaning over the steering wheel, she craned her neck to see to the windows for Ms. Burrows' apartment. A light popped on.

Rose needed to know who was in that room, but there was no way she could see from where she was sitting. Peering down the road, a plan came to mind. A sloping street intersected the one she had parked on, dead-ending at the building. If she moved up that hill, she might have an unobstructed line of sight into Julie's place. The curtains were open; she decided to try.

Exiting the car, she walked casually to the intersection, hugging the shadows. The view from the other side of the inclined street would be better. She scurried across and climbed the steep hill. At half the way up, she could see inside the apartment. The living room was empty.

She searched for a secluded place to observe without being seen. Positioning herself beneath a low-hanging pine, she settled in for the vigil. A gentle breeze made Rose's hair dance and the branches sway. The sweet scent of the evergreen filled the cool night bringing back scenes from her youth.

A child again, Rose was camping in the High Sierras with her mom and dad. She learned when she'd gotten older, after her dad passed, that her mom was the instigator for these escapes. While he loved the mountains, he always resisted leaving the city. 'Too much work' was the excuse. When her mom prevailed, as she frequently did, they'd drive to Yosemite for the weekend. Camping wasn't really her mom's thing but it was the only way she could get him away from the office. With no phones or computers within miles, the only thing he could do was relax with his little girl.

Rose laughed quietly to herself at a special memory from those times. Her dad had thought he'd outfoxed mom. Claiming they needed groceries, he packed everyone in the car and drove twenty miles to a lodge in the middle of nowhere. When the ladies came out with the supplies, they found him working from a pay phone attached to a lodgepole pine. His look was priceless. Her mom chewed him out, up one side and down the other. He never tried that again.

Movement in the apartment halted these reminiscences. Ms. Burrows had entered the lit room. Disappointed she hadn't found Anna, Rose was about to go back to the car when Julie turned and began talking. The unseen participant in this conversation was in an adjacent room.

While that space was darkened, Rose was in luck. Rock had given her night vision binoculars and the curtains were not drawn. Fishing the device from her purse, she fumbled with the controls. It came to life.

Under the prying eyes of the lenses, everything inside the room became clear with a greenish tint. A woman sat on a bed facing the room Julie occupied, turned away from the window. While Rose could not see her face, her build matched Anna's. "Look this way," she urged quietly into the night. The lady did not comply.

Julie switched off the living room light on her way to joining her companion on the mattress. The women shared an ardent kiss. Rose blushed. She was new to voyeurism. But she didn't look away, determined to see the visitor's face even if it meant being a Peeping Tom all night.

When they separated, the lady shuffled from the bed, disappearing into a bathroom.

"Damn!" Rose snapped, louder than she had intended.

While disappointed she hadn't confirmed Anna was there, Rose was relieved it was no longer uncomfortable to watch. Pressing the eyepieces to her face, she fixed a stare on the bathroom door anticipating the moment when the woman would return. With that look, Rose could finally leave.

Julie, however, didn't stick to the plan. Making it awkward again, she stood by the bed, stretched her back and tugged the belt of her housecoat. Disrobing with one smooth move, she tossed the covering to the floor then eased onto the edge of the mattress.

The sight of Julie wearing nothing but a smile caused Rose to flinch but she didn't put down the binoculars. She had a job to do. The plan remained the same. See the face; get out of there.

As the time passed, Rose's focus drifted to Julie waiting patiently for her guest to return. Then at the edge of her sight, something drew her attention. She pivoted the scope to the shadows.

On the far side of the room, a closet door inched open. Out crept a large man dressed in black. His face glowed green under the enhanced light.

Rose's heart raced.

Stalking closer, the intruder prowled toward Julie from behind. Her relaxed pose told she had no idea she was in danger.

When within reach, the man struck. His arms darted over Julie's head. A taut cord grabbed her by the neck, yanking her onto the bed. Julie's legs slashed air while she tugged at the binding.

Writhing and thrashing, she fought back. Flailing arms aimed balled fists over her shoulders. The glancing blows did nothing to diminish the ferocity of the assault.

With Julie's vigor ebbing, the bathroom door opened. The horror on Anna's face accompanied a scream Rose could only see. Anna dashed to Julie's aid.

Tying the noose, the man leapt from the bed and intercepted Anna. Holding her from behind, he restrained her while she shrieked at the sight of her lover struggling for life.

The end came with a few convulsive kicks. The murderer released his grip and Anna dove onto the bed. Cradling Julie's lifeless body, Anna shuddered while wailing.

Rose looked to the man. He was staring back. A beat later, he bolted from the room.

Fighting the urge to puke, Rose thrust a hand into a pocket. Extracting her phone, she stabbed the screen. Once, twice, three times - it remained black. The battery had died.

Panicking, she took off running. In two steps she was stumbling. Only snatching hold of a railing prevented her from tumbling to the bottom of the hill.

"Get a grip," she muttered. Heeding the advice, Rose steadied herself. Taking careful strides, she ran down the incline. At the corner she dashed across the intersection. The safety of her car was in sight.

Rose heard the attack before she saw it. Reaching the middle of the street, she turned her head in the direction of screeching tires. A dark sedan with no lights on shot from the building's underground parking. Accelerating, it took aim at her.

Looking away, Rose broke into a sprint. The bumper caught her on the hip. She heard a snap then felt excruciating pain. Airborne, everything went black.

While the vehicle sped off, Rose's limp body smashed through the window of a corner store.

# Chapter 23 – So Much Blood

"Come on, Terry, let's hit a club."

"It's midnight... three in the morning for my body clock. I got up at four today to catch my flight. I'd like to see how you'd be doing after two layovers and running around the city since noon. I'm beat."

"I told you to take the direct flight from BWI."

"You pay for it, Nicky, and I'll happily fly non-stop. You keep forgetting I only work part-time as an EMT. I had to pick up extra hours on the rescue squad to scrape together enough for the crappy connections I got."

"You should get a real job like I did."

"I'm not dropping out of Maryland with only a year to go. I worked my ass off to get in, I'm not giving up now."

"Then think of this as practice for your all-nighters. You pre-med guys pull a lot of those, right?"

"Yep, and I have to work harder than the other guy. I'm concerned that being twenty-six already makes me too old for many med schools. But even if I do get accepted, if I don't excel, I won't get the scholarships I need."

"I have every confidence you'll make it," Nicky encouraged.

"I'm amazed that I've come this far, but I have so much further to go. Still, not bad for a poor Black kid from inner-city Baltimore."

"Just don't forget your friends when you make it big."

"Never."

Terry Washington had arrived in San Francisco for a long weekend before his classes began at The University of Maryland. His studies always came first, but his Army buddy had talked him into coming out to relax. With his hectic last year about to start, this summer evening was dedicated to enjoying the quiet of the night with a friend on a walk home from dinner.

Their solitude was broken by hurried footsteps. A young lady appeared, darting across the street in front of them.

Terry saw everything. The sedan with no lights on blasting at full speed from the garage. The girl catching sight of it and dashing for the curb. When the car slammed her, she sailed into the air.

First the sound of metal on bone. Then shattering glass. All on top of the growl of the engine accelerating up the hill.

Before the silence of the night returned, the symphony of chaos began. Like the fortissimo first bar of Beethoven's Fifth, Terry yelled out, "Call nine-one-one!"

In a flash, Terry had crossed the street. At the girl's side within seconds, he discovered an expanding pool of blood. Every heartbeat mattered.

His Army medic training took over. He found the source. The cut was easy to spot, hard to control. It was bad. The window had torn a deep gash in her neck, slicing something major. Terry guessed the carotid. Nicked but not severed or she'd be dead already.

Terry worked franticly to stem the flow. The blood loss alone was becoming life threatening. He had no way of telling what else might require life-saving attention.

"Help's on the way," he comforted, the sound of the approaching sirens growing louder.

A minute later a paramedic joined Terry kneeling beside Rose. "What do we have?" the man yelled over the blaring security siren.

It had been howling since Terry arrived at Rose's side. With effort, the rescuers screamed questions and answers to each other. Terry remained unfazed. This was nothing compared to performing triage with shells exploding all around.

Motioning with his head, Terry shouted, "The carotid is cut. Deep wound under my hand. Can't let go to show you."

"Okay, hold on, the gurney is here. Think you can keep the pressure on while we move her?"

"Yes. We've got to go! Now!" Terry's answer was emphatic but not panicked.

Two paramedics and Terry hoisted Rose onto the stretcher, coordinating their movements like they'd worked together for years. Wheeling her to the van, the medic gave Terry a questioning look. "Are you with her?"

"No. Just got into town. Saw her get hit and reacted."

"Can you come along? We could use an extra pair of hands." It wasn't that they could use them, they needed them.

Terry yelled to his buddy being held back with the rest of the crowd by the police. "I'm going with! Be home as soon as I can."

The ride to the hospital was a short trip that seemed to take an eternity. Terry held tight to the wound, struggling to keep every drop he could in Rose's body. Her blood-smeared face was ghostly white. The paramedics were doing everything they could and more. Even with that, her vital signs were barely in the range of the living. Terry expected everything to go to shit any second.

A team of doctors and nurses met the ambulance at the entrance to the emergency room. They pounced into action the moment the wheels stopped rolling. A minute later, Terry stood alone watching the swarm surrounding Rose disappear through the ER doors.

He looked down at his bloody hands, then to the shirt and pants and shoes covered in the tacky essence that once flowed through Rose's body. He said a heartfelt prayer for the fragile young woman. Only God could save her now.

# Chapter 24 – More Work to Do

Michael sat alone in the study of his mansion on Nob Hill, the location in the heart of San Francisco where he always wanted to be. Once he'd amassed enough wealth, he bought a historic mansion and proceeded to totally gut it. He violated every rule and law associated with owning a home on the National Register of Historic Places, but he didn't care. The Historical Society was apoplectic over the wanton destruction of this city treasure, but the fines were paid and the bribes were made, and two years later Michael had the grand house he wanted and everyone else hated.

Tapping fingers nervously on the desktop, he glanced yet again to his cell phone. Only two people had the number - Anna and Red. He expected calls from both. After midnight, the phone rang. The screen registered 'blocked number'. That would be Red calling from his burner phone.

"Talk to me," Michael snapped, his impatience showing.

"There's one less carpet muncher in this world," Red quipped.

"Any problems?"

Silence answered.

"Well?"

"Nothing I couldn't handle."

"What'd you do, god damn it?" Michael wouldn't stand for another screw up. Not after the investigation into Alex's death.

"I did as you said. I made it look like an accident and we have something on Anna."

"How?"

"Everyone will think the dike died in some perverted sex romp. You know, the folks that like to be choked while they get off. SFPD gets a handful of these cases every year. An overly-horny couple ties a choke-knot too tight and someone buys the farm. It will look exactly like that. They'll investigate for an hour or two then let it drop, just some pervs who messed up."

"But they'll go to Anna. She'll make them keep digging. Then what?"

"She'll say the bitch deserved what she got for cheating on her. I made sure she'd say that when I made her watch Burrows die."

"You what?!"

"Relax. I told her she had to keep quiet about everything or she'd be the prime suspect. She couldn't deny she was there. If she points a finger at me, I tell the cops she's nuts. She killed her partner and is looking for some way out. They won't have anything but her word against mine. I staged it so all the evidence points to her. Trust me, she will be a clam after tonight."

"You had her watch Julie die?! Anna's going to go nuts and we'll both be screwed!"

"You worry like an old lady. I've managed far worse before and I'm still here."

Michael shook his head in disbelief. "Red, you're a fucking idiot."

The tension in his voice unmistakable, Red snarled, "Do you want me to lean on her?"

"No, stay away! I'll figure out how to deal with Anna."

"Whatever," Red huffed.

"Is that everything?" Michael barked.

A pause preceded, "There's something else. I think someone saw me do it." Hearing Michael's groan, he shot back, "I took care of it."

"Holy shit, what are you saying?!"

"The bitch was dead and I looked out the window. The lights were off but some young chick was standing up the street looking in at me like she'd seen it. Probably some degenerate who gets off watching folks do it. This city is full of wackos. I jumped in the car and got lucky when she was crossing the street as I came out of the garage. Nailed her good. Saw her fly through a store window."

"What if she talks?"

"The next time she does, it will be to an angel."

"You had a company car. There had to be security cameras. They caught it all. We're fucked!" Michael's shrill voice boomed into the phone.

"You're *worse* than an old lady," Red muttered. "The company cars look like thousands of other sedans in this city. I disabled the tracking device. It will show up in the system as never having left my house tonight. I have a chop shop in Oakland that will have the car in the junk yard by morning when I'll report it stolen. That will be the end of that.

"As for cameras, there was only one to worry about at the entrance to the garage and I knocked it out before I went in. They'll have some grainy footage of a car hitting a girl from the lobby camera and maybe one or two from the local shops, but everything will be too crude to get any leads. I had to dart out when I saw the chick, but I circled back while everyone was distracted with the mess out front. I made fast work of staging the bedroom to look like what I told you. In and out, and here I am."

"Was Anna there when you got back?"

"No. I'm sure she was long gone, probably left right after I did. Like I said, you have nothing to worry about with her. She's too concerned about saving her own hide to say a thing."

Michael considered Red a Neanderthal when it came to understanding human nature. The cretin knew how to take a life but didn't know much about the thoughts of the living. And Michael knew Anna. "You're wrong. I know you're wrong. I'm telling you, we're fucked!"

Red replied coolly, "I disagree, but do you want me to take care of her too? She can't be hard to track down."

Michael couldn't believe his ears. In Red's warped mind this was just more work to do, nothing more. Straining so hard his voice cracked, Michael screamed, "No you fucking moron, I've had enough of your screw ups! Just finish cleaning up the god-damn mess you made. *I'll handle her!*"

He stabbed the end button then hammered the phone onto the desk. Bolting from his chair, he dashed from the study to barrel along the hallway at a blistering pace. While crossing the grand entry, he caught sight of Lily staring down from the balcony.

"Get back in your room, bitch! This doesn't concern you," he yelled before disappearing through the door leading to the garage, slamming it behind him.

Once the echo had answered, the house fell deathly quiet.

# Chapter 25 – The Vigil Begins

Rock distracted himself after his dinner with Rose by reviewing the SBI flash drive, a mindless task to burn time until she called. He kept checking his watch between each file, as impatient as a parent waiting for a child late for curfew.

Even after this second look, the documents supported Michael's story. Everything but two random checks. Rock hadn't recalled seeing those when he reviewed the paper folder. They were curious, both in size – five million each – and transaction history - they were drawn from Michael's personal account, not a corporate one. While both checks were made out by Michael to Anna, she had signed them over to Julie. On the later check Anna had written the notation 'for services rendered' on the memo line. Rock made a mental note to follow up, but on this night, he was too preoccupied to do anything more.

His cell phone rang. He dove for it. Seeing the number was Lily's, Rock had mixed feelings - he wasn't in a mood to chat.

"Hello, Lily."

Before he could say any more, she cut him off. "Rock, I'm really scared," she blurted out, her voice quivering.

"What happened?" She had his undivided attention.

"I was in my bedroom thinking about all the things I still needed to handle when I heard Michael on the phone. He was in the study yelling his head off. This went on for a couple minutes and he kept getting louder and louder. Finally, I went out in the hall to see what was going on. I don't know who he was talking with and I couldn't hear what he was saying, except at the very end when he shouted, 'I'll handle her!' A second later he burst out of the study. He saw me, spewed some obscenities and then he was gone."

"How long ago was this?"

"About five minutes."

"Are you alone now?"

"I heard him leave in his old pickup truck."

"You're sure he's gone?"

"Positive. I've never seen him so mad." She lowered her voice. "You don't think he found out about the other night, do you?"

"You need to get out of there right now!"

"I know. But where can I go? I can't stay with you and I'm too afraid to go to a hotel all alone. What do I do?"

It took only a second for Rock to have a plan. "I'm sending the hotel limo to get you. You're at your place on Nob Hill, right?"

"Yes."

"It will be there in ten minutes. Grab only what you need for tonight, we can buy whatever else you will need tomorrow. I'm calling a friend of mine. You can stay with her a couple of nights until we make other arrangements."

"I hate to impose on anyone."

"I'm sure she'll be happy to help. It's just her and her daughter so she has plenty of room. You'll not be in their way at all."

"All right, if you think she won't mind."

"The driver will have her address. I'll call you back as soon as it's arranged. Now get going, I don't want you to stay there a minute longer than you must. Bye."

Rock didn't wait for a reply. Hanging up, he grabbed the room phone and dialed the front desk. Once the limo had been ordered he was on his cell phone to Rose's mom.

"Hi Hazel, this is Rock. I'm sorry to call so late but I need to ask a very large favor. I have a friend, a woman, who needs a place to stay for a few nights. She's having marital problems - very big marital problems - and she must get out of her place right away. Tonight."

Hazel finally had an opening to reply. "Yes, yes, Rock, that's no problem at all. I'll fix up the guest room. How soon can I expect her?"

Rock heard the same sweet caring voice he'd known for so many years. "You're an angel to help on such short notice. She'll be there in about a half hour. I'm sure she'll tell you more when she gets there, but I gotta go now, I need to call her back and tell her it's all arranged." Glad to have this decided, he remembered his other concern. "Is Rose home yet?"

"No, she isn't. She said she'd be late, but I expect her any time now," Hazel answered without a hint of worry. "Let me know if there is anything else you need."

"Thanks so much."

He hit the redial button for Lily.

She answered on the first ring.

"Everything is set. The limo will be there in less than five and the driver knows where to take you. I talked with the lady who you'll be staying with. She's happy to help. Call me when you get to her house. Oh, by the way, her name is Hazel and her daughter is Rose. You'll love being with them both."

"All right. Thanks."

When the line went silent, Rock sat down in a chair, relieved Lily would soon be out of harm's way. His thoughts turned to all the things to be done. The complexity of his relationship with Michael limited his options for involvement, but he didn't care about the risks, Rock would do everything it took to ensure Lily's safety.

Deep in thought, his phone rang. Rock didn't recognize the number. Assuming it was the limo driver with a question, he answered, "Robert Stone. What's up?"

"Mr. Stone, this is Officer Maloy of the San Francisco Police Department. I understand you're an acquaintance of Rose Chow. Is that correct?"

"Yes," Rock replied, clutching the arm of the chair. The tone of the officer's voice was unmistakable. "Is Rose okay?"

A long pause followed. "No, she's not. That's the reason for my call."

Rock's pulse quickened. Taking a deep breath, he forced out the questions he didn't want to know the answers to. "What happened? Where is she?"

"I want you to know we've been trying to reach her family. We'll continue our efforts, but we found your contact info in Ms. Chow's belongings. Could I ask for your help in tracking down a family member?"

"Of course," Rock replied, his mouth as dry as the desert. "That would be her mother, Hazel Chow."

"She's not answering her phone. We need to tell her that her daughter was the victim of a hit skip accident tonight."

Slumping into his chair, Rock swallowed hard before asking, "How is she?"

"For personal privacy reasons I cannot discuss her condition with you." The officer hesitated, then in a sympathetic voice he added, "Please don't delay in notifying her mother. Ms. Chow is in Mercy General near Fisherman's Wharf."

There was no use asking for more, the officer had shared all he legally could. "Thank you. I'll see what I can do."

Dropping the phone, Rock bent over, head in hands. Guilt overwhelmed him. If he hadn't given Rose the job, none of this would have happened. How could he make it up to her? Would he have the chance to? That thought was more than Rock could bear. A tear rolled down his cheek, then another. But those were the only ones he'd allow.

Straightening up, Rock dialed Hazel's number. When the answering machine picked up, he hung up. He couldn't leave this message. He called Lily.

"Hello -"

Rock interrupted before she could say another word. "How close are you to Hazel's house?" The question came out as a command.

"I'll ask the driver," she answered, her confusion apparent. A muffled exchange was followed by, "He says less than five minutes. What's wrong?"

Rock told her about the job he'd asked Rose to do, then about the call from the police. "They haven't been able to reach Hazel. I tried just now and I couldn't either. I don't know how I can ask you to do this, but you must tell her that Rose is in the hospital. She needs to get there right away. I'll meet her in the emergency room."

"She'll need help. I'll make sure she gets there."

Rock's relief at hearing Lily would be coming with Hazel came through in his voice. "I cannot thank you enough. Now, can you please hand your phone to the limo driver, I need to talk with him."

Rock was the first to arrive at the ER. The smell of bleach and alcohol assaulted his nose the moment he walked through the doors. Rushing to the reception, the nurse assured him a doctor would speak with him as soon as any news became available. Until then, he'd have to take a seat and wait.

Turning from the desk, Rock spied Lily helping Hazel through the entrance. Tears flowed freely down Hazel's cheeks. She looked as though she would collapse without Lily's support.

Rushing to Hazel's side, he practically carried her to the nearest chair. She dropped into her seat sobbing, bent and broken.

Rock focused on Lily's red damp eyes. "Thank you for getting her here."

"Of course," she replied, her voice quivering.

Easing into the space beside Hazel, Rock wrapped an arm around her, giving her a tender hug. He hushed, "They haven't told me anything yet. A doctor will be out shortly, then we'll find out more."

Hazel tilted her head against his. "I don't know what I'll do without her." Tears streamed down her cheeks as she buried her face into his chest. A tear fell from Rock's nose onto her head. He looked to Lily. She joined in their hug, adding her tears to theirs.

When a grim-looking doctor approached, Rock eased himself away from Hazel. Bracing for the worst, he asked, "Do you have any news about Rose Chow?"

"Good evening. I'm Doctor Singh. Is this Rose's mother?"

Hazel stared at the doctor but words wouldn't come.

"Yes," Rock answered for her.

"Thank you. Unfortunately, I don't have much to tell you. I understand the police have already informed you that Rose was struck by a car this evening. In addition to the trauma she received by being hit, she was thrown through a shop window. She sustained multiple lacerations. One cut in particular is life threatening."

Rock felt Hazel slump. Her face turned an even paler shade of white; her distracted gaze wandered to the ceiling. Rock pulled her close, holding her securely.

The doctor paused, waiting patiently until Hazel recovered her focus. "As I said, Rose's injuries are life threatening but she is alive and being operated on as we speak. I will not speculate on what they might find, but her condition is considered critical and not yet stable. I wish I had more encouraging news."

"When will we know more, doctor?" Rock asked for the stunned trio.

"I'm afraid it will be several hours. Until then, all you can do is wait and pray." Nodding in the direction of a disheveled young man sitting at the far end of the room, the doctor added, "I want you to know that if it hadn't been for the gentleman over there, I would be giving you worse news now. She's alive only because of his quick action. If that young lady has a guardian angel, he is surely it."

Without saying a word, Hazel wobbled to her feet and walked on trembling legs to Terry. He looked up with eyes barely open, exhaustion written on every aspect of his body. Bending down, Hazel wrapped him in a mother's hug. Through her soft sobs, she moaned, "Thank you for saving my baby."

# Chapter 26 – A Break

Rock and Lily followed Hazel, hanging back while she and Terry shared their moment. When she stood, Rock directed a look to Lily, his eyes motioning towards seats away from Terry.

"Hazel, let's sit closer to the reception desk so we can see the doctor when he comes back."

Secured in Lily's arms, Hazel shuffled toward the seat she had vacated. Once the ladies were beyond hearing range, Rock settled into the chair beside Terry. "I'm Robert Stone, a friend of the family. Your name is?"

The young man stared vacantly, the wheels in his brain turning slowly. Blinking hard, he replied with effort, "Terry. Terry Washington."

"Please, call me Rock. I want to thank you for everything. We can never repay you for all you've done."

Terry labored through his exhaustion. "I'm just glad I was there. I did what I could." He bowed his head, releasing a prolonged sigh. "Sorry I couldn't do more."

"According to the doctor, you kept her alive. That's all that matters."

Too tired to raise his head, he shrugged while staring at the floor.

Rock took the opportunity to look him over. Scanning the man from top to bottom, he noticed his clean set of scrubs. There was little else to see until his gaze reached the heavily soiled shoes. Rock shivered.

"Do you work here at the hospital?"

"Huh?"

Rock motioned to his shirt.

Glancing down, understanding crept in. "Oh… No. I just got into town today. I'm visiting with an Army buddy. The hospital gave me these, well...." His voice tapered off, leaving the sentence fall.

"She was lucky to have you close by. Did you see it happen?"

Terry took a couple deep breaths, the last one ending with an extended moan. Replaying the event, he laid out the details with analytical deliberation. "Yes, I saw it. A man in a black sedan came peeling out of the garage from across the street. The car didn't have its lights on. She saw it and sprinted toward the sidewalk, but she couldn't get out of the way. It caught her with the right front bumper. She was thrown about fifteen feet before crashing through a window." He looked to Rock. "I got to her as fast as I could."

"Did you see the driver?"

"No, everything happened so fast. I'm certain it was a guy driving, but that's about it. The lighting was low and he was by in an instant. Maybe my buddy got a better look." He paused, hesitating before saying, "I think the guy *tried* to hit her."

Rock didn't express any surprise when he asked, "Why do you say that?"

"He could have missed. Instead, he turned toward her."

"Thank you, that's very helpful. One more question. Can you tell me any more about the car?"

"It was a Ford Focus. I'm certain about that."

Across Terry's shoulder, Rock spied Agent Fuller coming through the ER doors. Motioning, he called, "Over here, Tim."

The agent quickened his pace and dropped into a chair across from the men. "I hurried here as fast as I could. Any word?"

"Alive and in the OR, that's it." Rock's look told Tim everything else he needed to know.

He had called Tim on the way to the hospital. While he couldn't spin this into official FBI business, Rock was hoping Tim would pull some strings with SFPD for more information on what had happened. He hadn't yet told him about the possible connection with Ms. Burrows and, by proxy, SBI.

Tim flipped an iPad out of its case. "I was able to get the security camera footage from the lobby of the apartment and the shop where Rose landed. Do you want to see it? It's pretty graphic."

Rock grimaced. "No, but I need to."

Ready to fire up the iPad, Tim discretely aimed a questioning look in Terry's direction.

Nodding Terry's way, Rock replied, "Tim, this is Terry Washington. He was there and helped the paramedics save Rose. It's okay, he can see it if he wants to."

Terry slid to sit straighter in his chair. "Sure," he sighed, "I might see something to help."

Moving to sit beside Rock, Tim cued the first video then held the screen so they all could watch. "Here's the footage from the lobby of the apartment. You can see the intersection through the front windows."

Rose appeared, racing down the hill. Terry and his buddy came into view across the street, walking in Rose's direction.

"That's me and Nicky," Terry offered, pointing to the screen.

A car appeared when Rose began crossing the road, emerging from the building's garage. Each man held his breath while watching the grainy video of the dark sedan. It accelerated across the street then swerved, catching Rose while she dashed for the curb. She disappeared from view when the impact flung her into the air. A few seconds more and the car was gone."

Rock forced himself to focus. He noticed everything, including Terry running at full speed the moment Rose was struck.

With a tap, Tim turned the iPad black. Rock pivoted to him. "You say there's another video?"

"Yep. Taken from through the store window."

Tim cued that tape. Rose entered the shot, running down the hill. Terry and his buddy couldn't be seen, they were blocked from view by the building across the street. The exit from the apartment garage, however, was visible.

Rose leapt into the street and darted across the crosswalk. The sedan exited the garage and accelerated. From this angle, it was even more apparent that the driver had veered to hit her. She disappeared from view when she went airborne, reappearing as she crashed sideways through the plate-glass window.

Terry came into sight, sprinting toward the camera. Within seconds, he hurdled the frame of the shattered window to land beside Rose's motionless body. A moment later he began applying the life-saving pressure.

The device went dark. "There's nothing more to see," Tim announced.

Rock's muscles had tensed tighter and tighter as the video shared its secrets. He held his stare on the screen a beat then turned to Terry. "Again, thank you," he offered, eyes moist.

Tim broke the ensuing silence. "Well, that's all we have. It's clear the guy wanted to hit her, but there are no shots of his face and I can't make out any license plate. The only lead we have is the make of the car."

Frowning, Rock asked, "You don't have video from the garage?"

"There isn't any."

"Every apartment these days records parking access. This one didn't?"

"They have a garage camera but it wasn't working. The cable had been cut earlier in the evening." Sharing an expression that told he too thought this strange, he groaned, "I don't get it."

"I may have an idea about that." Rock received the surprised look he expected.

"You do?"

"Yes. Rose was there to watch Julie Burrows' apartment. She's the analyst who's an expert on SBI stock." Rock allowed the significance of this information to sink in.

"You think this is related to that Gage guy's death, don't you?"

"It more than crossed my mind."

Tim gave a low whistle. "Well, it may be, but there's no hard evidence here to support that. Sorry, Rock, we've got nothing."

"Maybe so, but it might be worthwhile to watch the building for a couple days. It's possible that car will show up again." Rock was grasping at straws - the sedan was likely already on a scrap heap somewhere - but there might be more to learn by the FBI keeping an eye on the place.

"Seems like a long shot, but since we don't have any other leads, I'll see if I can get someone there tonight. Okay?"

"Thanks."

"Speaking of the Gage investigation, we got the analysis back on that gray powder. You were right, it is cigarette ash. Pretty curious, though. The results came back showing very high levels of arsenic."

"Does that narrow down the list of suspects?"

"It tells us the person wasn't smoking a domestic brand. Anything with that high an arsenic content doesn't get sold in the US. The lab guys checked the databases and found the only cigarettes known to have those levels are Turkish blends."

Rock's voice boomed in the quiet of the ER, "I know who did it!"

Tim's eyes narrowed. "You do?"

"Red McGregor, the head of SBI's security, smokes a Turkish blend. He told me just the other day he gets it imported specially from Istanbul. He has a violent past. I'm sure he's involved in both of these crimes."

Tim scoffed. "You know that's not enough for me to bring the guy in for questioning let alone arrest him. So he smokes foreign cigs. So what? That's what any judge and jury would say."

"But the circumstances, can't you make a case for probable cause to at least have him followed? It's possible you'll learn something from that."

"Sorry, Rock. No judge would buy it."

Rock was stymied. Poised to press harder, he halted when he noticed that Lily had joined them.

"I'm sorry to interrupt," she responded to his attention. "Hazel went to the bathroom and I thought I'd come see how you are doing."

"That's all right," Rock assured wearily. "We've been reviewing surveillance videos. Lily, this is FBI Special Agent Tim Fuller. Tim, this is Mrs. Schowalter."

Because of Tim's involvement with the SBI investigation, Rock had given him a heads up about Lily. He didn't want Tim surprised by the CEO's wife being at the hospital. But Rock only provided the background of her marital situation in the most general terms. He shared nothing about their previous night's encounter.

"It's very nice to meet you, Mrs. Schowalter."

"You, too, Agent Fuller. Please, call me Lily."

"And you can call me Tim," he answered politely. "As Rock said, we've been reviewing videos from around the building where Rose was hit."

"Any luck with who did it?"

Wagging his head, Tim answered, "No. The only thing we know for sure is some guy intentionally hit her. Slammed his Ford Focus into her."

Lily's eyes grew big. "What color was it?"

"Black. Why?"

"That's the same car they use in SBI's fleet. Half of the ones you see in the city are owned by the company."

Rock jumped on his opening. "There's your probable cause case, Tim. The guy not only gets his smokes from Turkey but he has access to the SBI corporate fleet. We have eye witnesses who swear the driver was a male and the car came from the building where the expert on SBI stock lives. If you can't get a warrant to tail the guy with that, then nothing will."

Tim pursed his lips. "I don't know. Maybe we can get a judge on board with following him for a couple days, but I'm not going to risk pissing some judge off by waking her for this tonight. If she does say yes, I'll have the warrant at seven and my guys will be watching Red by eight. That's the best I can do."

"All right. Thanks." Rock was hoping for something immediately but Tim was right, this wasn't a slam dunk so why make getting it any harder.

"Thank me when I have it. Now I'd better be going, I've got a lot to do. I'll give you a call in the morning." Tim was on his feet when he turned back to Rock. In a sympathetic voice, he encouraged, "She's in good hands here, don't give up hope."

"I'll try," Rock replied grimly. But guilt and despair left little room in his heart for hope.

# Chapter 27 – He Who Hesitates

Michael looked at his watch – one-thirty. He'd driven his old pickup truck around the city for more than an hour, taking the time to think.

'He who hesitates is lost.' He'd learned this adage as a teen and it had served him well for these many years. He had come to a decision – it was time to act. Michael would not lose now, not with everything he wanted so close within reach that he could taste it.

He had jumped into the pickup for two very specific reasons. First, the old heap had no electronics, not even the radio worked. No devices in the vehicle was very important for his plan. He could have nothing with him that might record his movements.

His cell phones had stayed at the house for this same reason. They would leave a trace through the cell towers they pinged, betraying the travels he wanted to remain unknown. But Michael felt naked without a phone. Even worse, now that the plan was coming together, he needed to make a call. Gathering his bearings, he realized his wanderings through the slumbering city had brought him close to the SBI offices.

The late-night security guard snapped to attention when he realized the beat-up pickup was driven by his boss' boss' boss' boss. There might even have been a few more levels between him and the CEO, he didn't rightly know. What he did know was Michael Schowalter was flashing his ID, impatient to enter the garage. The gate flipped up and the truck sped down the ramp out of sight.

Once in his office, Michael's first move was to pour a full glass of Scotch. He drained half in one gulp, set the tumbler down and topped it off. He was ready to make the call. Dropping into his desk chair, he dialed the number for the

153

one person who could provide the last bits of information he needed to pull off his scheme.

Michael had planted a mole in Anna's staff, one not even Red knew about. The phone rang - once, twice, three times - on the fourth she picked up. The voice on the other end of the line grunted, "Hello?"

"Jill, Michael here." He had been banging Anna's personal assistant for years. They'd been very discrete, and he managed to string her along on the misguided belief that she could be the next Mrs. Schowalter. She fed him details regarding Anna's activities. He'd been careful to make sure she never had any inkling as to what he was doing. For Jill's part, she happily shared what she considered innocuous scheduling information with her lover. Tonight, that info would be far from harmless.

"Sorry to wake you, but I was expecting to hear from Anna and she hasn't called. She's not answering my texts. I figured I'd check with you to see if everything was alright. While I have you, can you schedule time for me to meet with her first thing in the morning." Michael was throwing out a lot of threads to see what Jill might volunteer in return.

"Oh, sure. No problem," she answered wearily, her tone hinting at her relief that this wasn't a booty call. "Frankly, I'm worried about her. She had a terrible evening. She came back to the estate about an hour ago, I think, at least that's when she got me awake. She was all upset. Wouldn't tell me what had happened but I've never seen her so distraught. She ordered me to schedule a meeting with the investigator you hired, that Mr. Stone guy, for the first thing in the morning. She wouldn't leave me until I'd left a message with his secretary to set it up for eight."

"Is he coming there?" Michael asked casually, finding it difficult to keep concern from showing in his tone.

"No, she's meeting him at his hotel."

This was gold, exactly what he needed. It also fortified his resolve to go through with his plan. Anna had cracked, just as he'd thought she would. He had no time to waste. If she met with Rock, all would be lost.

"Is she still at the estate?"

"Yes. I know because I got her the sleeping pill she wanted and put her to bed."

"Did she say when she was heading to the city? I hope her driver or you will take her. She sounds way too upset to be alone." Michael said this with every hope the answer would be in the negative.

"I told her I'd take her but she insisted on driving herself. Said she needed the alone time to think."

"I hope she's careful. Those roads can be tricky in the dark."

"She isn't leaving until seven. It will be daylight by then."

"If she needs me to do anything, have her call."

"Okay, I will," Jill promised halfheartedly, a not-so-subtle signal she wanted to end the call.

"Thanks, babe." Michael had to throw her a bone, make her think she was still something special. "Get some rest."

"I will."

Michael hung up, satisfied with how clever he had been. While Jill was none the wiser, he now knew for certain that Anna planned to spill everything to Rock. He'd gotten lucky when she decided to go alone. That was critical. Knowing she wouldn't be leaving until seven gave him the luxury of catching a few hours of sleep.

After setting the alarm for five o'clock, Michael rolled onto the couch. Soon he was in a deep sleep, confident that within twenty-four hours everything would be back on track.

Michael jumped up when the clock buzzed, eager to solve his last problem. He needed to be in place by seven and he had some distance to cover. A quick stint in his private bathroom, a fresh change of clothes, and he was on his way.

Little traffic hindered him at that time of day. The tires of the truck hummed across the steel-grated surface of the Golden Gate Bridge. A few minutes later he was exiting the 101 Freeway onto the back roads leading to Anna's country estate. Michael drove relaxed, confident in the decision to kill Anna, his only option to solve the risk she posed. He wasn't going to lose that deal. Her life was a price he was willing to pay.

He had a foolproof plan. Michael expected to be a suspect in Anna's murder, he had no doubts about that, but he was being extremely careful. The scheme would leave no trail and no evidence that he had been anywhere near her when she was killed.

Michael had taken the necessary precaution of establishing an unbreakable alibi. He'd called one of his Russian whores and arranged for her to say he had been at her place the whole morning. It cost him a lot of money, enough that the hooker might permanently get off her back. But Michael knew sluts like her usually have an expensive drug habit. She'd likely be back in the business in no time, if she didn't kill herself overindulging on the windfall. He didn't care what happened to her, he only needed her to tell the lie and stick to it. Michael had no doubt she would never crack. She was Russian, after all, and those bitches know how to keep their mouths shut - no matter what.

The last detail was the gun. This was an easy decision. Only one would do, the .270 Winchester rifle from his youth in Pennsylvania. Michael had killed a lot of Bambi's with that gun. He was comfortable with it, it was deadly accurate, and most importantly it was untraceable. It had been handed down from his father and had never been registered.

He always kept it in a blanket behind the seat of the truck, the second reason he'd taken the pickup. This is where the gun had always been when he was a teen, and this is where it always stayed. Once a year Michael maintained it, cleaning and sighting-it-in away from prying eyes in the privacy of an open field on Anna's estate.

As he drove the country road with the hills and trees on both sides, it took Michael back to the fall days when he was in high school. The Pennsylvania schools treated the first day of deer season as a holiday. The hills and forests he had driven through in the state game lands weren't so different from these coastal California hills, if he looked past the giant redwoods and sequoias.

Michael pulled his thoughts back to the plan. He had a good idea about where he needed to be for the kill. A side road leading into the hills looked across a shallow valley to the entrance for the estate. From there it would be a shot of about two hundred yards, no distance at all with the precision scope. Low shrubs and grass covered the ridge, enough to conceal the pickup from traffic on the main road while allowing an unobstructed view to the gate.

He could control all the details for the plan except one - the weather. The crescent moon shone brightly in the clear skies of the dying night, but over the hills the weather could be completely different. Many a times Michael had driven that way on a clear day only to be surrounded by mist on the other side. He didn't need blue sky but he did need to see the two hundred yards.

The truck climbed the slope. Approaching the top, Michael began to worry. The coastal fog hung on the crest of the hill reflecting the dim predawn light.

Crossing the peak, he plunged into a thick haze. He turned on the truck's fog lights, slowing to a crawl while descending toward the ocean. Michael's heart sank. He couldn't see to take the shot in this soup.

He continued on, maneuvering the switchbacks leading down the steepest stretch of road. The fog thinned the lower he went. By the time he passed the gate to the estate, it hung as a hazy sheen over the landscape. While the sun had risen, only the white glow all around told him that it had. Now that the visibility would be good enough, Michael welcomed the additional cover the fog provided.

He drove along the country road for another half mile then turned onto the side road. Pulling to the berm, he slowed the truck to a crawl while straining his eyes to find the gate between shrubs. With fifteen minutes until Anna would come through the exit, he needed to set up in a hurry.

At last, Michael found the perfect spot. He stopped and cut the engine. Grabbing the crank for the window, he wound it down. The damp air rolled inside the cab, chilling his legs.

The gun rested behind the seat bundled in a blanket. Reaching back, Michael carefully fished it out. With steady hands, he unwrapped then loaded the weapon. The bullet slipped easily into the chamber. With a push of the bolt, he moved the cartridge into position. He loaded only one round. He would get just one chance.

He remained inside the cab. Better for cover; better for a quick getaway. He slid across the bench seat then propped the gun barrel on the ledge of the open window. The metal on metal seemed awkward, the rifle wanted to slide. Michael draped the blanket over the sill, nesting the weapon in its soft folds. Perfect. Sitting sideways on the bench with the weight resting on the door, he could hold this position all day. He wouldn't need to.

He twisted his wrist to see his watch. Five minutes until seven. Michael had known Anna a long time, and for all her faults, being late was not one of them. The rustic barrier would begin opening any minute.

Staring at the entrance, Michael visualized the sequence. The gate would open by swinging away from him. When it reached half way, he'd have an unobstructed view down the lane. Anna would be driving directly towards him. She'd slow for the stop at the country road. He'd take the shot.

Michael had made much harder kills than this. His mind wandered, replaying those he'd nailed on big game drives.

He had satisfied his blood-lust on nearly every continent. Only the biggest and most ferocious beasts enticed him. Killing pheasants in Pennsylvania bored the hell out of him. If the thing he killed couldn't kill him, he wasn't interested.

While his mind kept him entertained, he held an eye tight to the scope, focused on the prize. Absentmindedly, he caressed the stock.

The barrier began moving. It opened more slowly than he'd remembered. Like watching a striptease, his anticipation built. The gate parted; a white Audi approached. It slowed.

Gripping the gun's handle, Michael eased the scope toward the driver's side. Anna came into view. He steadied himself. "Patience," he whispered.

The car coasted at a walking pace, nearing the end of the lane. Anna's face occupied the center of the sight. Her head turned, checking for traffic.

Michael lowered the cross hairs. Her breasts looked nice. He drew a slow breath. Holding it, he squeezed the trigger.

# Chapter 28 – Sunrise

Rock looked to Hazel sleeping on a bench, lying still at last after hours of thrashing about. Lily too was asleep, her head resting on his lap. She had been curled up in the fetal position across three chairs for half the night. The padding on those seats was thin. Rock knew from the hours he sat awake while his ass slept. He'd lost feeling in his leg long ago but wasn't going to move. Enjoying Lily so close, he would cut it off before he disturbed her.

He scanned the quiet waiting room, likely the slowest night the ER had experienced in years. A parade of patients had come and gone, but on the whole a mundane group. After Rose, not a one came crashing through the doors with an entourage of frantic doctors and nurses yelling commands. No gang fights continued to follow their victims into the lobby. A peaceful night when Hazel and Lily found a few minutes of uncomfortable sleep.

Terry didn't last long after talking with Rock and Tim. He'd passed out while they said their goodbyes. By the time Rock returned, Terry slept slumped sideways in a chair with his head mashed against the wall. Looking at Terry this early morning, Rock could see he hadn't moved since then. Had an ambulance crashed through the windows, it wouldn't have roused him.

Rock, however, had seen every tick of the clock mounted above the reception desk. His thoughts had fixed on the events of the previous day, but mostly he kept coming back to his decision to allow Rose to do the job. Every second not knowing she would be okay drove the idea deeper and deeper into his mind that this was all his fault. His exhaustion didn't help. The dark feelings grew and grew.

The big hand had jerked to the two while the little hand inched past the seven when the door below the clock opened.

160

The movement drew Rock's focus. Doctor Singh turned toward him. Rock sat straighter, anticipating the worst.

Lily stirred, turning her head to Rock. "Is everything all right?"

"The doctor is here."

This was enough to set her fighting to get fully awake.

Lumbering to them, Dr. Singh made no effort to waken Hazel. Rock could not read good or bad in his stare, only fatigue. Lily sat up while the doctor took the chair beside Rock.

Exhaling deeply, the surgeon hushed, "Well, Ms. Chow is out of the OR. She is stable and we believe we were successful in stopping all the bleeding. As we'd assessed on her arrival, the carotid was nicked. We repaired that first. Then there was significant internal bleeding to be addressed. In the process we removed her spleen. Fortunately, no major organs were damaged."

Impatient with the checklist, Rock interrupted, "Will she live?"

Another sigh led to a pregnant pause. "We don't know."

Rock flinched. Lily grasped his hands, squeezing tightly.

"Her vitals are stable but very weak. I'll be honest, she's received more units of blood than anyone I've seen in a long time, at least for someone who lived. But she's young and healthy, which gives her a fighting chance. The next twenty-four hours are critical. If she makes it until tomorrow when the sun rises her odds go way up. Then there will be many more months and many more operations before she can hopefully make a full recovery. I'm sorry for being brutally honest. I really want you to hope for the best, but you must be prepared for the worst."

Lily looked in shock. Rock answered for them both. "We appreciate everything the team has been doing for Rose. Please thank all the doctors and nurses for us."

"I will." Glancing to Hazel, he added, "I know this has been hard on her. When she wakes up, would you give her the update?"

"She'll want to know if she can see her daughter."

"Rose has been moved to intensive care. I expect her to be there for at least a week. Assuming Rose doesn't have any setbacks, her mother may be allowed to visit later this afternoon. It's best if you encourage her to go home and get some sleep. She can plan to come back, but she needs to call first. I'll contact you immediately if Rose's condition changes."

"Thank you, doctor," Rock answered, "that sounds like good advice. We all need some rest."

While Dr. Singh exited, Rock noticed that Terry was awake and intently listening. "Were you able to hear all that?"

"Yes. There was a lot of bad, but I prefer to focus on the good. She's still alive."

Rock and Lily nodded.

Watching Terry gather his things, Rock asked, "What are your plans? You said you're visiting a buddy. Are you staying with him or are you in a hotel? I will arrange for my hotel's limo to take you wherever you want to go."

"That would be nice. I'm bunking at Nicky's. I'll crash on his couch and probably sleep until my flight on Monday."

"You need some rest but you'll never get it on a couch. I'm getting a room for you at my hotel. You can have it for the whole time you're here."

"That's okay, all my stuff's at his place."

"Don't worry about that. The limo driver will take you to get it."

"Thanks, but I'll be fine where I am."

"I insist. And if you're worried about the cost, don't. I'm picking up the tab. I need to do something to repay you for all you've done."

Rock was never going to give up. Terry relented. "The thought of a comfortable bed in a quiet room sounds really nice."

"Excellent." Rock would make sure the manager gave him a suite as grand as his just down the hall. And anything else Terry wanted. He also had in mind a special surprise for the young man. With the help of the hotel's personal shopper, Rock would buy Terry new sneakers to replace the pair of Nike's that had been ruined.

Turning from Terry, Rock focused on Hazel. "Now that we have that settled, we should wake her." Kneeling beside the bench, he softly called her name.

Hazel needed a full minute until she recognized where she was. "Hasn't the doctor been back yet?"

"He was just here but you were sleeping so soundly he didn't want to wake you. Rose made it through the surgery and is recovering in the ICU."

"Thank God she's going to be okay!"

"It's still too early to say for sure," Rock offered as gently as he could.

"I don't understand."

Rock and Lily replayed the doctor's report, putting as much positive spin on it as they could without unreasonably building up her hopes.

Hazel rose from her chair, demanding, "I want to see her."

Rock wagged his head. "The doctor said maybe this afternoon. Right now, Rose needs to rest. And so do you. You won't be any good to her if you make yourself sick, too."

Hazel looked to Lily. Lily nodded her agreement with Rock.

"All right. But you must promise to bring me back this afternoon."

"We will," they assured.

Rock wrapped an arm around Hazel and eased her in the direction of the exit. "It's time to get some rest."

While they approached the doors, Agent Fuller hustled in.

Tim hurried to Rock wearing the stone-cold face of a seasoned FBI agent. In a somber tone, Tim commanded, "We need to talk."

"Is there news?"

"A lot."

# Chapter 29 – Body Count

"All right, but first I need to get Hazel and Lily on their way home," Rock answered, tipping his head in the direction of the women watching with riveted attentiveness.

"Have you found who hit Rose?" Hazel blurted out.

"No, Mrs. Chow, I'm sorry but we haven't."

Hazel's energy instantly faded, her body slumping back to its previous state.

Tim turned to Lily. "Actually, I'd like to talk with you as well. Can you stay here for a little longer? I have some questions, if you don't mind." While stated as a request, Tim's tone left no doubt there was only one right answer.

Noting Lily's surprise, Rock expressed his concern. "These ladies need rest. Can't it wait?"

"No, and you'll understand why once I give you the update."

Reluctantly, Rock changed the plans. "Terry, can you see that Hazel gets home okay? The limo will take you both to her house then the driver will get you to the hotel. He can swing by your buddy's place to get your stuff on the way. Would that work for you?"

Terry had hung back while Rock walked the ladies to the door but quickly sprang to Hazel's side. "No problem. Come on, Mrs. Chow, I see the limo is right outside. Let's get some rest." He looked to Rock. "Don't worry, I've got this."

Rock knew Hazel was in good hands.

Once the pair had started toward the exit, Rock's focus returned to Tim and Lily. "I want to hear everything, but first I need some very strong coffee. The receptionist told me there's a coffee bar at the main entrance. Let's go there to talk. You guys in?"

"I think we all could use a jolt of caffeine. It was a short night," Tim grunted, leading the way from the ER.

Ten minutes later they settled into a table in a far corner of the lobby, away from as much of the morning foot traffic as possible. Rock dumped two packs of brown sugar into his cup hoping it would spike his energy. The slow-motion swirls of the spoon with tired muscles felt like mixing concrete. Taking a quick sip, he got more than he'd intended of the steaming drink, burning his tongue. He backed off, blew the brew, and immediately went in for more. The reward was worth the risk.

Tim spoke first. "Like I said, I have a lot of news. But first, how's Rose?"

"She's alive and stable. That's about all the good news we have. They tell us the next twenty-four hours are critical. She's far from out of the woods," Rock replied wearily, forcing the words from his mouth. His anguished look shared his feelings. "Any leads on the car or driver yet?" he prodded, eager to change the subject.

"No, nothing, but we were able to get the judge to authorize the tail on Red. More about that in a bit, but first let me tell you why I wanted to talk with Lily. I got a call on my way here that Ms. Belaire was murdered."

"What?!" Lily's shout turned every head in the lobby. She lowered her voice. "How? Where?"

"She was shot through the chest as she left her country estate. It must have happened around seven. A delivery truck driver saw the back end of her car sticking out of the brush across the road from the entrance. He found her dead body in the running car. The police have been on the scene for nearly an hour now. They interviewed Ms. Belaire's personal assistant and she told them her boss had left just before seven for a meeting in the city."

Directing a questioning look to Rock, Tim continued, "That meeting was to be with you. Do you know anything about this?"

"No," Rock answered wide-eyed. "My phone was turned off all night, since I got here." He tapped the screen and stared, impatient for it to come to life. As it did, it began pinging like a pinball machine. When it finally quieted, Rock saw he had twenty texts and three voicemail messages. "John's been trying to reach me."

A quick scan of the texts confirmed the scheduled meeting with Anna. The frantic efforts to reach Rock built to a final two-word text. 'CALL ME!!!!!!' Rock then listened to the voicemails, the essence of which were, 'Anna urgently wants to meet with you at eight in the morning at your hotel. Call me as soon as you get this message!'

Rock shared all with Tim. It was clear John wouldn't have any more information. "I'll call him back when we're done, please continue," Rock moaned, exasperated that in all the confusion of the night he'd forgotten to let John know where he was or what had happened.

"That explains why she was on the road at that time. The investigators' working assumption is someone was waiting for her on the hill across the road, but how close or far away they don't have any idea yet. From the preliminary inspection of the car and the body, they know she was shot with a high-powered rifle. The killer could have been as far away as several hundred yards. It will take the police all day to search the brush for evidence."

"Any suspects?" Rock had his candidate.

Tim shook his head. "Sorry Rock, it wasn't Red. I told you we got the okay to tail him at seven. My guys anticipated the go-ahead so they tracked him down overnight. They found him at his gym where he always works out early in the morning. Must be his military training. They had eyes on him by seven-ten. There's no way he could have shot Ms. Belaire at her estate and gotten to the gym by that time."

Rock stared in disbelief.

"That's the reason I wanted to talk with Lily," Tim continued, pivoting to her. "Our next person of interest is your husband. I know you were here all night, but can you tell us what he was doing last evening? It will help us piece together his movements when we talk with him today."

Lily proceeded to recount the story she'd told Rock when she called him in a panic. Tim's eyebrows raised when she told him about Michael yelling, "I'll handle her." She confessed she had no idea where he went when he left in the pickup.

"Thank you. That was very helpful. Do you have any idea where he might be now?"

"If he's not at the office, I really don't know. But my best guess is he's with one of the many whores he keeps employed. Michael doesn't give me their contact information. I doubt, anyway, if my phone's memory would be big enough to store them all." Her voice was filled more with disgust than anger.

"We'll start with his secretary. Hopefully she knows how to reach him."

Tim folded his notepad, readying to wrap up the interview, when his phone rang. He looked at the screen. "I need to take this." He answered, "Yep, what's up?" Listening intently, a scowl formed. "Don't let anyone touch anything! I'll be there in five."

Tim hung up, his thoughts holding him lingering over the call while shaking his head. He raised his focus to Rock and Lily. "That was Joe. He's on the stakeout of the Burrows apartment. The cleaning lady just found her dead in bed. Joe's with the police on the scene. Looks like she was accidentally strangled, a kinky sex act gone wrong."

Lily shouted out exactly what Rock was thinking. "You don't buy that, do you?"

"No, I don't. That's why I need to leave you guys right now. Joe's holding everyone back. I must see everything exactly the way the cleaning lady found it." Standing, Tim quickly gathered up his notepad and pen. Grabbing his coat from the back of the chair, he snapped, "I need to talk with the both of you sometime later today. Can we get together early this afternoon?"

"Meet us at one in my hotel room. Good luck and thanks," Rock called to the back of Tim's head.

Tim tossed his harried reply over a shoulder while dashing away. "Great. Get some rest."

Rock and Lily sat at the coffee table in stunned silence a minute before she spoke. "I'd better be getting to Hazel's house. I need some rest and I want to check to make sure she's okay."

"You're coming to the hotel with me. Until we know what's going on, I'm not letting you out of my sight. Terry got Hazel home and she's asleep by now. I need to make sure you stay safe until we have more answers."

Rock had thought for a brief second about going with Tim to the crime scene, but he wasn't going to leave Lily and he couldn't chance her seeing something disturbing there. "We'll go to my place and try for a few hours of sleep. We desperately need it if we're going to make it through the rest of this day."

"Okay. I guess she'll be fine," Lily replied, relief apparent in her voice. When she rose, she stood unsteadily, clutching the back of her chair.

Rock leapt to her aid. He knew the events of the last twelve hours had shaken her to her core, even before the body count began to rise. Helping her toward the exit, he soothed, "You'll be better after some sleep."

At nine o'clock, the pair entered Rock's hotel room. He'd called John on the way there. With that piece of business completed, Rock could rest. "You take the bed. I'll take the couch."

Lily came over and wrapped her arms gently around Rock's waist. Laying her head softly on his chest, she said quietly, "I don't know how I'd be handling this if it weren't for you." Releasing the embrace, she trudged away to the bedroom.

He watched until she disappeared behind the door. After ordering a noon wake-up call and a light lunch to be delivered at twelve-thirty, he made a beeline to the couch. He collapsed without removing anything but his shoes.

He was asleep before his head hit the pillow.

# Chapter 30 – The Gumshoe Work

Tim stood in the middle of the bedroom with his back to the front windows, the best angle to take in the full scope of the scene. Julie's corpse sat against the headboard of a Victorian bed, arms spread wide with wrists lashed to bedposts. A nylon stocking knotted around her neck dangled down covering one of the naked breasts. Her head lolled to the side, a black tongue protruded, vacant eyes stared.

Tim struggled to ignore the stench. Urine and feces coated the body from the waist down, soiling the sheets. It had been a ghastly end for the woman.

The filth, the smell, the gruesomeness, all of it struck Tim as looking exactly the way it should. The common ingredients of a violent death. But to his expert eye, it appeared just a little too perfect. Maybe his perspective was colored by the events of the last two days. The bra on the floor by the bed, frilly white panties wadded up on the corner of the bedspread, the whole place felt staged. Nothing wrong but everything *too* right.

He strolled closer to inspect the lingerie on the cover. Without disturbing it, he could see a light-pink streak. "Hey Joe, come over here. What do you make of this?"

Joe moved from blocking the doorway to peer where Tim was pointing. "Looks like a stain. Maybe lipstick?"

"My thoughts exactly. Make sure the lab gets that analyzed right away. See if they can get a brand and color, this may be our only lead for her partner." *If there was one.*

"Will do."

Tim scanned the room one last time then turned to leave. "I've seen all I need to. The guys can come in. I'm going to SBI headquarters to start working the Belaire murder. Call if you find anything else."

\*   \*   \*

Staring down into the rigid face of Michael's executive assistant, Tim growled, "Well then, do you have a *guess* when Mr. Schowalter might be getting in?"

It was mid-morning and Tim was having a hard time accepting that the secretary to the CEO of a major corporation didn't have at least some idea as to when her boss would arrive.

Before Nancy could squeeze out her next unhelpful answer the doors to the executive suite snapped open. Michael came sweeping in.

Leaping to attention, she called out the thinly-veiled warning, "Michael, Agent Fuller is here from the FBI. He'd like to talk with you."

Michael strutted toward the agent. "Mr. Fuller, is it? How can I be of service?" He reached out and gave Tim a firm handshake. His body language presented a perfectly relaxed persona.

"I apologize for interrupting your day, but I need to talk with you about your ex-wife." The agent was being purposefully vague, looking for any reaction this might provoke.

"Really? What about?"

Tim saw only a questioning look. "I take it you've not been told. She was murdered this morning."

"Oh my God! What happened? Do they know who did it?"

Tim noted Michael's flawless shocked and alarmed look. His sixth sense, honed by years of FBI interrogations, was nominating Michael for an Oscar. "She was shot as she left her estate at about seven this morning. And no, we don't have any leads. That's why I'm here. I need to ask you some questions."

"I'm happy to help however I can. Come in my office." Leading the way, he scurried to the bar. "This is horrible, I need a drink. Can I get you one?"

"No," Tim replied, following Michael into the room.

Slumping into a chair, Michael downed most of the pour with two gulps. Waiving his drink-hand at the seat next to him, he sighed, "Please sit. What would you like to know?"

Tim eased into the cushions then flipped open his notepad. He began with the usual line of questioning. Did Anna have any enemies? Did she mention any concerns for her safety? Had anything curious happen to her recently? These and so many more, lasting for several minutes. The answers were without variation either, "I don't know," or "Maybe Anna's assistant can answer that."

With these basics completed, Tim turned to the questions he really wanted answered. He prefaced them by saying, "As I'm sure you can appreciate, we need to take statements from everyone close to Ms. Belaire regarding where they were when she was murdered."

At this, Michael presented the appropriate amount of indignation. "You can't possibly think I'm somehow involved?"

"I'm sorry, but it's standard procedure when we're investigating a homicide. If you'd like, I'll stop and allow you to have your lawyer present."

"That won't be necessary. I have nothing to hide," Michael answered casually, taking a sip of his drink. "Go ahead."

"Let me start by asking where you were last night."

"I was here in the office working. I arrived around midnight, maybe later, one o'clock. The night guard will have the exact time. The building security system will show when I swiped my key card to get in."

Tim thought for a second about inquiring why he had yelled, "I'll handle her", but he didn't want to let on he'd talked with Lily. He would see what Michael might volunteer before tipping his hand, so he followed where Michael was leading. "And what time did you leave the office this morning?"

"About five o'clock. I don't know for sure whether the guard saw me, but I tapped my card to exit the garage. That will provide the exact time."

"What vehicle were you driving?"

"I have an old pickup truck. I felt like taking that last evening when I left the house. You'll find it in my parking space if you want to look at it."

"Maybe later." Tim would want to check it out, but first he had more questions. So far the story was consistent with what he already knew from Lily. "And where were you between five and when you returned to the building?"

"With a friend."

"Would you be more specific?"

"A lady friend," he answered, flashing a sly smile. "I think you know what I mean."

"And would you mind giving me her name? You realize we'll need to follow up with her to corroborate your story." Tim was getting nervous this line of questioning might encourage Michael to reconsider not having his lawyer present.

Michael remained eager to help. "Oh, of course. But I do expect that what I'm telling you is solely to help your investigation. None of this can become public knowledge."

"I can't promise that," Tim countered, "but if you don't volunteer it, I will get a court order and force you."

Frowning, Michael answered. "Her name is Tatiana Federzinski. Here's her address and phone number." He pulled a slip of paper and pen from the adjacent table then jotted a few lines.

Tim glanced at the proffered sheet. "Would you provide the details regarding what you did with Ms. Federzinski?"

"We talked." Another sly smile.

"Mr. Schowalter, I will be asking your lady friend the same questions. You do not need to offer any more specifics, but please realize that any inconsistencies between your accounts of the morning you spent together will only create issues for you. So again, would you like to tell me what you two did?"

Michael relaxed into his chair. "I got there about five-thirty and we got right at it. By that, I mean we had sex. For about the next hour, maybe a little longer. After that I took a nice long shower. When I came out, Tatiana had made coffee and bagels for breakfast. We ate together then we had more sex. First on the table, then across the table, then on the living room floor, ending in the bedroom. We took a shower together, then I came to work. She will corroborate every detail."

Tim looked Michael over, noting his damp hair. "Thank you, Mr. Schowalter, you have been very helpful. I have no additional questions, but please contact me if you think of anything." Tim decided to not explore what Lily had heard, at least not until after talking with Michael's lady friend.

"I certainly will," Michael assured, rising from his chair. "I'll do whatever I can to help catch poor Anna's killer."

Tim stood, joining Michael in walking toward the door. "I'd like to look at your truck now. Can you have someone take me or would you like to come along?"

"I'm late for a meeting but my Executive Assistant will show you to it. No need for the key, it's unlocked."

Halting in the doorway, Tim turned to Michael. "One last thing. Would you happen to know how we might reach your head of security, Mr. McGregor? He's not in his office today and I need to talk with him."

This request noticeably surprised Michael. "No, I'm sorry I don't. We had a long day yesterday. We didn't arrive back from a trip until late, so I assume he's still resting at home. You might want to ask his assistant, she may know his plans."

"Certainly.  Thank you again."

Tim followed Nancy to the truck.  Once there, he searched it from top to bottom, inside and out.  When finished, he walked away having found exactly what he'd expected - an immaculate vehicle smelling of cleaning products.


Michael poured another drink then fell into a chair, relishing how smooth he'd been.  He knew Tatiana would back up every detail of the story.  The vague first hours were part of the concocted alibi.  She'd give the same general 'sex, shower, breakfast' story.  The detailed second part would be easier still since it actually happened that way.

After they practiced the script, they went at it like horny teenagers.  Michael figured she was throwing him a freebee for all the money he was giving her.  The amount of that cash payment put more than the usual enthusiasm into her performance.  For Michael's part, the thrill of the kill had worked him up into a fine lather.

The only damper on the morning was the question about Red.  Michael could only hope the guy hadn't fucked up yet again.  He took another generous pull of Scotch wondering how he could get to Red first.

# Chapter 31 – Now What?

"Rock, time to get up… It's after noon… Lunch will be here soon."

Lily quietly doled out the details hoping one might spark in his brain.

Rolling onto his side, with effort Rock opened his eyes. Just to slits. The room was dark even though the curtains were open. The gentle patter of rain on the windowpanes, the distant roll of thunder - perfect conditions to sleep the day away. Grunting, he pulled the blanket tighter, sealing his eyelids.

"Come on, hon-… Rock," she stammered, catching herself, "lunch will soon be here and Tim is coming at one."

He found her voice soothing. All he wanted was to enjoy it while drifting off into peaceful slumbers.

Rubbing his hand, Lily hushed, "I'm sorry, but you need to wake up. We have a lot to get done today."

Her warm touch was the key. Opening his eyes, he gave her a relaxed smile. "You know I could stay here all day. The only thing missing is you cuddled up against me."

Rock turned red the instant he said it. Not that he didn't mean it - he did - but this is not how friends talk to each other. Lily's face colored, too. He'd said too much. "I'm sorry, I'm just so tired. I didn't mean to embarrass you." Or himself.

He searched his brain for an out. Nothing came. He'd said it, so the best course of action was to just ignore it. "Okay, I'm up," he announced lightly while sitting. "Thanks for waking me, I must have slept through the call. I see it's gotten pretty crappy outside." Rock stretched, turning away from her to peer out the windows.

"Yes, it has." Grinning, Lily turned away to fish in her purse. With brush in hand, she busied herself with her hair.

Watching the lack of progress in a mirror, she groaned, "I don't have any of my makeup or clothes or anything I need to be presentable. I don't even have a toothbrush. Look at me. I'm a mess."

Rock accepted the invitation to gaze her way. "I don't know, you look lovely to me. I just won't stand too close to you." His smirk broke the tension.

"That's very kind of you, but I do need to get my stuff from Hazel's if I'm going to be here tonight. Either that or go shopping. Preferably both." Giving a last frustrated tug on the brush, she surrendered.

Accompanied by a knock, the waiter called out, "Room service." Rock opened the door and the man wheeled in the food cart. "May I set the table?"

"Yes, please." Rock's stomach began to growl the moment the aromas wafted into the room. He hoped he'd ordered enough.

The server was as efficient as always. Once he'd departed, the pair slid into facing chairs and dug into their lunch.

Between bites, Rock picked up the conversation. "I've been thinking. There are too many coincidences here. Red has to have been involved in murdering Alex and Julie. And my gut tells me he was the one driving the car that hit Rose. The problem is, I'm equally sure he's covered his tracks well enough that he could get away with all of this."

Lily frowned. "You're forgetting about Anna. Don't you think he was involved there as well?"

"I would, except I must accept hard facts. Red was nowhere near the place at the time she was shot. Plus, considering the two murders I'm sure he did commit, Anna's is pretty unsophisticated. Red seems to like deception, the finely crafted staging of events, whereas Anna's murder was a sledgehammer. No finesse at all."

"Then who?"

"My prime suspect is Michael. I thought about what you overheard him yell. I'm convinced he was talking about Anna. If that's the case, I'm even more adamant that you stay close to me. I certainly don't want you alone with him. It's too dangerous."

"I just can't believe he's capable of that, but I'm terrified of him now. I'll never set foot in that house again."

"If anyone can solve these homicides, Tim can. I hope he's made progress this morning."

"Me too," Lily replied gloomily, stirring in her soup.

"Eat up, you need to keep up your strength," he encouraged, giving her a forced smile.

"Okay." But she barely touched a thing after that.

Tim knocked on the door at one o'clock.

"Come in," Rock greeted, "have a seat." He directed the agent to the couch. "I know it's too much to think you've solved three murders in four hours, but have you made progress?" Optimism tinted Rock's voice.

Agent Fuller did not wear the look of a happy man. "Where do I start? It's not been a good day."

"Fill us in," Rock urged, his tone now subdued.

"Well, first thing, we lost our tail on Red."

"What?!" Lily blurted out. Fear instantly replaced her relaxed look.

"They had him at the gym but he must have spotted my guys. He gave them the slip. He's not been seen since nine," Tim growled, shifting in his seat. "I doubt that he's taken off. But I'm very concerned about what he might do next, especially if he's still in the city." He focused a narrow-eyed stare on Lily. "I don't want you out of Rock's sight until we find this guy." Wheeling a concerned frown to Rock, he added, "And you, watch your back. I'm positive Red has figured out you're the one who put us onto him for Alex's murder. Be careful."

"You bet. I'll sleep with one eye open," Rock quipped uncomfortably. "So, what about Anna's murder. Any breaks there?"

"Yes. We know she was killed with a two-seventy Winchester rifle. The shot was taken from about two hundred yards away, from the hill opposite the entrance. We found fresh tire marks along a road up there. Unfortunately, the tracks aren't clean enough to make out any details of the tread. They scoured the place but found no casings and no footprints. That tells me the killer fired from inside the vehicle."

Brows furrowed, Rock replied, "That's not an impossible shot, but it takes some marksmanship to pull that off. The strange thing is, a two-seventy Winchester doesn't strike me as the weapon of choice for a sniper."

"Exactly my thought. I've been bugged by that ever since I got the ballistics report. Something doesn't add up."

"Michael is an avid hunter," Rock noted. "He'd have the skills to make that shot. But again, the rifle is all wrong. I'd have expected him to grab a high-powered gun he uses for big game. It would be more accurate."

Tim shook his head. "Michael is a dead-end. I talked with him and he has an airtight alibi. He was nowhere near the estate when Anna was shot. We have a sworn statement corroborating that."

"Who?!" Lily snapped.

"I'm not at liberty to provide information from an ongoing federal investigation."

"One of his whores, I bet."

"I can neither confirm nor deny that."

"So I'm right," Lily shot back.

Rock jumped in. "You know that's fabricated, don't you?"

"Of course I do. But unless the witness cracks, and I seriously doubt this one will, we are left with nothing but a bullet and a dead body as our evidence. Neither of those point to Michael being the murderer."

"He can't get away with this. He just can't," Lily moaned.

"Sorry, Lily," Tim countered, "but I'm afraid he can. Big-name trial, if it ever got to that, with this flimsy evidence and lawyered up to the hilt with all the money he has at his disposal, I give better odds to the snowflake in hell than winning a conviction against him under these circumstances. The only way we will have any chance of pinning this on him is literally finding the smoking gun."

"Then let's do it," she challenged.

Slouching into his chair, Rock gave Lily a resigned look. "I don't see any chance of that. The gun is long gone to the bottom of the ocean or melted down to a block of steel."

She leaned in, urgency coloring her reply. "But we've got to try. Can't you get a search warrant to go through the house, check all his guns? You can match the bullet with the murder weapon, right? We find the gun, we match the bullet, and he goes to jail."

Tim's demeanor mirrored Rock's. "I'm sorry, but I agree with Rock. That gun is long gone. Plus, no judge would grant a warrant to search his house with what I have. I can't even try. My superiors would have my head for going after a man as powerful as your husband with less than nothing to go on."

"But we've got to try," Lily pleaded, tears welling up. "For Anna."

Rock couldn't stand to see her this way, and he hated the thought of the bastard remaining free to harass her – or worse.

"I have an idea," he offered, sharing a hint of optimism, "one I admit I really don't like, but I think we need to chance it. Lily can invite us into the mansion where we can check out Michael's guns." Rock focused on her. "Is it easy to get a look at them?"

"Yes," she answered excitedly, "he keeps them on display in cases in his study. He loves to show them off."

"Hold on, guys. Rock, I know you practiced law for only a couple years and didn't do criminal law, but you did go to law school and you did take the bar exam. Somewhere along the way you must have learned about illegal search and seizure. I can't go one step inside his place looking for evidence, even if you invite me. And if we do get extremely lucky and the gun is still there, everything I find will be inadmissible as evidence. I'm sorry, this is not an option."

"I do recall some things from those days. You may not be able to go in, but we can. Lily still lives there and I'm a private citizen. Plus, the guns are on display in plain sight. While I can't get the rifling to match the bullet, I can tell if any are the right caliber and if it was recently fired. When I find it, I tell you and that alone should be enough to convince a judge to at least allow the ballistics testing. Michael will fight it tooth and nail, but it's so non-invasive I don't see any judge saying he doesn't need to surrender the weapon for one test. It's a million-to-one chance, but I agree with Lily, we need to try."

Tim groaned a deep sigh. "All right, but be very careful. If the guy is guilty, you two could be next. Let me know when you're going in. I can't join you but I sure as hell will be in the neighborhood if you need me. And for God's sake, if he finds you there, get out immediately!"

"I agree," Rock replied. "A cornered Michael would likely kill us then argue it was a crime of passion before taking his chances on getting arrested for Anna's murder." He pivoted to Lily. "It's now or never."

Her eyes grew big. Then setting her jaw, she focused a determined stare. "We can't wait another minute. The gun is there, I know it is, but it won't be for long."

"I'm not on board, I think it's too risky," Tim muttered, "but I know Michael is at his office so the house should be empty. Get in and get out before he comes home."

Rock jumped to his feet. "We're ready."

# Chapter 32 – You're Out!

They disarmed the security system at exactly two o'clock. By two-fifteen they planned to be done. No longer. Rock expected to make speedy work of inspecting the collection. If a gun matching the one used to kill Anna was there, he'd find it in that time.

Lily held his arm while leading the way through the ornately decorated hallway. Rock paid attention to every door they passed, his head cocked listening for any signs of life.

"Nobody is here at this time of day," Lily assured. "The kitchen staff will be back at five. Until then, we have the place to ourselves."

"Good to hear," he replied, no less wary.

Rock hadn't appreciated the size of the mansion. Michael's study was on the first floor near the grand entrance but they had to enter through a side door of a wing. When they finally arrived at the room, Rock checked his watch. Two minutes gone of the allotted fifteen. At this pace, he would have ten minutes tops with the collection. He'd not asked how many rifles Michael owned. More than thirty would be a challenge to stay on time.

Lily grabbed the handle and pushed. "It's locked!"

"Does the cleaning crew have a spare key?"

"Yes. They keep it in the security office. I know the codes."

"Let's go, there's no time to waste."

They scurried along the hall toward the kitchen. The office occupied a small room next to the servants' entrance. Lily tapped the keypad then pressed the 'unlock' button.

Nothing.

"Slow down and try it again," Rock encouraged patiently.

She re-entered the code, more deliberately this time. While pushing the last button, she unconsciously held her breath. The pad buzzed; the lock clicked.

They hurried into a room barely bigger than a storage closet. Rushing to a lockbox on the wall, Lily lined up four digits then yanked the handle. The opened door revealed rows of keys, each one tagged by a ring. She grabbed the one labeled 'study' then slammed the cover. Turning toward Rock, she pulled up short. "What?"

Rock's face shared a look of mild amusement. "Really? The code is one-two-three-four?"

"What can I tell you, Michael doesn't hire smart security."

With the box and room locked, they sprinted to the study. Lily engaged the key and twisted. The bolt snapped. Rock gave a quiet sigh of relief when the door swung away. While Lily sealed the room, he glanced at his watch. Half of the fifteen minutes had passed.

She rushed toward the far side of the room. Reaching three large glass-topped cases, she announced with a wave of her arms, "Here are all his guns."

Rock's heart sank. Each one held fifteen rifles of all caliber lined up one next to the other. He dove in.

He assessed the first case faster than he'd expected. All were large-bore Rigby rifles, the ones Michael used for hunting big game like elephants. Those could never be mistaken for the gun used to kill Anna.

The next case, however, was a different story. Each muzzle and stock required careful inspection. There were .30-06 Springfield's, .308 Winchester's, even the odd .30-30 Winchester. But no .270 Winchester.

The last display was the same, a painstaking effort. He checked it twice then straightened up.

Lily leaned close, anxious anticipation written on her face. "Well?"

Turning, Rock groaned, "It's not here."

From the direction of the door, a voice filled with malice growled, "I could have told you that."

Rock and Lily spun around.

Michael stood in the doorway, a sinister smirk on his face. His beady eyes were barely visible through narrowed slits.

"Well, Mr. Stone, I'd asked if I can help you, but I understand you've already helped yourself to my wife," he snarled. "You didn't expect I'd be watching the house. When I got the notice the alarm system was turned off, I knew she had come sneaking back. But having you here with her, this is a surprise." He prowled in their direction as he spoke.

Lily's quivering voice pleaded, "Michael…"

Cutting her off, he shot back, "Shut up, bitch! I wasn't talking to you. Can't you see the men are working?!" Spittle sprayed from his tightly set mouth. The muscles of his clenched jaw twitched; dark eyes fixed a piercing stare.

"Don't talk to her like that," Rock demanded, his voice low and steady. The flame of hate burned in his eyes.

Jerking his glare to Rock, Michael gave a harsh chuckle. "You know, she was a good fuck once. You should have had her when she was young. You can have her now, I'm done with her. But I doubt you'll be interested," he noted dismissively, his tone filled with disgust.

"You bastard!" Lily shrieked, tears forming.

Her feeble curse drew Michael's attention. "Ah, I may be a bastard, but I'm a rich one. Soon I will be free of you. But only after I've taken every last thing you love."

Turning his loathsome focus to Rock, Michael scoffed, "And you, my pain-in-the-ass mistake. I'll sue you for all you own. When my lawyers are done, I'll have everything you've ever held dear and your balls will be in a jar on my mantle."

While talking, Michael had worked his way across the room. Halting in front of the couple, he gave the rack of guns a furtive glance.

Lily sobbed.

Rock laughed. A true, hearty laugh.

Michael's look of surprise morphed to one of uncontrolled fury. Flushing a dark shade of red, he screamed, "This is funny to you?!"

In a relaxed, even tone, Rock replied, "I've been around enough bullies and blowhards to know when the only thing they have is piss and wind. And you, my giant asshole, are filled to the brim with both. Nothing more."

His body tensing, Michael shook as his anger consumed him. "I know you came here looking for the gun that killed Anna," he hissed through clenched teeth. "I'm sure you know by now there's no two-seventy Winchester in those cases. In this house. Get the fuck out, *now*, or-"

"Or what, you impotent prick?" Rock taunted.

Standing toe-to-toe with Rock, Michael looked up at him, his crimson face pinched with rage ready to explode.

"I got it!" Lily yelled, pivoting to Rock. "I know where the gun is!"

Michael wheeled his glare to Lily.

"You do?" Rock responded, not taking his focus off of Michael.

"It's in his pickup. He keeps a rifle in there behind the seat. I saw it once, a long time ago. I bet that's it!" she declared triumphantly.

Michael's eyes widened. His nostrils flared. Releasing a guttural roar, he spewed, "You fucking bitch. I'll kill you!"

Thrusting his clenched fists high, Michael sprung at her.

Lily screamed. Covering her head, she ducked and spun away.

Rock's uppercut caught Michael square on the jaw. His head whipped to the side. Spit and snot flew. The force of the blow lifted him to his toes. The dark eyes disappeared; only the whites remained.

Teetering for the briefest of moments, Michael dropped like a giant tree lopped off at its base. Slowly at first, then picking up speed, he fell until his face slammed the floor. Bouncing once, his entire mass shook. When he stopped quivering, he was out cold.

Rock stood over the motionless body gloating. "That's strike three, asshole!"

"How's he doing? Do we need to get him to the ER?"

Leaning over for another look, Agent Fuller spoke to the paramedic evaluating Michael, unconscious where he'd fallen more than fifteen minutes before. Michael's jaw was swollen and bruised. Tim watched the efforts to revive him, worried that he would have to wait until his prisoner spent a night in the hospital before he could book him.

Michael groaned while his arms and legs began moving. Turning his head toward the man tending to him, his eyes tried to focus.

The EMT looked up at Tim. "He's starting to come around."

Regaining consciousness, Michael peered first at the medic then with effort directed an expressionless gaze to Tim. But when a nerdy-looking officer wearing rubber surgical gloves appeared holding a rifle, Michael's face lost all of what little color it had left.

"Here's the gun. We found it in the pickup behind the seat. It's a two-seventy Winchester and it's been recently fired," the man announced, holding it out for Tim to inspect.

Tim gave a satisfied nod. "Get it to the lab, I want the ballistics asap. I need to know if it's a match with the one that killed Ms. Belaire before the end of the day."

"You'll have it in an hour, sir." The officer cradled the stock then made a bee-line exit from the study.

With this exchange, Michael watched the gun and the rest of his free life leave the room.

"Looks like he's coherent, Agent Fuller," the paramedic declared.

Tim knelt next to the prisoner. "I'm glad to see Mr. Stone didn't hit you too hard. Just lay back and relax, I have a little story to read to you." Tim fished in his pocket and pulled out his Miranda sheet. He knew it by heart but he wanted to make sure he could testify under oath that he'd read Michael his rights word-for-word without any mistake. "You have the right to remain silent...."

Rock and Lily positioned themselves inside the front door to watch the FBI agents lead Michael from the mansion into the heavy rain. The hateful glare he gave them when he passed did nothing to dampen the joy and relief they felt seeing him hauled off in handcuffs. While Michael watched, Rock pulled Lily close. Waving an exaggerated goodbye, Rock offered the jolly farewell, "Have a nice day."

Lily beamed when Michael huffed, "Fuck you."

# Chapter 33 – Catching a Break

The day remained dark and dismal, but inside Rock's hotel room everything was sunny. Rock relaxed in a chair cradling a glass of bourbon, his feet propped on the coffee table. Lily leaned against the arm of the couch closest to him with legs curled up on the cushions.

"I can't stop smiling," she giggled.

"I know. Ever since we found the gun, it feels like a weight has been lifted. The whole thing was a rush. A terrifying one, but a rush nonetheless."

Her happy expression dimmed. "I nearly had a heart attack when I saw Michael standing in the doorway. I had no idea he could track when I turned off the alarm."

"In retrospect, our lucky break was him coming after you. The rifle wouldn't have been in the house if he hadn't."

Sliding from the couch, Lily eased onto Rock's lap and wrapped him in a tight embrace. "Thank you again for stopping him from hitting me."

"I think that's the hundredth time you've hugged me. But I'm not complaining. I kinda like it." He flashed her a sweet smile.

"You'd better, or I'll just keep doing it until you do."

"While I could do this all night, I'm getting hungry. Knocking the crap out of that prick took a lot of energy. Any thoughts on where we should go for dinner?"

Before Lily could answer, Rock's cell phone rang.

He swapped his drink for the phone on the side table. "Hello?"

"Rock, Tim here."

He mouthed "Tim" to answer Lily's questioning look.

"I'll start freshening up," she whispered, sliding from the chair.

While she disappeared into the bedroom, Rock directed his attention to the call. "Sorry, you caught us making dinner plans. How are things going?"

"We got a break. Michael ratted out Red for the murders of Alex and Julie. He also confirmed that Red hit Rose."

"That's great! Do you have him in custody? I hope the bastard fries." Rock's grasp of the phone tightened, strangling Red by proxy.

"No. But we know where he is. That's why I'm calling." Tim's voice hinted that not everything was under control.

"Why? What's up?"

The agent exhaled deeply. "We didn't have a clue where he was until we located his phone signal. Using the cell towers, we found him hiding in a barn on Ms. Belaire's estate. He's holed up, taking potshots at us. I've got snipers in place to take him out but he's too smart. We're never going to get a clean shot. He says he'll come out on one condition."

"What's that?"

A pregnant pause preceded, "He wants you to come here so he can talk with you."

"Did you say he wants to talk with *me*? In person? About what?"

"Yes, yes, and I have no idea," Tim muttered. "Look, I really don't like this, but I have no other choice. I know I can't force you to help, but I'm hoping if he gets to talk with you then he'll give up. Frankly, I'm concerned if we go in with force, we'll get him but only after a couple of my guys get hurt. Maybe killed. If there's a chance to avoid that risk, I'm all in. But I realize it's not my call."

Rock drew a long breath, then released a protracted sigh. "You know I'll do it. I'll be right there."

"There's a car on the way to pick you up. A helicopter is waiting to zip you over here. At least you won't have to fight the bridge traffic," Tim offered, his weak attempt at lightening the mood.

Rock gave a humorless chuckle. "Knew I'd say yes, did ya?"

"Not for certain, but you would have surprised me if you didn't. Thanks for stepping up. I'll owe you."

"Just keep me alive so I can collect, okay?"

"It's a deal. See you soon."

"Yep," Rock grunted, hanging up as Lily returned from the other room.

On standing, he turned his sullen look to her. "I'll need to take a raincheck on dinner."

"Why, what's happening?"

"Tim has Red cornered. He'll only give up if he can talk with me."

"Why you?"

"I don't know."

"Don't do it," Lily demanded, her voice quivering, "it's a trap."

"I think it is too, but Tim's certain his guys will get hurt if they have to go in after him. Even if it's a small chance that he'll surrender, I need to try."

"Please don't." Tears moistened her lashes.

"If I don't and someone gets killed, I'll never be able to look at myself in the mirror."

Walking over, Lily wrapped her arms around him. "Okay, I know you need to do this. But *please* be extremely careful. That man is a cold-blooded killer. He's up to something, I know it with every fiber in my body. I just hope when it's all over, if anyone is dead, it's him."

The room phone rang. Lily reluctantly released her grip so Rock could answer.

"Hello? …. I'll be right down."

Rock hung up then focused a determined look on Lily. "I'll be fine. Stay here, relax, and I'll be back in no time. Then we'll celebrate. I promise."

"I'm holding you to that, mister." Her attempt at sounding confident was betrayed by her trembling voice.

Hugging him one more time, she held tight until he gently eased her away.

Kissing Lily softly on the forehead, Rock assured as solemnly as an oath before God, "I'll be back."

Within a half hour of leaving the room, the chopper descended toward a sodden field on the estate well away from the action. Visibility was poor, the ride was rough, and Rock was not a fan of helicopters. He didn't relax until the craft was resting safely on terra firma.

Bent low, Tim ran below the whirling blades to the door. Helping Rock to exit, he hollered over the thumping, "Thanks for coming."

Scurrying across the slick grass, they dashed to an idling Suburban. Tim struggled to hold the car door open against the rush of wind while Rock led the way into the back seat. Sliding in after him, the agent closed them in and the SUV peeled out.

While the vehicle bounced down a tractor lane, Tim produced an aerial photo of the estate on his iPad. "Here's what we've got. As I told you on the phone, he's in the barn." His finger landed on a long rectangular building. "A big tractor shed, really. Anna hasn't had animals on the estate for years. Because there are two gasoline reservoirs, a thousand-gallon propane tank, and a fuel oil depot next to the structure, we've had to be careful returning fire." He zoomed in on the hazards ringing the barn. "As you can see, the tanks aren't very close to the residence but a number of outbuildings are nearby. If anything blows, they're all gone plus every window on this side of the manor house."

"You said he wanted to talk to me in person, so I'll need to get close to the barn, right?"

"Right."

"Here's my first request for your team. Don't shoot the tanks!" Rock quipped, smiling nervously.

Tim's stern demeanor softened. "Noted. Any others?"

"Just one.  Get me home alive."

"Double check.  We've been working on a plan to do just that."

# Chapter 34 – The Boy Scout

Tim hunkered down beside his Suburban adjusting the microphone inside Rock's raincoat. He looked to the SUV parked ahead of his. "Can you hear me, Joe?"

Sitting by video monitors, his partner gave a thumbs up.

Pivoting to Rock, Tim announced, "All set. We haven't been able to track Red with the infrared scopes. Lure him to a window so the snipers can get a bead on him. They won't shoot unless he pulls something. If he does, yell and we'll open fire."

"You can bet your sweet ass I'll be yelling. What's my exit strategy?"

"We'll cover you while you hightail it back here. Remember, run to the gap between the SUV's. We'll be shooting on either side of that alley. It's your direct path to safety. If you deviate, you could get hit by friendly fire. Got it?"

"Yep." Rock wiped the moister from his brow, not sure if it was rain or sweat. Peering across the hood, he steeled his nerves for the hundred-yard walk to the spot where Red had demanded he stand for the meeting.

"Any last questions?"

"Yeah. Tell me again why I'm doing this?" Rock joked morosely, a hint of nervousness sneaking into his tone.

"Good luck. We're going to keep you safe."

Joe called over, "Okay guys, he says it's time. Send Rock out."

Nearly sunset, daylight was quickly dimming, hastened by the persistent clouds spitting a light rain. Rock squeezed between the Suburbans, hands held in plain sight. He walked slowly, careful to avoid sudden movements. He didn't want to give Red any reason to start shooting.

Rock's heart raced. Sucking a deep breath, he worked to steady his nerves. The adrenaline rush had his body supercharged.

Shuffling along, he considered his escape. That was simple - run like hell. Easier said than done. The wet grass – higher than a lawn yet shorter than a field – would present a challenge for speed.

He arrived at the meeting point.

"That's far enough, Stone," Red snarled.

Rock heard the voice but couldn't see the man. "I thought you wanted to talk face-to-face? We could have done this on the phone."

"Through the window."

Brows furrowed, Rock stared at the building. "Where?"

"Look closer. I see you just fine," Red growled.

Peering through the closest panes, Rock spied a face in a mirror.

Red tipped a nod. "I'd be happy to meet in the open, but I can't make it too easy for your buddies."

Fixing his attention on the building's interior, Rock spotted a second mirror. Red could be anywhere inside. "Pretty clever using two mirrors," he called matter-of-factly, a bit louder than needed.

"I thought so, too. I hope Agent Fuller heard his guys won't have a clean shot. I know you're mic'd. That's okay, I want him to hear."

"What do you want?" Rock snapped, not hiding his impatience. His bad feeling about this whole thing had jumped to another level. He'd stay for a brief chat then bolt.

"I had to look you in the face this one last time. The prick who fucked everything up for Michael and me. I told him you were too sharp, but he said he needed someone the Japanese would respect. God damn Alex had slipped you onto the list and I didn't have time to nix you. Pissed me off big time."

"Is that why you killed him?" Seeing the guy was in a talkative mood, Rock figured he'd fish for an admission. It would come in handy if Red lived.

"That's why I was happy to kill him, but Michael calls the shots. He gave the go ahead and left the details to me. By the way, what tipped you off with Alex?"

"You dropped cigarette ash on the bathroom floor. That, and the cane was too far from the tub. Pretty sloppy for a professional," Rock taunted.

"Damn observant of you. And you're right, that wasn't my best work. But that Burrows chick, now that was perfect. Well, except for your little friend and Anna."

Rock's stomach churned at the mention of Rose. He forced the thought from his mind. "Is that why you killed Anna?" Rock still suspected Red had a hand in her death.

"I had nothing to do with that. Michael did her. He should have left it to the pro, but he ran off half-cocked and tried doing it himself. Never send a boy to do a man's job."

"Maybe you two will end up being cell mates. Then you can let him know how badly he fucked up. He'll probably like making you his bitch in there, too," Rock sneered, releasing a sarcastic chuckle.

Scratching deeper at Rock's raw nerve, Red asked, "By the way, you sent your little friend to the apartment that night, right?"

"Yeah." The word stuck in his throat.

"Pretty unlucky for her that she saw everything. Tell me, is she dead yet?" Red goaded.

"No," Rock barked. "I'm sure she'll be around when they hook up your IVs." Unrestrained hatred colored the tone of his reply.

"By what I heard, she's still touch and go. My money is on dead by sunrise. Want in on the action?" Red jeered, laughing cruelly.

"If she dies, I'll be the one doing your injections. Then I'll shit on your grave."

"Oh, I seriously doubt that," Red purred maliciously. Moving from view, he boasted, "I'll outlive you both."

Blue steel glistened in the mirror. Rock spun to flee. With his first step, a gunshot rang out.

The impact of the bullet threw Rock to the ground. Gut-wrenching pain seared his side. The next shots whizzed by his head.

Then all hell broke loose.

The agents opened fire with everything they had. A barrage of bullets peppered the building, turning the barn wall into Swiss cheese.

Under cover of the assault, Rock struggled to his feet. He fought through the pain to retreat. Slumped over clutching his side, he used his free arm for support. He ran beneath a crisscrossing hail of bullets limping like a three-legged dog.

Absorbed into the chaos was his scream, "Don't hit the tanks!"

The time it took to traverse the open field felt like an eternity. With shots pinging off bullet-proof plating, Rock split the gap between the SUVs. Diving for safety, he slid past Tim on the wet grass. Darting back, he collapsed by his side.

Tim stopped firing and bent over Rock. Pulling back the raincoat, he fumbled underneath in search of wounds.

Rock lay gasping for breath, holding his side. "Jesus H Christ, Tim, how much does this fucking vest weigh?" Every word punctuated his agony.

"About twenty-five pounds," Tim replied, maintaining focus on his evaluation.

"Well, it felt like I was carrying an elephant," he shot back, breathing hard to endure the pain.

"Move your hands! I need to see where he got you."

Rock reluctantly complied.

Finding a hole in the body armor, Tim probed its depth. At the bottom, he discovered a bullet buried in the vest's mass.

"That elephant saved your life," the agent noted happily. "You have no serious injuries that I can find."

"Are you sure? My ribs hurt like hell!"

"The slug packed a powerful punch. Your side will throb for a while, but other than that, you'll be okay. Good thing you had it on, otherwise we'd be finding your guts all over the field. We'd better...."

If Tim finished the sentence, Rock never heard it. A bright flash lit the agent's face then the Suburban and everything around it rocked from the concussion of a blast. A beat later, another explosion.

Rock glimpsed the second on the video monitor. Both gasoline tanks went up in balls of fire. A plume of smoke billowed to the sky atop a mushroom cap of flames. With debris raining down, the agents ran for cover.

Soon all was quiet except for the crackling sound of flames consuming what remained of the outbuildings. The barn was totally gone. The blasts had pushed the Suburbans several inches.

Standing to lean across the hood, Tim surveyed the devastation muttering, "What the fuck just happened?"

More than an hour had passed before the fires were finally under control. Tim called out directions to the expanded team of firefighters and EMTs. He needed to secure the site and conduct the investigation. It would be a long night with a mountain of paperwork to follow.

He detoured to check on Rock. The paramedic was finishing up as Tim approached. The ten second synopsis given to Rock concluded, "No broken ribs, but that bruise is going to look a lot worse in the morning. Ice it for a day, then hot compresses. It will be weeks before you're feeling normal again." With that not-so-cheery diagnosis, the medic moved on to tend to cuts the agents received from flying debris.

"Well, it could have been far worse," Tim offered when he arrived, trying to sound positive. His lingering concern registered in his tone.

"I know. Thanks for keeping me alive."

"You're welcome." He drew a bracing breath, exhaling deeply. "I'm sorry for all of this."

"I know you are. I'm just glad nobody but Red was killed."

Giving a weary nod, Tim urged, "You'd better get going. Rest up and call me tomorrow to tell me how you're feeling." Turning to leave, he threw back, "I need to check on the guys. See you later."

Tim trudged sloped-shouldered across the field until he got within earshot of his team. There, he straightened up and began barking orders.

Rock remembered he hadn't called Lily to let her know he was okay. It was late. She would be about crazy.

She answered on the first ring. "Are you alright?!" Her question registered somewhere between frantic and panicked.

"Yep, fine. I got a bruised side but that's all," Rock answered as casually as he could. Maybe someday he'd tell her the whole story, but for tonight it was less than nothing. "I'll be fine."

"Thank God, I've been worried sick all evening. Did you get Red?"

"He's dead," Rock assured without any hint of regret.

"So, the Boy Scout is dead," Lily sighed, sharing her relief.

"Huh? Did you say boy scout?"

"Yeah. Michael called Red 'the Boy Scout'."

"Funny name for him. He didn't seem courteous or kind or helpful or any of the other things the Scouts encourage."

"No, Michael called him that because he was always prepared. Michael said the guy was thinking three moves ahead of everyone else. Red had contingency plans for contingency plans. I never thought he'd get caught, let alone killed."

"I gotta go!" Rock shouted, hanging up.

Sprinting in Tim's direction, he yelled at the top of his lungs, "We need to talk! Now!"

# Chapter 35 – His Muse

The lingering smoke hung thick in the air, mixing with the worsening fog to drop a white blanket over the estate.

"Over here!"

Rock heard Joe's nearby cry but could barely see his flashlight on the other side of the hedge. When he approached, he spied the agent bent over, pulling at the ground. Rock added his light to the effort. "Did you find it?"

"Yep. Here it is. Footprints lead up the hill toward that ridge." Joe flicked his beam along a path.

"I bet you'll find a road on the other side. Fresh tire marks as well," Rock moaned.

After an exhaustive search of the grounds, they'd finally found what Rock knew for certain existed. Red had an escape tunnel from the barn.

When the FBI arrived to capture Red, they'd ringed the building a hundred yards out, inside the hedge row bordering the property. But Red had access to a tunnel extending beyond that boundary. While the agents scattered to avoid the raining debris created by the explosions, in the ensuing confusion, he'd slipped from the hatch. Scurrying over the nearby mound, Red had fled in a car he'd secreted along the dirt road on the other side.

Rock realized only too late how badly he had underestimated Red. It was Lily's comment that changed the way he viewed the man.

Tim came running up. "God damn it, you were right. He's got at least a three-hour head start and we don't have any idea what vehicle he's driving. At least we know he's headed south."

"Yep, he's running to Mexico," Joe chimed in. "It's the closest border. My guess is he'll stay off the main roads, but even with that he'll be there by tomorrow night."

"He'll likely cross on land," Tim noted, "but we'd better watch the ocean too. We'll need to get the Coast Guard on alert."

While the two agents reinforced each other, Rock wagged his head.

Tim noticed. "What's wrong?"

"We've been two steps behind him all along. Leading us one way while he goes the other. I just can't see him changing now, choosing the obvious option. He's cleverer than that," Rock scoffed.

"You're overthinking it," Tim shot back. "He believes we know he's dead. He probably thinks he could walk there before we'd find anything that would make us question that. If we ever would. Sorry, but the easy answer is the only one. The challenge is guessing his route, nothing more."

Rock cut Tim off when his phone rang. "Hold that thought, I've got to take this. Lily's probably ready to kill me."

Pulling the phone from his pocket, he was surprised to see 'blocked number' on the screen. He answered, "Yeah?"

"The reports of my death have been greatly exaggerated."

Rock held a finger to his lips. Motioning for the agents to gather closer, he tapped the speaker button. "So where are you now, Red?"

"That's for me to know and you to find out," he sneered. "But since you're not in your hotel room, I know you're still at the estate. I also know I'm on the speaker. Hello, Agent Fuller. You do love to listen in on our conversations." The honeyed voice carried a taunting edge.

"Fuck off," Tim barked.

"Have you found it yet?" Red queried, his tone relaxed.

"Yes. How long have you been planning this?"

"Ever since they built the place. Ms. Belaire hired me to consult on security for the estate. That gave me opportunities to make some, shall I say, modifications to the construction plans. One was to add a tunnel from the barn. It was easy enough to disguise it as a sewer line. Nobody ever questioned when it wasn't connected to any system. I am surprised you found it so fast. Frankly, I was certain you'd never figure it out. You continue to find new ways to amaze me, Mr. Stone. But this really does spoil the surprise of my call. I do feel a bit foolish now with my greeting. Fortunately, I have another shocker for you."

"Yeah, you're giving yourself up."

"No, definitely something better," Red replied, sounding almost giddy. Background noise joined the call when he engaged the speaker phone. "You can speak now, missy."

"Rock..." Lily spoke this helpless, pleading word.

Rock's heart stopped. "How?... Why?"

"You left her alone at the hotel. It was easy enough to convince her to join me," he joshed, releasing a perverse laugh. "As for why, this, Mr. Stone, is all your fault and yours alone. Had you only died as I'd intended tonight, this lovely lady would be mourning your passing in the solitude of that hotel room. But since I couldn't end your life, I thought it only fitting to make you regret surviving."

Rock could hear Lily sobbing violently. They both understood how this ride would end.

"Shut up, bitch! Can't you see the men are working?!" Red's demand was accompanied by a sharp crack.

His blood boiling, Rock needed to gather himself. Losing control wouldn't help Lily and he could learn more if he kept Red talking.

Then it struck him. "How long have you had Michael's study bugged?" These were the same words Michael had yelled at Lily when he had caught them.

"Very good. A long time, actually. I wouldn't be an effective head of corporate security if I didn't know what the

CEO was doing. I'm very glad I had. That's how I knew it was time to retire. Did you gentlemen enjoy my party tonight?"

The laughter riled Rock but he kept his cool. "I only wish I could have given you the gift of lead."

"That's not very nice," Red replied, feigning disappointment. "But I've allowed myself to be distracted. I really called for another reason. Are you a fan of Edgar Allen Poe, Mr. Stone?"

"What is wrong with you?" Rock couldn't form a more coherent response to such a bizarre question.

"Oh, I'm sure quite a bit, but the reason I ask is because I have found Poe to be my muse. His works have inspired me to be creative in my killings." Red's manner had become whimsical.

"I didn't picture you as the reading type. More the crayoning type."

"Oh, I'm really not," Red continued playfully, "but my pain-in-the-ass high school English teacher made us read all kinds of shit. Crap like *Lord of the Flies* and fluff like *A Christmas Carol*. Classics my ass. But when she made us read a couple of Poe's works, I found my calling."

"So you like Poe. Why should I care?"

"Because I've decided Mrs. Showalter's death will be a page out of one of Poe's stories."

Lily began sobbing, this time even harder.

Red permitted her to continue. His explanation was having the intended effect.

In a more serious tone, Red continued, "Personally, I love *The Pit and the Pendulum*, but it's really hard to find a giant, razor-sharp pendulum these days. I guess they stopped making them at the end of the Inquisition. What a shame," he muttered. "I confess, I have always been disappointed by the ending. I mean really, freeing the prisoner? That's not the ending I would have written. But by far Poe's best story is *The Cask of Amontillado.* Do you remember that one, Mr. Stone?"

Rock had an immediate shiver of recognition, anticipating what Red would say next.

"I take from your silence that you do. Being walled up alive is everyone's nightmare. Well, I have decided to pay tribute to Poe's greatness by ending this lady's life in a similar fashion. I say *similar* because I wouldn't be expressing my creativity by slavishly copying Poe. Instead, I'll put a modern twist on it. You'll enjoy the video I send you. I may even live-stream it. That would be novel."

"You're a very sick bastard." Rock had never been more filled with hatred for another human being than at that moment.

"Thank you, I take that as a high compliment. Now, I do need to focus. I have more driving to do and I'd hate to be in an accident and injure someone," he said jokingly. "Any last words you'd like to say to Mr. Stone, missy?"

"Rock…." Overcome by emotion, Lily's choked attempt at saying goodbye ended in sobs.

Rock understood everything that existed between them in the way she said his name. He didn't need to hear any more. "I know, Lily. Be strong. I promise, I'll come for you."

Red gave a harsh laugh, growling, "I think not. But if it helps ease your conscience, then go ahead and give the bitch false hope. Now I really must go."

But Lily cut Red off before he hung up, pleading urgently, "Rock, tell my Aunt Nord to pray for me!"

Red scoffed, "You'll need more than prayers. Goodbye forever, Mr. Stone, from the both of us."

Silence returned to the woods.

# Chapter 36 – The Long Shot

Rock, Tim and Joe ran to the command center. The rain had stopped but the smog had grown thicker. The men couldn't see beyond the glowing beams of their flashlights. The whole way, Rock played the call over and over in his mind. So much troubled him, but what he kept coming back to was Lily's plea. Deliver a message to her aunt? Suddenly, he understood.

Tim reached the tent first. Throwing the canvas screen aside, he darted inside. Joe then Rock followed in his wake.

"How far can a car driving to Mexico get in three hours?" Tim barked at the team.

His men returned blank stares.

"We know Red is alive. He has a three-hour head-start on us. I need to know how far he's gotten. Come on, I need this now!"

"No! He's headed to Canada," Rock challenged.

Tim spun. Focusing his pissed-off glare, he confronted Rock. "This is no time to play hunches. We don't have enough resources as it is." Tim wheeled to the team. "Tell me where he might be heading south!"

The agents dove for their computers.

"*Stop!*" Rock yelled with such force that every agent halted. "It's not a guess. Lily told us."

Tim's red face shared his boiling ire. Through clenched teeth, he let Rock have it. "God damn it, Rock. I'd listened to the call, too. She did not. Now shut up or get out!"

Rock didn't back down. In a calm even voice, he explained, "Lily doesn't have an Aunt Nord. Nord is French for north."

The wheels of the jet touched down at the airport north of Kalispell, Montana at five in the morning. More than a day had passed since Rock last heard Lily's voice. The memory fueled him like nothing else could. He hadn't slept more than two hours in the last two days, but his passion to save her and kill Red was a potent stimulant.

For the majority of the flight, Rock reviewed the report John had prepared. Roused from a dead sleep in the middle of the night by Rock's call twenty-four hours earlier, John had worked nonstop ever since. The first twelve hours searching for a lead on where Red might be headed produced nothing. The break came when John found Red owned a cabin inside Glacier National Park. Its relationship to Red was well concealed by a holding company of a holding company. That was the first clue.

Michael provided the second. Looking to curry favor to avoid the death penalty, he was being particularly cooperative. He was familiar with the camp, having hunted bear with Red there once. He described it as a compound armed to the teeth with every modern security measure. The razor-wire-topped fence ensured hikers wouldn't visit. That and so many more obstacles would present formidable barriers to an assault. Most importantly, the place was stocked with enough weapons to fend off an army.

Rock supplied the last. He'd been to Glacier many times. A quick look at a map confirmed what he suspected. The cabin was on the northern side of Lake McDonald, a half-day hike from Waterton Lake, a lake spanning the Canadian border. In the summer, a ferry connects the park with the town of Waterton in Alberta, Canada. It is used mainly by tourists taking round-trip sightseeing tours, but it also transports one-way passengers across the border. Rock had ridden that boat once from Waterton and was surprised to find on the U.S. side a border-crossing station. In a cabin at the dock, hikers are processed to enter and leave the country. Rock could not imagine a more secluded place where Red could slip away.

The jet rolled up to a hanger and parked on the tarmac in front. Alongside the building, three FBI Suburbans and four state police cars sat idling. The plane door opened and a dozen agents scurried off to load weapons and gear into the vehicles. Rock watched them fill the SUVs with enough equipment to outfit a platoon. Would it be enough to save Lily?

Tim noticed Rock's worried look. "The agents who arrived last night have set up the command center. We'll join them in an hour. From there, it's a mile walk to Red's compound. He won't hear us coming."

Looking no less fraught, Rock replied, "We need to surround his cabin as soon as possible. Red had a twenty-hour drive to get here. He couldn't have arrived in time to cross the border yesterday, but he'll be leaving today, by mid-morning at the latest. Any later and he won't catch the last ferry. I just hope he didn't take off at sunrise," Rock moaned, looking east to the sun peaking over the horizon.

"We're about ready to go. We'll get there in time."

"We must. If we don't stop Red at the compound, we'll have no chance of saving Lily. Your agents might grab him at the border, but by then she'll be dead. Or worse." Rock shuddered at the thought of Lily trapped in a cave somewhere, left to suffer an excruciatingly slow death.

"Let's roll!" Tim's command jolted Rock from this horrifying vision.

The caravan moved out.


Motion on one of the screens in the bank of video monitors caught Red's attention. The main entrance to the airport showed activity. A parade of Suburbans and state police cars rolled out of the airport then turned onto U.S. Highway 2, heading north. The show ended when the last of the vehicles rolled off the screen.

"We need to prepare a proper welcome, missy."

# Chapter 37 – Can She be Saved?

The agents set out for Red's compound as soon as they arrived at the command cabin. The sun had risen into a glorious Montana morning above the canopy of the park's forest. Below, where sullen shadows hung deep, the men had the cover needed to move into position.

Tim dispersed the local resources to watch the roads. If Red made a run for it, they'd intercept him. He positioned his men two hundred yards out, at all twelve numbers of the clock. Each could eyeball the man to his left and right. Tim wasn't taking any chances Red would escape this time.

Pointing to a tree deep in the woods, Tim told Rock, "You'd better hang back. I can't risk having you get hurt again. You know how hard it was for me to convince my superiors to let you come along. You get hurt and my ass is grass," he sighed, offering an apologetic smile.

While the truth, Rock had also assured Tim that he was going to be there one way or the other. It was just a matter of how. "Okay. Tell me the moment you know anything."

Rock wasn't happy, but he had no say in this operation. Tim was doing everything in his power to save Lily. Now that he had helped find Red's cabin, Rock would only be in the way. His job was to wait.

Settling into his assigned spot, Rock peered through a narrow opening in the trees watching Joe adjust the equipment. Tim hung over his partner's shoulder pointing to the screens. A slight breeze blew the leaves, occasionally obscuring Rock's view of the pair. Once all the agents assumed their positions, the operation would commence. Rock said a prayer for Lily.

"Don't move."

Rock heard Red's command barely above a whisper at the same time he felt the cold round tip of a silencer press the base of his skull.

"Good boy," Red growled. "Now, hand over your cell phone."

Rock complied.

"And the tracking device."

Rock hesitated.

"Don't make me wait," Red snarled, grinding the gun into Rock's skin.

He had hoped Red wouldn't know to look for the tracker. Tim had given it to him just in case things turned chaotic and they got separated. Rock fished it from his pocket.

Red disabled both devices then yanked Rock's arm. "Come on, we're going this way." With the pistol pushing the back of Rock's head, Red herded him away from the compound.

"How'd you know?" Rock's heart was in his shoes.

"How could I miss the line of cop cars coming from the airport? I tapped into the security system of the restaurant across from the exit. The camera to the parking lot gave me the perfect view. I rigged it on my way through last night. While ordinarily I wouldn't have bothered, I've come to realize I shouldn't underestimate you. My caution has rewarded me nicely."

"Where's Lily?" he demanded.

"She's alive. That's what you really want to know. At least for now. Whether she stays that way depends on what Agent Fuller does. I hope it isn't anything stupid."

From the corner of his eye, Rock saw Red flash a sinister smile.

"So where is she?" Rock harbored the slimmest of hopes that he could save her.

"The cabin."

"Where are we going?" Rock now had the urge to go to the compound. Red, however, kept leading him deeper into the forest.

"Once again, Mr. Stone, you've forced me to change my plans. Thankfully this will be the last time. Still, I am glad you came today. It allows us to finish the conversation cut short at the estate."

"Go ahead, it's your show," Rock replied, eager to keep the man talking. The longer Red did, the longer Rock stayed alive.

"You really screwed up a good thing I had going with Michael. But I do need to put some of the blame on him. If only he had let me handle Anna, we'd still be sitting fat and happy. The irony is, I had the perfect plan figured out. I just couldn't reach him."

Red tugged Rock's arm, leading him onto a trail. "I give Michael credit, however, he almost pulled it off. The alibi with the Russian whore was perfectly executed. The shooting, too, was a masterpiece. He only needed to get rid of the gun and he would have been golden."

"Maybe." But Rock knew he was right.

"No, he would have. I called him after Agent Fuller interviewed him. He told me everything, including that he still had the gun. He'd stashed it at the slut's place. Said it had too much sentimental value to pitch away. Kept insisting nobody would find it. I finally convinced him to throw it in the ocean, but once he retrieved it, he did a dumb-ass thing. On his way to dump it, he saw Lily was at the house. I'd told him about your night with her. In a rage, he went there with the gun in the truck."

Rock's eyes narrowed. "You knew about Lily coming to my room? You had her tailed?"

"I've always kept a close eye on her. Until that night, she took whatever Michael dished out and eventually went home alone. Not this time."

"So, her coming to me started the chain that ended with Michael and you getting caught. Now I know it was the best night ever."

"And the chain that will lead to your death," Red scoffed. "Don't forget about that. Still the best night?"

"Yes," Rock answered without hesitation.

Red shook his head.

"Again, where are we going?" Rock asked casually, but he needed to know in order to plan Lily's rescue.

"I had to move out of the compound when I saw you coming. Very inconvenient. It will cost me a half-day's delay in crossing the border. But having you here to see your lover die and allowing me to kill you myself, when I thought I'd lost that opportunity, the delay is well worth it."

"You have me now. Let Lily go." Rock didn't intend to give Red the satisfaction of hearing him beg, but an unintended hint of pleading carried in his request.

"I don't think so. I want you to suffer to the end knowing you caused her death."

Rock's mind raced, desperately searching for any option that might lead to saving Lily. He found none.

"Keep going. We've got another fifteen minutes," Red grunted, pushing harder with the gun.

Nearing the end of their trek they emerged from the forest into a small clearing. The first thing to draw Rock's eyes was a nearby sewage treatment plant. Two large open reservoirs were visible. One was the solid waste settling pool – basically a shit pond. The other contained the system for cleaning up the water. Rock instantly recognized where he was. This was the waste treatment facility for Lake McDonald Lodge.

Red noted Rock's gaze. "Tourists' shit's got to go somewhere. Just be glad the wind is blowing away from us today. Some days it's unbearable in there." He pointed to a small building close to the ponds. "Get going."

Poking Rock with the muzzle, Red urged him toward the door.

Tim's preoccupation with coordinating the assault prevented him from noticing Rock had disappeared. His attention was fixed on Joe, watching him adjust the monitor for the heat-sensing camera aimed at the cabin. "Do you see anything?"

"Looks like someone is on the first floor, front room, but I can't be sure. The source isn't moving."

"Could it be Lily? She might be tied to something." Tim peered at the monitor. "Any other signs of life?"

"Haven't found anything else. The snipers can't see anyone through the windows either, but Red knows how to be careful. We saw that at the estate."

Tim nodded. "Can we get the drone in place to look? Maybe take it in high with the trees around and drop it down to peek in. These shadows will make it really hard for him to see it."

"We need to try. We can't go in blind, he'll have all the advantage."

"Okay, go ahead."

Joe pulled the drone out of its bag. With both video and infra-red capabilities, it could scope out a building with minimal chance of being detected. Its propulsion system was as quiet as a whisper. The light color and small size made it hard to spot.

Easing the drone into the air, Joe expertly guided it through the trees until it was above the front of the two-story cabin. He lowered it slowly, looking for a high angle view into the second-floor rooms. Tim watched the video feed over Joe's shoulder, searching for any signs of life.

Joe brought the drone to a stop, hovering above a window. The camera peered down onto a bed.

"Anything?" Tim asked.

"Nope," Joe muttered. Deftly maneuvering the joystick, he lowered the drone to linger at the top of the window. The entire bedroom came into view.

Both men saw it. Tim asked, "What's that?"

When panicked recognition dawned, Joe yelled, "Shit!"

The red light of the motion-detector flicked on, visible for just an instant before the video feed went black. Diving to the ground, both men hit the moss-covered earth at the same time. A fraction of a second later the explosion tore through the trees around them. Shrubs were uprooted while debris whisked through the forest. When the dust settled, the cabin no longer existed.

Rock and Red were approaching the door when the roar of the blast broke the quiet of the morning. Rock's heart sank at the sound. Red smiled at his reaction. "Seems like Agent Fuller did something stupid."

# Chapter 38 – A Sharp Knife

Tim confirmed all his agents were accounted for. Except for a few cuts and bruises, everyone was unharmed. Rock, however, was nowhere to be found.

"I can't even locate his tracking device," Joe grumbled, fiddling with the settings on the equipment. "I hoped I was missing something, but everything is working. Maybe it got broken in the blast."

"Great," Tim huffed, "I should have known better than to bring him along."

After making one last quick scan of the place, Tim grunted, "We'll look later. We don't have time to search for him now."

Pulling out his radio, he called to his troops. "Close in on the remains of the compound. Keep an eye out for Red while you advance, I don't want him sneaking through our net. Once you reach the fence, halt for additional orders. Nobody crosses into the compound until we're sure there aren't other booby traps. The bastard likely set up trip wires with more explosives. And let me know if you find Stone."

"You sadistic son-of-a-bitch!" Rock barked, looking from Lily to Red when he spied her strapped to a chair.

"Rock!" Lily greeted excitedly.

"I said she was in the cabin," Red answered wearing an evil smile. "Pull that chair beside hers. I have a lot to do and can't have you in my way."

Rock trudged toward the seat, unable to take his eyes off of Red.

"Guten Morgen, Herr Stone. Mein name ist Dirk Werner." Red pronounced the 'W' as a 'V' and everything else with a perfect German accent.

On the march to the cabin, Rock had not gotten a look at Red. But seeing him face-on, Rock knew the voice but everything else about him was unrecognizable.

The thin red hair on Red's head was now a thick black mane. The graying highlights rounded the edges of his angular head. A bushy salt-and-pepper mustache obscured the upper lip of his tanned face. Even his build was different, the result of a girdle and padded body suit. Lifts in his boots added a good two inches to his height. In addition to making Red appear more than ten years older, the overall effect concealed his Irish heritage behind a Western European façade.

Then there was Red's German. Rock was fluent in the language and what he'd heard him speak was impeccable. "So, you're Dirk Werner now?"

"You like my transformation?" Red chuckled, enjoying the stunned look on Rock's face. "You didn't think I'd walk up to the border looking like me, did you?"

Red backed away. Motioning with the pistol to the chair next to Lily, he commanded, "Sit down and put these zip ties on your legs and arm." He threw three at Rock, growling, "Come on, get moving."

Rock lingered to survey the new Red before binding his legs at the ankles to the sturdy furniture. He then fastened a wrist to the armrest.

Approaching cautiously with the final strap, Red warned, "You move, I shoot her." Training the gun on Lily, with his free hand Red made quick work of lashing Rock's other wrist to the chair."

Even on close inspection, Rock found the new Red appeared so unlike the man he had come to know. And if he couldn't identify him, he wondered how the border guards would. But Red would be traveling alone. That should tip them off. At least that's what Rock hoped. "They'll be waiting for you at the border; they'll still know it's you.

How many older hikers will cross alone into Canada this week? You'll stand out like a sore thumb."

"Who said I will be going alone? I've paid a handful of my mercenary buddies to join me. It will be Dirk Werner and his German hiking club who show up at the border. On our way from Glacier to continue trekking in Waterton Park after the fourth week of our five-week holiday. Such a nice way for me to get away from Frankfurt and the stress of selling Mercedes-Benz in Kronberg."

Red patted his vest pocket. "My German passport is authentic, a perk I was able to keep after a previous employment. And as you heard, my German is perfect."

Kneeling in front of Rock, Red double-checked the leg restraints while continuing, "Our Canadian tour guide, another of my buddies, will meet us with the ferry from Waterton. He'll buy out the last trip of the day to ensure we have the boat to ourselves. But on the slim chance I am recognized, we will go to plan B. We shoot everyone in the head and sail ourselves across the lake. By the time someone finds what the bears haven't eaten, we'll have scattered to the four winds. I will be free to enjoy a long life while you will be dead."

A self-satisfied grin bloomed on Red's face. Giving a tug on the last zip tie, Red stood, holstering his gun.

Rock accepted that Red was right. The bastard would slip away undiscovered if he didn't stop him. This realization added fuel to Rock's resolve to find a way to save Lily and take Red down. Whether Rock survived was irrelevant.

Sitting straighter, Rock responded, "I admit I'd misread you, and I don't often do that. I had you pegged as a blunt instrument, nothing more. But you're surprisingly resourceful." There was no hint of surrender in his voice.

"What is a person more cautious around, a dull knife or a sharp one? I don't mind being viewed as a 'blunt instrument', as you say, then people like you are less careful around me. They wrongly assume they have the upper hand.

A mistake you will only have a short while longer to regret. Now, as I said, I still have a lot to do. Feel free to say your goodbyes while I wrap up the last details."

After re-examining their bindings, Red hustled from the cabin.

# Chapter 39 – The Cask of Amontillado

Rock and Lily faced each other in the quiet of the cabin. He paused until Red's footsteps faded away before whispering the question he was eagerly waiting to ask. "Are you okay?"

"Other than my mouth hurting where he punched me, I'm good." Grimacing, she flexed her jaw. "He gave me something that knocked me out soon afterwards. I came around in his cabin during the night. After sunrise he brought me here." Lily anticipated the next question. "He didn't do anything else to me."

Rock's tensed demeanor softened. "I'm glad you're all right." Fixing eyes on the door, he continued in a hushed voice, "I may have an idea for how we can get away."

"Isn't the FBI coming?"

"I doubt it. I'm sure they think Red and you are dead in the explosion. While they've discovered I'm missing, their first priority will be to secure his compound. They won't start looking for me for hours. This cabin is a good two miles away so it will be days until they search this far out. By then, it will be too late. No, it's up to us to save ourselves." Rock spoke without any trace of fear, he had the start of a plan. This filled him with renewed hope.

But his candid assessment frightened Lily. "How?" Her voice quivered.

"I'm not completely sure yet. But I know some things about this cabin that I'm assuming Red doesn't." Rock's eyes stayed locked on the door while he whispered, "John's report gave details of the properties surrounding Red's compound. The FBI needed a cabin nearby to use as the staging area for the assault. I was surprised to see a sewage treatment plant in the middle of a national park. Why someone would build a cabin so close to it had me stumped until I read that the plant was built in the late sixties *after* the cabin. The Park Service acquired the property in order to build the plant."

Rock's focus flit to Lily to make sure she was keeping up.

She nodded. "Got it. But how does that help us?"

Looking back to the door, he answered, "The cabin was built in the fifties. It caught my eye because of a unique notation on the description of the property. It was designed to include a bomb shelter. If we can get away from Red, maybe we can slip into the bunker and hide out until he leaves."

"So where is the entrance?"

Rock hesitated. "I don't know." Locking eyes with hers, he muttered, "The property report didn't confirm that it had been built. It only said it was zoned for a shelter." He pressed on, not allowing the possibility that it didn't exist to diminish his optimism. "Did you see anything around the cabin when you got here? Maybe a cement cap nearby or access to a cellar?"

"No, nothing like that. Could it be somewhere in here?" Her gaze surveyed the Spartan interior.

Shaking his head, Rock answered, "It's a one-room cabin. We can see every inch of the place. Nothing looks like it leads to a bomb shelter," he grumbled, frustration sneaking into his voice. "The walls are bare except for the shelves back there, the joints of the floor boards are too tight to be hiding a trap door, and there's no furniture except for the chairs we're strapped to. I'm not seeing anything that might be the entrance."

Lily wouldn't give up. "I visited the Greenbrier Hotel in West Virginia once. It has a bomb shelter in the basement built to house Congress during the Cold War. I remember it so well because the entrance was hidden in plain sight behind a false wall. Any chance they did something like that here?"

Rock examined their surroundings again. "I don't see anything. The dimensions of the cabin outside look the same as inside. There doesn't appear to be room for a hidden space behind any of the walls." But as Rock's gaze traveled past the pine rafters to the peaked ceiling, he spied something unusual. He studied it hard, then blurted out, "I know where it is!"

Lily leaned forward, her wide eyes searching the space Rock was focused on. "Where?"

"It's under the potbelly stove," he cheered in a hushed voice, nodding to the squat wood-burner near the back wall. "Look up there, the flue is strange. It's hinged near the roof. That kind of pipe would only be used if it needs to flex. I'm not exactly sure how the stove is attached to the floor, but it must move to expose a shaft leading into the bomb shelter. There's got to be a lever somewhere on the side or bottom that releases it. Once in the tunnel, it can be moved back into place sealing the entrance, something like the way a hatch is closed on a submarine." Rock was guessing at ninety percent of this, but the hinged piping convinced him their path to a hideout was under that heater.

"How do we get loose to get down there?"

Lily had hit on the part of the plan that stymied Rock. He gave her a brooding look. "I don't know."

Struggling silently against his bindings, Rock flexed his arms and jerked his legs. He couldn't detect the slightest weakness in his restraints. His frustration built as he continued fighting for freedom. The chair took small hops across the floor with each futile spasm.

"Rock, stop," Lily chided, focusing sad eyes on the trickle of blood coming from under one of his arm ties. Two crimson drops speckled the floor by his chair.

He relaxed, resting his chin on his chest. He didn't look at her when he spoke. "I'm sorry. They're too strong to break and the chairs are too sturdy. We need to wait until Red unties us. We'll look for our chance then." Drawing a deep breath, he released a long sigh before demanding, "When it comes, don't wait for me. Get to safety whether I'm there or not. Do you understand?"

She didn't respond.

Lifting his head, he added urgency to his gloomy directive. *"Promise* me you'll do this."

"No, I can't," Lily replied defiantly, her eyes filling with tears.

"I'll join you if I can, but if I can't, you must go. Please... do this for me," he pleaded, his voice tapering off. His look implored her.

Lily hung her head. Reluctantly, she nodded.

With the plan made, they sat in silence, deep in their thoughts.

The latch rattled when the cabin door opened. Red lumbered in carrying four long metal posts with wires leading from them. A satchel hung from a shoulder.

"I'm happy to say everything is about ready. I hope you've completed your goodbyes because the time for you to part is just about here." Red stood the posts on their base by Lily then dropped the bag.

"I guess you'd like to know how this will end. I could keep you in suspense, but I find the anticipation of knowing what horrible future awaits adds a little extra to the experience." Red was giddy at the prospect of executing his plan. "These four poles are my modern twist on Poe's story."

Rock and Lily's expressions showed they weren't following.

"Keep up, now, I don't have time to repeat myself. In *The Cask of Amontillado*, the victim was walled up alive in the cellar. Left to die a horrific death. I could have found a cave and sealed missy in it to die, but simply copying Poe involves no creativity at all. That just won't do. Fortunately, modern technology allows me to make walls to accomplish the same result."

Rock and Lily listened intently, anticipating the worse to come.

"These four poles are equipped with laser sensors. I'll place them around missy like this." Red moved the poles to the four corners forming a square around her chair. "When I hook the sensors to the transmitter and turn on the lasers, I've created an invisible box around her. If she goes in any direction between any of the poles, she will break a beam and activate the transmitter."

Rock shuddered. He knew where this was leading. "Then boom," he groaned.

"Exactly, Mr. Stone! Well put!" Red beamed. "I've placed explosives on the outside of the building, enough to level it and kill anyone within forty yards. If by chance Agent Fuller does find this place before missy triggers the blast, I want to make sure she and a couple agents go together. In addition to these sensors, I've rigged the outside of the building with detectors to detonate the charges if agents close in."

Red stood in silence radiating a satisfied glow. Shaking his head to revive his focus, he mumbled, "But I digressed. Where was I? Oh yes, I need to replicate the essence of Poe's story."

He looked at Lily. "I will allow you to be free inside this electronic box. Just on the other side of these infinitely small laser beams I will leave food and water." He pulled from his sack a water bottle and clear tub containing an apple and bag of nuts. "All the things you need to sustain your life will be in sight but unattainable. You'll starve to death or reach through the beam putting yourself out of your misery. Either way, you die a truly ghastly death as Poe envisioned."

Red took a bow, proud of his creativity.

Lily sobbed softly.

"What's the plan for me?" Rock growled through clenched teeth. His hatred for the man had risen to its full fury.

"I thought about having you watch her die. If you hadn't been so kind as to join me today, I would have live-streamed the video of her sitting in my compound. You could have watched her waste away or end it all. But now that you're here, I'm satisfied with you knowing how badly this will end for her. I need the instant gratification of seeing you die by my own hands. I am going to shoot you in the head and dump your body in the shit pond. The place where you truly deserve to spend eternity."

Rock hung his head.

# Chapter 40 – It's Time

Red made the finishing touches to the invisible walls. Attaching the wires to the transmitter, he flipped the switch and red-eyed lasers came to life.

Constructed right before her eyes, Lily stared in horror at the means for her death. But the tears no longer came. Only when Red put out the bait did she realize she hadn't eaten since being taken. Dehydrated and famished, the food fueled her hunger as powerful as a junkie in need of a fix. She would not last long in the box.

After double-checking the preparations, Red returned his attention to his captives. "When I push the button on this remote, the stage is set to play out my version of *The Cask of Amontillado*. A masterpiece. Truly my best work," he gushed, self-satisfaction written on every aspect of his body. "And now, it's time."

He moved to Lily. The serrated steel of his switchblade snapped out in front of her face. She jerked away, expecting the sting of a cut. Instead, he reached to her ankles and severed the zip-ties. He then removed the ones securing her arms.

She flexed her stiff limbs in sweet relief.

"Now undo Mr. Stone," Red demanded. With the pistol aimed between her eyes, he handed her the knife. Focusing a menacing look on Rock, he warned, "Don't make any sudden moves. She dies first."

Fumbling to cut the bindings from Rock, she nearly slit his wrist. She drew a deep breath, steadying her nerves. The razor-sharp blade slid through with an easy pull.

"Now the legs." Red held the cocked pistol at her head.

Lily bent, locking eyes with Rock. Should they try something desperate? It might be now or never. Miniscule furrowing of his brow gave the answer. She clipped the ties and eased away.

"Good decision," Red sneered. "Now throw the knife toward the door and sit down."

Obeying orders, Lily collapsed into the chair rigged to kill her.

Red circled behind Rock. Training the gun on him, he commanded, "Get up, Mr. Stone, I'd like you to join me outside."

Rock leaned heavily on the arms of the chair, considering his odds. Was he quick enough to get Red before he fired a lethal shot? Rock didn't mind dying, but he needed to live long enough to kill Red. He rapidly calculated the angles, the possible moves, the permutations and variations of the available options. All ended with him dead on the floor and Red still alive. He had to bide his time.

"Come on, don't drag your feet. I didn't expect you to be afraid to die," Red mocked. "Get your ass up and head to the door." He positioned himself directly behind while Rock lumbered to his feet.

Rock trudged to the exit, the muzzle kissing his head. Easing it open, ready to step into the sunlight, he realized Lily was untied and her box was not armed. She could slip into the bunker while Red was off killing him. The relief that she would be saved lifted him.

"Hold up," Red snapped, halting in the doorway. He looked to Lily. Her tears would not come but her body shook with the sobs that expressed her infinite sorrow. "Don't go anywhere, missy, I'm turning on the sensors." He pushed on the remote.

Rock swallowed hard to keep from puking.

"Go." Red shoved Rock through the door then slammed it shut. "That way," he directed, gesturing toward the pond.

Rock's pace was slow but steady. He'd accepted that he was about to die, but he wouldn't go without trying to take

Red with him. The thoughts came fast and furious, but nothing had any reasonable possibility for success.

When half-way to the pond, out of earshot of the cabin, Red leaned to Rock's ear. He whispered in a conspiratorial tone, "Want to know a secret? You have to promise not to tell Lily or I'll put a bullet in her head. I didn't arm the sensors," he snickered. "Funny thing, she could eat and drink if she wanted, but she won't. Is that called irony or pathos? I'm not sure what the right word is, but for me, it's *fun.*"

Rock readied to call him a sick bastard or some other warped-prick term but he held his tongue. Whatever he'd call him, Red would take it as a compliment.

With a few more steps they reached the top of a short hill leading to the sludge below. Spying the narrow ledge separating the ground from the tank, Rock had an idea. If he got Red there, he'd yank his killer with him into the shit and hold on. They'd both be dead but Lily would be free. It was the only plan that had any chance.

"I assume you'll want me to stand on the rim when you shoot me. Have me fall in so you don't get dirty."

"That's the plan. Why drag a body when gravity can do the work?"

Looking down, Rock surveyed the terrain. A steep slope fell away to the pond. Slick damp grass coated the incline. He'd use this to his advantage. Twisting Red off balance, they'd tumble together into the muck.

Rock began his descent. When he did, Red stopped. The separation between them grew. Looking back, Rock slowed his pace.

"Keep walking," Red demanded, his shooting arm fully extended. The muzzle targeted Rock's chest.

Rock stared in hopeless desperation.

Suddenly, Red's shoulder jerked. His body twisted. The crack of a rifle accompanied his cry.

Off balance, Red dove for cover. Stumbling, he swung the gun toward Rock.

Rock bolted. Red fired.

The bullet missed.

Red rolled down while Rock sprinted up. Reaching the rim, Rock heard two soft puffs. Neither shot found its mark.

Adrenaline fueled Rock's dash to the cabin. He needed to get Lily to safety. Red still had the detonator.

*"Lily, run!"*

She couldn't hear him. The boom of rifle blasts drowned out his screams. FBI agents were laying down cover for his escape.

Rock burst through the cabin door.

Red slid to a stop by the pond. Looking up, he spied Rock cresting the hill. He popped off two more shots.

Scrambling to his feet, he scurried after. Bullets pelting the grass at the summit halted him. He hugged the slope, shielded from the agents.

He needed to get away. His only hope - set off the explosives. He'd disappear during the chaos.

Pulling the remote, he hit the button.

Nothing.

He stabbed it again, then again.

Still nothing.

Red stared at the controls. "What the fuck?!" Then recognition dawned. "Shit! The hill."

With head down, he crept up the incline. Holding the trigger in front, he inched higher. Repeatedly fingering the switch, he growled, "Blow, God damn it!"

Nearing the rim, his attempts continued to fail. That's when he heard the cabin door slam. He could see, without seeing, Rock rushing in. He still had a chance to kill the bastard and his bitch.

Red crouched below the bullets singing overhead. A cluster of slugs sprayed the ground, showering him with dirt.

Pulling a deep breath, he leapt to his feet, thrusting the remote into the air. With arm held high, he pressed the button.

The concussion radiated a wall of force across all three-hundred-and-sixty degrees.

# Chapter 41 – For the Third Time

"Get him out of that crap!" Tim barked. "Come on, move, move, get him out of there."

Joe chuckled, "The asshole blew himself into the shit pond."

"I can't believe he's still alive," Tim moaned.

"Throw him a rope," Joe called to the agents by the tank, "but be careful!"

Tim leaned over the slope watching the line slap the muck next to Red. "Quit flailing and grab it, dickhead."

Red held tight while two agents struggled to pull him across the viscous pond. Miraculously, he was relatively unharmed. In addition to the shoulder wound, Red was cut and bleeding, but nothing was life-threatening.

The lowest-ranking agent received the honors of cuffing the prisoner's filth-covered wrists. He also won the lottery to ride along to the hospital. Tim knew he needed to find a way to make it up to the poor guy, but he couldn't begin to think of anything big enough.

Once Red was on his way, Tim forced himself to address the difficult task of finding what remained of his friends. For the third time in forty-eight hours, he stood looking at the wreckage of something Red had blown up. The previous two times he'd approached the task hoping society was ridden of a truly horrible person. This time it was with the reality that the world had lost two special people.

The cabin was leveled. Everything had been scoured away by the blast. The floorboards were lifted up and scattered about like random Lincoln Logs. A few roof timbers had fallen into the heart of the building. Little else remained.

Tim stood near the site with a handful of men. In the distance the whining of the ambulance was fading away.

Around the perimeter, held back by a couple agents, were the crime scene investigators and coroner waiting to claim whatever they recovered of Rock and Lily. Small groups were talking, planning their next steps.

"What's that?" Tim's eyes widened. "Joe, did you hear that?!"

"No, what?"

"Shut up! Everyone, *shut up!*" Tim screamed.

The murmur slowly became silence.

Tim cocked his head. His gaze narrowed while he concentrated on his hearing. "There, did you hear that?"

Grinning, Joe answered, "Yeah." He pointed to the middle of the jumble. "It's coming from over there. Sounds like someone crying for help."

Very faintly, Tim heard a woman yelling, "Down here."

"Holy shit, that's Lily!" Tim's voice cracked with excitement. Dashing into the scattered mess, he called back to Joe, "Quick, get in here, we need to move these timbers."

Picking his way through the devastation, Tim listened, trying to get a bearing on where the sound was coming from. Standing in the thick of it, he spied a partially-exposed rim for a concrete slab.

"Over there." Hopping planks and beams, Tim reached the block. "Give me a hand."

Joe stumbled to his side. Together they pulled and pushed a massive log. "This thing weighs a fucking ton," Joe groaned, putting his shoulder into the effort.

"Keep pushing, it's moving," Tim grunted.

Nudging the obstacle a few inches, Joe huffed, "Hold up. Take a look at that." Standing away sucking deep breaths, he pointed to a metal disk that looked like a hatch. From the narrow opening between metal and concrete, they heard Lily's cries more clearly.

"We're here, Lily," Tim called. "Get back. We need to move more wood." Turning to an agent on the perimeter, he yelled, "Get a tire iron over here right away!"

Tim and several agents struggled to remove the obstructions from the cover. Once cleared, he put the tire iron to use. Wedging it between the plate and rim, he pulled and tugged until he was drenched in sweat. The cap wouldn't budge.

"Out of the way!" he snarled at the agents coming to lend a hand. With one end of the bar inside the hatch and the middle over a beam, Tim jumped on the other end. The cover popped open with an ear-piercing screech.

Regaining his balance, he darted to straddle the opening. Joe stood by his side shining a flashlight into the shaft. The beam penetrated to the bottom. Lily's smiling dirt-covered face peered up at them.

Tim was thrilled to see her alive. His joy, however, was dampened by not knowing what had happened to Rock.

Before he could ask, a grimy grin appeared next to hers. "Hi guys, thanks for dropping in."

Rock watched the paramedic drape the last strip of tape around his sprained ankle. His leg throbbed and his ribs stung, but he never felt better in his life. Lily was alive.

She stayed with him from the moment he was hoisted from the bunker. In no uncertain terms, she told every person who urged her to get checked out or make herself more comfortable that she wasn't leaving his side. Rock didn't try to change her mind. He wanted her there.

Trudging into the command tent, Tim sat across from them while Lily finished her second bottle of water. Rock's tired look couldn't have been happier. Tim broke the silence. "I don't know where to start. I guess you want to know if we got him. We did."

The couple's smiles said it all.

"Is he dead?" Lily asked.

"No. He's in a bad way, but he'll live. Long enough to be executed."

"Can't be soon enough for me. The explosion should have finished him," Rock growled.

"We had to fish him out of the shit pond. I suspect he'll smell like that until the day he dies. Seems fitting for the piece of shit he is," Tim chuckled roughly.

Rock wagged his head. "Why didn't you just kill him when you had the chance? That would have saved me from running for my life and almost getting blown up."

Tim grimaced. "I was lucky I hit him at all."

"What? Why?" Rock's voice shared his confusion. And his concern.

"We were coming down the lane toward the cabin, sneaking along the berm hidden by the trees, when I saw him bring you out. Fortunately, he didn't see us when he turned you toward the pond. I was at least two hundred yards away and didn't have a clean shot, he was standing too close to you. I hurried after but couldn't run without making noise. He would have killed you right then if he'd spotted us."

"I'm sure of it," Rock chipped in.

"When you got to the hill and he started hanging back with the gun extended, I knew I'd run out of time. I dropped to the ground, drew a bead on the biggest part of him I could put in the scope, and pulled the trigger. When he fell and you ran, my guys started laying down cover fire. The goal at that point wasn't to kill Red but to not hit you."

"Thank you for that."

"You're welcome, buddy," Tim responded, nudging Rock lightly. "But you sure confused me when you headed to the cabin. Then I figured it out - Lily was with you. We kept Red pinned down until you made it inside. That's when he surprised the hell out of us. He jumped up but before we could tap him, the building exploded. I saw the blast throw him into the pond but none of us saw you escape. I was certain you both were dead."

Tim focused narrowed eyes on Rock. "It couldn't have been more than five seconds between the time you went in and the boom. How the hell did you survive?"

"Lily saved us," he answered, tipping his head in her direction.

She beamed.

Turning to Lily, Tim joked, "He's never been good at taking care of himself. But how did you know the shelter was there?"

Lily squeezed Rock's hand. "He's the one who found it."

"I'd read in John's report that the cabin might have a bunker. We suspected the entrance was concealed in plain sight under a potbelly stove, but we couldn't slip in because we were tied up."

Tim interrupted. "You weren't sure it was there?"

"No, but thank God we were right. When I broke through the door, Lily was already standing inside the shaft yelling for me to hurry." Rock pivoted his attention to her. "By the way, how *did* you move the stove?"

"You called it. The door handle was the release. The whole thing slid away from the hatch. I heard the shots, then you yelling, so I figured I needed to take the chance. When I didn't get blown up, I knew I'd chosen wisely. The hatch was easy to lift - before a cabin fell on it," she teased Tim. "I crawled in and watched the door."

Peering lovingly at Rock, she sighed, "I knew you'd come back for me."

"You can't get rid of me that easily," Rock kidded.

Returning his attention to Tim, Rock continued, "She disappeared while I slid for the opening, skidding like I'm stealing home plate. When my feet hit the hatch, I dropped into the shaft. Time was running out. I grabbed the levers for the cover and jumped, pulling the lid closed with me. Catching a rung of the ladder with a foot, I kept from tumbling to the bottom. I had just enough time to seal the opening before the cabin went up."

Frowning, Rock glanced to his bandaged ankle. "The ground shook so hard I fell into the bunker. When I landed, I thought I'd broken my leg. We waited to call for help. If the explosion had started fires, we wanted to give you time to put them out before we raised the cover. My leg was too messed up to climb so Lily had to. When she tried opening the hatch, it was blocked. She finally forced it up a crack and started yelling. It was a long time before you heard her. We were starting to panic you might leave us there."

Sitting back, Tim let a low whistle escape. "Wow, that's some story. Had Red triggered the blast a second sooner… Or you'd been a second slower."

Rock focused on Lily. Reaching an arm over her shoulders, he drew her into a hug. "If you hadn't had the hatch open, I would have been done. Thank you," he whispered tenderly. Leaning in, he kissed her.

The couple lingered in the embrace until Tim's polite cough reminded them that they were not alone.

Easing away, Lily opened her eyes. Her flushed cheeks directed a sweet smile to Rock. "You can repay me later," she purred.

After soaking it in, Rock turned to Tim. "Now I get to ask a question. How did you find us?"

Tim shrugged. "You know, I'm not quite sure. I was planning to ask John that, too. He's the one who did. I texted him you're alright but let's give him a call."

He dialed, hitting the speaker button when John said hello. "Hi John, Tim here. I have you on the speaker. Rock and Lily are with me."

"Hi John," the couple's happy voices replied in unison.

Rock took the phone. "I hear you're the one who found the cabin. How in the world did you manage that? You saved our lives."

"When Tim called and said you were missing, we agreed you wouldn't have just walked off. The fact that your tracker had stopped made us certain Red had gotten to you. I decided I needed to think like Red if I wanted to find you. I know, it's a scary thought that I can do that. I knew he'd head north toward the border. He also wouldn't take you more than a mile or two away from his compound. Those two assumptions helped me narrow down the options."

"That still had to leave you with at least fifty places to check. How did you decide on the right one?" Rock was sure John had discovered some amazing clue.

"I guessed."

"What?!" Rock blurted out.

"Well, it was an educated guess. The sewage treatment plant made me pick that cabin. Red needed an unused and secluded place. The building had been abandoned for decades and I imagined the smell around it would discourage visitors. Of the remaining twenty-some options, I figured this one would be the most likely."

Rock stared at the phone in disbelief. "It was a damn good guess. Well done! Remind me to give you a bonus and a raise."

"Just having you around is good enough for me. You know how I hate looking for new jobs," John joshed.

Tim wrapped up the call. "We must go. I need to start my report and these two need a bath and a meal before I take their statements. Thanks again."

Once the call ended, Rock jumped in to prevent Tim from saying anything else. "Before I do one more official act, I need you to get us two rooms at the Lake McDonald Lodge. Make sure they're the nicest in the place looking over the water. We'll clean up, eat in the restaurant and then have huckleberry margaritas in front of the lobby fireplace. When we've finished, you'll have one hour with us. After that, I plan to sleep for a full day. How about you, Lily, you in?"

She laid her head gently on his shoulder. "I like the way you think, Mr. Stone."

# Chapter 42 – First Sight

Through drawn shades, the setting sun stole into Rose's dimly-lit hospital room casting a crimson hue on the scene. Visiting hours had ended; the hallways were finally quiet. The constant rhythm of her heart monitor was the only sound disturbing the otherwise peaceful silence.

Hazel combed fingers lovingly through her daughter's hair. The long dark locks cascaded down the pillow framing a serene face. Hazel leaned in, kissing Rose's forehead. Tilting close to an ear, she whispered, "I love you, baby. Please wake up."

Rose had not regained consciousness since the accident eight days before. The doctors were at a loss to explain why. For the first few days, they blamed the coma on her concussion and the shock of all she had been through. But once the weekend passed, the lack of improvement heightened their concerns. While all the tests had come back with reassuring results, she remained comatose. Doctors hate medical mysteries.

While Hazel backed away, the door eased open. Light from the hallway swept slowly across the bed.

"I'm sorry I couldn't be here sooner," Rock hushed. "The follow up with Tim is endless and Lily needed my help. How's she doing?" His tone was tired but hopeful.

"She's been resting peacefully since you left, but there's been no change." She understood what he really wanted to know. Her despondent reply spoke louder than her words.

"Has Doctor Singh stopped by yet with the most recent results?" he asked casually, but his concern was unmistakable.

"He came by earlier to say they won't be available until the end of the day. He promised to check in before we left with an update. Terry has been keeping me good company."

She nodded toward the darkest corner of the room. Offering a shallow grin, she teased, "I brought him along so he'd stop cleaning the house."

Rock looked over his shoulder. "Oh, hi. You've been here all day again I see. Thanks so much for moving your flight back a week. I can't tell you how much I appreciate your help."

"He's been a God-send," Hazel added. "I don't know how I'd be surviving if I didn't have him with me. The house would be so lonely," she moaned, choking up.

"Hi, Rock, I was happy to do it," Terry answered from his chair, tipping into the light to share a welcoming smile. "We had a pleasant visit with Rose today. We talked nonstop but figured she needed some quiet time. She's probably sick of hearing us gabbing on and on."

Rock marveled at Terry's ability to remain upbeat. This sustained Hazel more than anything else could.

"Terry and I had a very nice chat today. Did you know he's studying to become a doctor? He did really well on the entrance exams."

"Yep, I'm pretty proud of my MCAT scores, if I must say so myself. They're competitive for the best schools. Now all I need to do is convince one of them to take me."

"That's more than half the battle," Rock encouraged. "If you need a letter of recommendation, I'd be happy to write one."

"Thanks, I'll likely take you up on that."

A voice accompanied a gentle rap on the opening door. "May I come in?"

Rock turned his attention to the visitor. "Hi Doctor Singh, please do."

Terry rose from his chair, joining Rock and Hazel to hear the update. They allowed the doctor time to enter before Rock asked the question they all had. "Any news?"

"The results are back. We still don't see any reason why she remains in a coma. There are some other tests the team would like to run. Don't worry, they're just to confirm everything we've seen so far. Given the circumstances, we think it's best to double-check we're not missing anything. Let's step outside and I'll show you the list. We need Hazel's consent before we can proceed."

Rock wrapped a comforting arm around the slumping Hazel. "Sure," he sighed, the tone sharing his disappointment with the continuing lack of progress.

Terry remained where he stood while they exited. "You go ahead without me. This is a family discussion."

Settling into a chair, he closed his eyes.

"Who are you?"

Rose's raspy challenge interrupted Terry's introspection. His eyelids popped open to find her focusing a confused look on him.

He bounded from his seat to stand beside her. In a voice charged with excitement he comforted, "It's okay, you're in the hospital. Your mom and Rock are just outside."

Pivoting toward the door, he halted when she began fingering her cords. "I'll have the nurse bring them in," he soothed.

Terry scurried around the bed toward the call button, watching to make sure she didn't unhook anything. When he moved from the shadows, the golden glow of twilight illuminated his kind, caring face. Rose relaxed.

"What time is it?" she forced out, her hoarse voice cracking.

While rounding the foot of the bed, he replied, "A little before nine."

"I've been out all night?"

He answered as nonchalantly as he could, "No, not in the morning. It's nine o'clock at night."

"The whole day?!"

Seeing Rose's alarm, Terry could only imagine how poorly she'd react when she found out her one night was actually eight days. "Your mom and doctors will tell you everything. Lay back and rest. They'll be right in."

Becoming more aware of where she was, she focused on her wires and tubes. With each passing second, she grew more and more agitated.

Terry gently gathered her hands into his. "It's all right. You're going to be fine." His warm hands, his soft voice instantly calmed her.

He pressed the call button. A moment later, the door flew open. Doctor Singh rushed in with Hazel and Rock on his heels.

Before anyone else could say a word, Hazel exploded with joy. "Rose! You're awake!" She dashed past the doctor and dove for her daughter, crying a river.

"Mom!" Rose packed all her love into that one word.

The men watched the mother-daughter reunion in silence for the longest time. Finally, Doctor Singh eased closer to the pair. "Hazel, I hate to interrupt your special moment, but I need to evaluate Rose."

Hazel released her hug but kept petting Rose's head like she never wanted to leave her daughter ever again. Reluctantly, she pulled away and staggered into Rock's arms.

The doctor moved to Rose's side. "Hello Rose, I'm Doctor Singh. I've been caring for you after your accident." Pouring water into a plastic cup, he offered, "Please, have a drink. I'd like to ask you a couple of questions, then you can continue visiting with your family."

Rose drained the container. Licking her cracked lips, she looked to him wearing a weary but happy expression on her tear-moistened face. "Thanks."

"I promise this won't take long. First, do you know where you are?"

"A hospital."

"That's right. Do you remember anything about what happened that brought you here?"

"No. I had dinner. After that… nothing."

"You don't recall being struck by a car?"

"I don't," she groaned, shuddering.

Hazel gasped.

"That's all right. It's normal to not remember a traumatic event," he assured.

The woman's nervous demeanor relaxed.

"Now, can you tell me the names of your visitors?"

"This is my mom, Hazel." She gave her mother a weak smile. Moving her focus, she noted, "Rock. My godfather." But when she turned her attention to Terry, she became anxious. "I… don't remember."

Recognizing her distress, Rock jumped in. "It's okay, honey, you've not met. This is Terry Washington. He's your guardian angel."

# Chapter 43 – His Fifty-First

Rock sat alone at the desk in his study. Another birthday, his fifty-first, had begun. He leaned back in the chair as far as its springs would tolerate. With eyes closed, he did what he did every year. He thought. But for the first time, he wasn't thinking about getting older, or being alone, or being bored. On this day, he focused on the past year. None of the bad, only the good. And for the first time in a long, long time, he smiled on his birthday.

A rap on the door roused him. "Come in."

The entry eased open and Lily's twinkling eyes peeked in. "Can we join you?"

"Of course!"

She entered holding baby Violet. Right behind them appeared Rose.

"There are my Flower Girls," Rock welcomed, his pet name for the three of them. "And how's my baby? Say da da," he babbled in his best baby talk.

"Rock, babies don't talk at three months old," Lily playfully scoffed.

"She would if she took after her mother," he joshed. "That's what I love about her mommy."

"Nice save," Rose quipped, pulling up beside Lily.

The parade of guests didn't end there. Terry followed behind Rose, joined by Sam. Then while Rock stretched his neck to see who else might arrive, Tim and John slid in. John shut the door for the assembled reunion.

"Thanks for coming, but this many people must violate some fire code," Rock chuckled. Tipping forward, he looked up to Lily. "Since everyone is here, we might as well have the ceremony right now. Why wait until this afternoon?"

"No sir," she answered lightly, wagging her head, "there are a hundred other guests coming who want to see me claim you for my own. They tell me they won't believe it until they see it. The end of the bachelor years for Robert Stone. Besides, the garden is looking so lovely. Won't that be better than your messy study?"

"If you do it here, mom will kill you," Rose chimed in, "she hasn't left the wedding planner's side all morning. Every flower is exactly where it should be."

Lily caressed Rock's cheek. "You wouldn't do that to Hazel, would you? And admit it, with the views of the Napa vineyards, it's your favorite place."

"Oh, okay," he sighed, feigning disappointment. "But isn't it bad luck to see the bride before the nuptials?"

"Most couples don't have their three-month-old daughter at their wedding. I think we've already decided to be non-traditional." Bending to her cooing baby, she kissed Violet on her bald head.

"Good, I hate being conventional."

Rock scanned the room. "Thanks again everyone for being here. You are the people Lily and I wanted to share our home and this day with the most."

"I for one wouldn't have missed it. It's going to be quite the soiree," Tim chuckled, putting on his most pretentious airs.

Rock nodded. "It sure will be. That's because we have a lot to celebrate. Our wedding, our baby, and the great things that have happened for all of us this past year. And let's not forget. It's my birthday!"

"Well thank God, you're finally having one where I don't need to put you on suicide watch," John kidded. "I've never seen you happy on your birthday. It's a good look for you."

Jumping in, Rose noted cheerily, "It's been a terrific year. Except for this cane and the nasty scar on my neck, nothing remains of the bad, only the good." Her eyes fixed on Terry.

Rock also looked to him. "So, when do your med school classes start?"

"Two weeks. And thanks again so much. How can I ever repay you guys? Arranging to cover all of my medical school expenses is way too generous."

"Lily and I agree it's the least we can do for what you did for Rose. We're glad to do it, the world needs another talented doctor. Just don't get too distracted, Rose can be a big pain," Rock teased, turning an impish expression on her.

Rose gave Terry's hand a squeeze. "He's very happy we're living together, aren't you, hon? It's been nearly a month and we haven't killed each other yet, so I think it's going to last. And you should be the one to talk. Don't make me tell Lily the things I know, so close to you being married," she giggled, giving Rock a playful wink.

Sam leaned around Rose for a view of the bride. "So, Lily, what are you going to do with yourself? You'll finally have some free time to enjoy life. And very well deserved, too, I might add."

"I can relax and do whatever I want knowing you have the CEO job well in hand. SBI couldn't be doing any better than it is. I will make a day available every couple of months for my Board responsibilities, but other than that, I am one-hundred-and-ten-percent devoted to being a loving wife and mother."

"Even though you hold the controlling shares of SBI, I realize you had to work hard to convince the Board to give me the job. I won't let you down."

"I'm just glad Michael agreed to the quickie divorce. I confess, I still find it shocking that he gave me everything."

"Not me," Rock interjected. "It makes perfect sense. Turning it all over to you was his only chance to save SBI. It was and still is his baby. He knew he wasn't going to see the light of day outside of prison ever again. If he wanted to prevent the company he'd created - the only thing he ever truly loved - from going to ruin, he had to give you control."

Lily turned to Rock. "You'll recall he didn't give me his shares without strings attached. His conditions that I become

Chairwoman of the Board and pick the next CEO required a ton of work. But SBI's new leader was an easy decision. Sam was the only person who could right the ship."

"I hate Michael with a passion," Rock grumbled, "and I'm glad he's going to spend the rest of his life behind bars, but I must give him credit for doing the right thing by assigning his shares to you."

"I know he didn't give me everything out of the kindness of his heart," she sneered, "or that he has even the smallest bit of remorse for treating me so badly. Still, even though it has meant months of sleepless nights, I'm glad he gave me the opportunity to help turn things around at SBI. Now, I really need to make some time for me and my family." She pivoted to Sam. "I'm confident I can do that with you in charge."

"You're going to do great things," Rock seconded, "I'm sure of it. Sato-san wouldn't close the deal with Michael for the one reason Michael could never accept - he just didn't trust him. Making you the head guy was exactly what Sato-san needed to see to make him comfortable with selling his favorite division to SBI." Looking to Lily, he added, "Babe, that was a stroke of genius, you two going to visit Sato-san right after Sam became CEO. A day later the deal was signed."

"In all modesty," Sam responded, "I have to agree that making me CEO was exactly what SBI needed. But I also know that given my past, not everyone was excited about putting me in this position. Thank you, Lily, for trusting in me."

"The others couldn't see what I do," she replied, "you were the obvious choice. You've proven the naysayers wrong. And what's more, you've turned the morale around at the company. I didn't recognize the executive suite when I visited the other day. People are actually enjoying their jobs."

"My first official act was to send Nancy packing. I convinced Del to be my Executive Assistant and she has been a breath of fresh air for the entire floor now that she runs it. I really enjoy working with her. She's great!"

"I love Del," Rock agreed heartily. "I can't wait to see her today. But you have to admit, folks are also happier now that the company is doing well. Look at the stock price. It has gone through the roof since the acquisition."

Sam reacted with a satisfied smile that morphed into a questioning look aimed at Rock. "Speaking of the stock, there's one thing I never understood about this whole affair. Was Michael guilty of insider trading or not?"

"Michael manipulated the stock price with the help of Anna and Julie. He was telling the truth when he said all the trades had been arranged a long time in advance. And as he contended, the sale of the stock was a part of the divorce agreement."

Tenting his fingers, Rock leaned back in his chair. "But the purchase of the property from Anna had *two* options. One to buy half and one to acquire it all. The real estate he bought is an exclusive golf resort near Carmel. Buying half was a lot of money, but purchasing it outright put his control of SBI at risk. In spite of having to give up so many shares, he decided to acquire the resort so he could sell it to Sato-san. That was the side deal Michael was dangling to entice him to go through with divesting the Seattle division."

"Okay, so many questions," Tim interrupted. "Why did Anna and Julie help him, what did they do, and why does Mr. Sato want a golf resort?"

"All good questions, Agent Fuller," Rock replied grinning. The investigator in Tim was coming out even at a social event. "First, Anna did it for the money. She stood to make a whole lot more from the sale of the resort when Michael bought it all. He leveraged her greed and her romantic relationship with Julie to pull Julie into the scheme.

"It was critical for Michael's plans that Julie issue her analyses at the right time to influence the stock price. The first of her reports made it fall. Michael needed uncertainty around SBI's future to scare off investors looking to take over the company. He recovered his controlling interest when he exercised his stock options, but Michael wanted more - better terms for the deal with Sato-san. The higher valuation of SBI resulting from Julie's second report accomplished this."

Rock's expression turned gloomy. "Anna and Julie are the classic tale of star-crossed lovers. Julie made good money off the transactions, ten million in total. Michael funneled the payments to her through Anna. But I'm convinced that Julie didn't do it for the money. She was in love with Anna and would have done anything for her. Anna realized only too late how much she loved Julie or she never would have used her like she did."

Shaking off his sullen look, Rock declared, "Red killing Julie was the start of the end for him and Michael. Anna was going to tell me everything the next day. She was concerned enough for her life that she had written me a letter detailing the whole plan. She gave it to her assistant to mail when she left the country estate that fateful morning. I got it after arriving back from Montana."

"Is it true what I heard about the way Red died?" Rose asked, sounding hopeful. "That he went crazy and died yelling and screaming?"

"Turns out his wounds got infected," Tim answered. "Imagine that, after swimming in a pool of shit. Sorry, ladies. Lily, hold Violet's ears. But that's what it was. A week later he was in the hospital running a one-hundred-and-five-degree fever. Whatever caused it was nasty and he couldn't be cured. During his last twenty-four hours, Red kept howling, 'Eat shit and die!' The doctors described it as a truly horrific death. I think Satan was calling him home and the fever was preparing Red for the heat."

Rose's expression shared her satisfaction.

"Red got what he deserved," Rock muttered. Stirring himself from these gruesome thoughts, he directed his attention to Tim. "You also asked about the golf resort and Sato-san. He had told me when I worked for him that he was planning to retire. His dream for his golden years was to own a great American golf course. He wanted to play on the links all day and entertain his many friends at night.

"Michael found this out. That's when he decided to acquire all of the property from Anna. By owning it, he could leverage the resort to lure Sato-san into closing the deal. But again, Michael had to take a big risk and we know how that ended."

Lily groaned, "Sadly, yes. His greed hurt many people, including a large number of SBI shareholders. What a mess he left for the lawyers and me to clean up. He nearly killed his baby, but I'm happy to say we've put all those lawsuits to bed. We settled the last one this week. Best wedding present I could have gotten. Now I can relax."

Looking to Rock, she added, "You and I can do that together while golfing. Sato-san already sent us our wedding gift - we have lifetime memberships in his resort. Please remember to thank him when you see him today."

"I will. John, remind me to do that." He gave John a sneaky smile knowing how he'd react.

Chuckling, he replied, "You forget, I only work part-time for you now that you cut back on your jobs. Today is not your day."

"Admit it, you were glad to follow me when I decided to move out here. Gets you back to your old stomping grounds with your computer buddies. The business you started doing projects for them will make you ten times what you made with me."

"Twenty times more. You really didn't pay me very well," John teased.

"Okay, okay, does anyone else want to insult the birthday boy?" He paused to look around, pretending to be hurt but unable to keep from grinning. Catching sight of Lily soothing a fussing Violet, he gave her a knowing nod. "Hearing no takers, I think we all need to get ready for the wedding. So if you would please leave me alone, maybe enough oxygen will return to the room to allow me to think."

Easing forward in his chair, Rock concluded sincerely, "But one last thing before you go. You've made this the best birthday I could have ever hoped for. Thank you all."

# Epilogue – Family

Lily leaned her head through the doorway, eyes searching the darkened nursery. She spied Rock sitting at the end of the couch wearing his tux, the bowtie hanging undone. Violet slept peacefully cradled in his arm. Lily could see her baby's face; the little one couldn't have been more content. Easing the door open, it creaked softly.

Rock looked up.

"There you are," she whispered. "The party is still going strong. What are you doing in here?"

He hushed, "It's my birthday. I wanted to play with my favorite gift."

His sweet smile made Lily love him even more, if that were possible.

"Come, sit with us," he invited, patting the cushion. "The guests will be fine without their hosts."

She stole into the room. Slipping off her shoes, she snuggled up against him. While she settled in, he wrapped an arm gently around her shoulders. Pulling her close, he sighed, "Now I can cuddle both my ladies."

"And your ladies are loving it." She gave him a soft peck on the chin.

He looked down at Violet for the longest time. Lily was happy just watching him love their daughter. When his gaze returned to her, his expression told he had something serious on his mind. They'd not been together long, but from day one they both could read each other's emotions like an open book.

"What is it, honey? Is there something wrong?"

"Now that we are married, I have a confession."

Her look of concern deepened.

"No, no, nothing terrible," he added quickly. "But I do need to get some things off my chest."

Her muscles release some of their tension. "So, what's this not terrible confession? Are you sure it's something I need to hear?"

"I need to tell you why I wanted to get married on my birthday."

"You had me worried," Lily groaned, her voice louder than she'd intended.

Violet stirred. Rock soothed her and she quieted.

"No, I need to tell you. I had two reasons. One selfish. One unselfish. Now that we're married, I feel you should know."

"Okay then, how were you selfish?"

"I wanted to finally have a birthday I enjoyed."

"Honey, that's not much of a confession." All remaining tension left her body.

"No, I know you had other dates you wanted and other places grander than our new home. But I've never had a truly good birthday in my life. Even as a kid, something always went wrong. I made myself sick eating too much cake, it rained on the party, the dog I got ran away. As an adult, all I wanted was to be somewhere else, to be doing something else. I even called the feeling my *itch*. Ask John sometime about it. He'll tell you how bad those days were."

"I'm so sorry. That sounds horrible."

"It was. Every birthday was like that for fifty years. When you agreed to marry me and I knew we'd have a beautiful baby by this birthday, I decided to give myself a present by making you my wife on this day. More than that, giving myself a family. And I was right. This has been the best birthday I, or anyone, could ever hope for. Thank you for making it happen."

"Sweetie, I'm glad I could give you this wedding present. It's one for me, too." She leaned close, kissing him tenderly on the cheek. "You said there was an unselfish reason. What in the world could that be?"

Rock paused, drawing a deep breath. Swallowing hard, he continued, "I wanted to give you time to change your mind."

Lily gaped; her eyes grew wide. "Didn't you want to marry me?!"

"No, no, no. Just the opposite, I wasn't sure you really wanted to marry me."

"You think I don't love you?" she moaned, her voice cracking.

"I know you love me," he stammered. "I was afraid I wasn't being fair to you. You told me you were pregnant and I jumped at the opportunity to make you my wife. I really want this family. I couldn't love you more, you mean everything to me. I would have gladly married you on the day I proposed, but you'd just finalized the divorce, you were trying to handle all the complexities of SBI, and you were figuring out what a baby would mean for you."

Rock shifted uncomfortably. "After you said yes, I was afraid one day you'd wake up feeling I'd tricked you into marrying me. You were stuck with a man ten years older who you really didn't love. I needed to give you time," he pleaded, his tone strained.

"Robert, you're an idiot. And I mean that in the most loving way I can. Never once did I doubt my decision. No amount of waiting would have changed my mind. You've given me the life and family I've always dreamed of. I've loved you from our first night together, I love you now, and I'll love you until the end of time. You are my rock."

With those heartfelt words she gave him a long, passionate kiss.

While she eased away, through a devilish grin Rock whispered, "Beautiful, you've still got it."

Lily beamed. Snuggling close to his ear, she purred, "And I always will."

# About the Author

Kim practiced Intellectual Property Law at a Fortune 100 company for thirty-one years. In retirement, he discovered his passion for creating fiction novels across multiple genres, including crime, science fiction and fantasy. When not traveling the world, he and his wife, Christine, live in Cincinnati where they love being with their two daughters, sons-in-law, granddaughter, and a multitude of cats and dogs. Kim enjoys building Legos, venturing anywhere his wife can take photos of animals and nature, and playing a sport that only roughly resembles what others call golf.

# Acknowledgement

It is impossible for me to thank everyone who has supported my enthusiasm for writing or contributed to making this story better, but I would be remiss if I didn't try. First, to my wife, Christine, and my mother, Mary, I want to recognize the loving encouragement they provided when reading the earliest drafts. By kindly overlooking the many flaws, they gave me the confidence I needed to keep trying.

Next, I greatly appreciate the support I receive from my daughters, Tiffany and Megan. Hopefully the reading of stories that expose a side of their father they never knew could exist hasn't traumatized them (too much).

Then there are my many friends who have been so kind to read this or other of my projects. I name but a few when I mention Suzette Roof, Jeff Hamner, Bill Pearlman, Mary Ralles, Debbie Troutman, John Evans, Donna Kaminski, Jim Haus and Sharon Haus. Your feedback has helped more than I can express. One person in particular, Kathleen Miller, has gone above and beyond to encourage me along my journey. I'm indebted to her not only for her guidance over the years but for her patience with my propensity to want to discuss writing every time we get together.

Finally, I need to thank my friend and editor, Valerie Gower. As an editor, her skill at catching holes in my plots, helping me tweak dialog, fixing grammar, and identifying typos is unsurpassed. She has taught me to be a better writer. As a friend, her positivity when things aren't going the way I want is invaluable.

Thank you, all.

Made in the USA
Columbia, SC
31 August 2024

40876198R00157